inbetween

a Kissed by Death novel

inbetween

a Kissed by Death novel

tara fuller

Entangled Publishing, LLC
2614 South Timberline Road
Suite 109
Fort Collins, CO 80525
Visit our website at www.entangledpublishing.com.

Edited by Heather Howland
Cover design by Heather Howland

Print ISBN   978-1-62061-083-1
Ebook ISBN   978-1-62061-084-8

Manufactured in the United States of America

First Edition August 2012

The author acknowledges the copyrighted or trademarked status and trademark owners of the following wordmarks mentioned in this work of fiction: Camaro, Jeep Wrangler, Ouija, Red Hots, Dixie, Bronco, YouTube, Ancestry.com, Google, Chevy, Jell-O, Sheetrock, F-150, Bubble Wrap, Windbreaker, *Back to the Future*, Gap, Photoshop, *Lethal Weapon*, "The Very Thought of You," Spider-Man, Kit Kat, Honda, Coke, Volkswagen, ChapStick

For Heather Howland, who makes dreams come true.
This book would not be without you.

Prologue

Finn

"Tell me again. How did you miss the mark?" I shoved my hands in my pockets and pressed my lips together to keep from grinning. "I swear, Anaya, this is the last time I follow one of you Heaven reapers anywhere."

Anaya and I walked down a two-lane strip of asphalt that glistened with puddles of leftover rain. Somewhere in the distance, a second round of clouds let out a hungry rumble. Anaya silently kept pace beside me, the gold band around her biceps glinting with each feather-soft footstep.

She turned her nose up into the air. "I never miss a mark."

"Then would you mind explaining why I'm walking up a mountain to get to our reap? We could've just flashed there."

She squinted at her surroundings, hesitating. I knew we

were close, but it was way too fun messing with her to let this one go. "It's okay to admit you're losing your touch," I said. "I'd be happy to take the lead on this one."

Anaya held up her hand, ignoring me. "Do you hear that?"

I stopped, listening to the mangled wail of a horn in the distance. As if pulled in by the sound, a black blur, like a cloud of ink, whipped past us before disappearing around the bend.

Shadows. Scavengers from the outskirts of Hell. Souls that weren't chosen to start again, had escaped their reaper, or hadn't earned their way into Heaven, so they'd been left to decay and rot. They were soulless beings that craved the scent of death. The taste of a soul.

I hated them. But I hated the memories they brought back even more.

Every shadow that blurred across my vision was a cold reminder of Allison, the love of my afterlife. What I'd done to her. What I'd almost let her become. Her name tumbling around in my skull made my chest ache.

But I couldn't change it. I'd never be able to change it. I'd pushed her into a world where we'd never be together again and nearly gotten myself banished to Hell in the process. The shadows would never let me forget it. After fifteen years of penance, Balthazar wasn't likely to let me forget it either. A sick feeling started to brew in my gut, so I shook it off and watched another black blur zip past us. At least they always led us to our targets.

"See." Anaya smiled and skipped ahead. "We're here."

Sure enough, around the last bend, a candy-apple-red Camaro lay upside down, crumpled like a discarded Coke can at the tree line. The horn blared, the sound careering off the rock wall and slamming back into the cliffside forest where it splintered into a thousand echoes between the branches. If I had to guess, the car had taken a similar journey. A ringlet of white smoke seeped from under the ruined hood and twirled up into the air.

"Looks like we have a winner." Anaya pulled her pearl-handled scythe from the leather belt she wore around her white dress, and twirled it in her hand. The twelve-inch blade, with its efficient, palm-sized handle, gleamed like it had never been used.

I glanced down at my sad excuse for a scythe with its plain iron handle and dingy blade. Heaven's reapers got all the perks. I may have been a slave to the Inbetween, but I was still a reaper, for God's sake. We were supposed to be the stuff of nightmare and legend. You'd think they'd at least give me a decent scythe. "Hey, what do you think the chances are of me scoring one of those?"

"Keep dreaming, Finn."

I stopped, leaving a few feet of distance between the car and me. Whoever was in there wasn't ready for me. Not yet. A slow warmth, an ache, spread through my chest, and drove sparks through my veins. Not the impatient icy burn I would have expected from a reap at all.

That…was different.

Anaya strolled past me, the shimmery brown plaits that hung down to her waist swaying behind her. "Look at the bright side," she said. "At least they did away with those awful cloaks."

She gripped the scythe and looked to the heavens. Her lips moved around the words to a prayer, one she'd never let me hear. Then, with a graceful sweeping motion, the blade of her scythe sliced through the car. She tugged once, twice, and yanked her glittery prize from the wreckage. Anaya shoved her scythe back into the leather belt at her hip and pulled the man to his feet. The shadows were on him in an instant, hissing and swirling like smoke around his legs and waist, just waiting for us to make a mistake. They were desperate. Hungry. Of course, their reaction wasn't really a surprise. Balthazar had loaded the territories with reapers, cutting off their food supply—souls rarely slipped through the cracks anymore.

Anaya turned around, tucking the soul behind her, and swung out her scythe. The shadows shrank back before dissolving into an oily spot on the pavement. She scowled and shoved her scythe back in its holster. "Vermin."

Vermin. I'd almost doomed Allison to be vermin. I couldn't look away from the dark spot on the pavement.

"Emma?" The soul babbled, rubbing his head. His eyes swam dizzily in his skull as he tried to regain his bearings. "Emma. You have to help Emma. Have you called an ambulance?"

I closed my eyes, trying to block him out. I didn't want to know her name.

"It's going to be fine, sir. She's going to a very…nice place. Don't worry." Anaya looked up at me, her odd golden eyes begging me to back up her lie.

I couldn't give him what he needed. What he needed was to hear that his daughter was going to live a long, happy life. All I offered was death. I wouldn't lie to him. The fact that I was about to take his little girl to the Inbetween was bad enough.

If she ever decided she was ready, that is. I glanced back at the car, waiting for the icy pull to kick in. Something still didn't feel right about this.

"Dad!" a girl's broken voice cried from the inside the crumpled car.

"Help her!" the man cried, trying to scrabble toward the car. Anaya easily held his shimmering form back. "For the love of God, she's only fifteen years old. You should have helped her first."

Now the pull kicked in. Except, *this* pull was dizzying and familiar in an unfamiliar way. And getting stronger by the second. My head spun with the force of it. Something was wrong here. Nothing about this felt like a standard reap. But I'd swear I felt this before. Once…

Memories pulsed through my mind in blinding flashes as I inched toward the vehicle. Soft-as-satin lips, warm whispers against my neck, smiles like the sun… The pull intensified, like a pounding in my chest, and my knees buckled. I knelt down to the broken window. Something like hope surged through me, followed by a cold rush of fear. I could only think of one other time that it had felt like this. Back when I'd peeled the soul from a frail, bloody body, packed in snow. The day that had changed me forever.

No. It couldn't be her. Not again, and not like this. Blond hair lay matted with blood against the girl's cheek. I reached through the window and traced the path of a tear that had fallen from her closed eyelids, my fingers scattering like mist. Her skin was petal-soft, deadly cold. A warm spot pooled in my hand where we touched, then traveled up my arm, down my neck where the heat exploded in my chest. Connection throbbed beneath my ribs. Certainty pounded in my temples.

Allison…

I jerked my hand back and scrambled away from the car. It was her. After all these years…*it was her.*

"What's wrong with you?" Anaya sounded annoyed.

"Dad?" the girl whimpered again, weaker this time. Or maybe that was the gray, gauzy feeling that was suffocating me. Fifteen years. Fifteen years of wondering if I'd done the right thing, and this is what I find? A girl halfway to death, clutching a bloody backpack? *No. No. No!* I shut my eyes and focused, touching my scythe to be certain. It wasn't there. No burning pull. No clawing need to take her soul. She could still be okay. Unless—

"Finn?" Anaya crouched down in front of me. "I don't know what is going on with you, but if you are incapable of handling this, I will."

I blinked until Anaya's blurry face slowly came into focus. I bolted upright. "Is she yours? Are you here for both of them? Because it's not me." A cold, throbbing panic took up residency in my chest. When she just stared at me, confused, I snapped. "Answer the damn question, Anaya!"

Realization slowly replaced the confusion in her eyes. Anaya shook her head and stared up through the spiky treetops where a crow swam across the turbulent lavender sky. "It's her."

It wasn't even a question. I couldn't hide this. Couldn't shove the secret into the dark safety of my pocket and walk away. Anaya knew.

She glanced back at the car, and then her gaze settled on me. "Walk away," she said, her voice just a whisper of breath. "If you have any sense left in you, you'll walk away from this and forget it happened, Finn. Don't screw this up. You've worked too hard to go back now."

I still had *some* sense. I must have, because part of me knew she was right. That I should walk away right now before this went any further. I blinked at the car, trying so hard to ignore the pull tugging me to her, warm and urgent like the need to breathe. The pull telling me I was here for a reason, even if that reason wasn't to take her soul. I didn't admit that to Anaya, though. Instead, I nodded, not trusting the words tumbling around in my mouth.

Anaya wrapped her fingers around her charge's hand and smiled at him. The air behind her rippled like a silk curtain, then erupted with light. His eyes went wide as he glanced at Anaya, then to me.

"I'm…I'm…" He stopped when Anaya patted the back of his hand, the word *dead* hanging among us.

"Yes," she said.

"And my daughter?" His shimmer dimmed as he watched the car teeter ineptly on the cliff's sharp drop-off.

"I'll take care of her," I said. "I swear."

I swallowed, realizing I meant it. What were the odds that I'd find her again like this? What were the odds that out of all of the places in the world she could have been reborn, she'd end up in California? I'd reaped this territory for years, and she'd been right under my nose. There had to be a reason.

Anaya shot me a sharp look, but didn't get a chance to follow through with her usual rant. Glittery tendrils of light reached out and wrapped around her and the soul in tow. A gust of balmy air exploded from the porthole, blowing Anaya's braids in every direction. It fluffed her white skirt until she looked like she was floating on a cotton mushroom top, then spun them around until they were just a swirl of blinding color.

When they were gone, the wind died, and the light dimmed and dissolved into the murky blue twilight.

Something cracked.

The tree that held the wreckage in place swayed. I looked up. A brilliant flash of red bounced on a branch, as if begging it to snap.

Maeve.

The soul whose second chance I'd stolen fifteen years ago when I pushed Allison through the portal in her place.

And all at once, I realized what fate wanted me to do.

"Don't!" I scrambled for the car. It wobbled on the one tire that hadn't gone flat, threatening to go over any second and take the girl inside with it.

"I knew following you around would eventually pay off." Her voice echoed through the treetops, followed by a mocking laugh. "I realize this is bittersweet, so I'll let you say a quick good-bye before I kill her and ruin your sad excuse for an existence."

I wriggled through the window, closed my eyes, and gave into gravity. Cells connected. The air sizzled. I flexed my fingers, only a breath away from being fully corporeal.

No.

I stopped myself, fighting the urge to slip my arms around Allison's limp frame, and pictured Balthazar, the second in command to the Almighty, ruler of reapers. He'd feel me go corporeal and would know I'd found her again. I punched the ceiling and let my skin scatter like sparks against the gray felt. I couldn't afford that kind of hell right now.

She groaned and something like relief flooded me. Yes, definitely still alive. But not for long. The tree swayed again, this time allowing a little of the car to slip through its hold. I glanced out the window and watched a few rocks spring loose from the cliff and roll to the bottom.

"Finn, come out of there," Maeve sang. She bounced again,

rocking the car. "Just give in to this and we'll call it a day. She was going to die anyway. You'd just be doing your job."

She was *not* going to die. I wouldn't let her.

"Come on, Allison." I leaned in close and watched her eyelids twitch, then crack open one at a time. Thank God. "I know you're scared, but I need you to trust me."

Her eyes darted back and forth, wide and afraid, before settling on me. "Who are you? Where's my dad?"

When she leaned up to try to see in the front seat I moved in front of her to block her view. "He's fine. Don't worry about him right now," I said, softly. "I need you to get up. See that window?" I pointed to the upside down broken window and she nodded.

The car lurched again.

"You need to crawl through there. And you need to do it fast."

She tried to sit up, then winced and fell back. "I can't. It hurts."

I plastered a smile on my face and had to force myself not to touch her, to brush the hair out of her face, to grab her arm and pull her the hell out of there. "Yes, you can. You're tough. I can tell."

She shook her head. "No, I'm not. Really. I didn't even make it through one week of softball before I sprained my ankle."

I laughed in spite of myself. "I have a feeling you're a lot tougher than you give yourself credit for. Now come on." The car rocked and I tensed. "Get out of the car."

She looked into my eyes for a long moment, then pushed herself up and inched toward the window. I crawled out first, coaxing her to follow.

The car shifted. Groaned. I heard more rocks break loose from the cliff to tumble over the edge.

"You're making this unbearably complicated, Finn. Really, why not just pull her out of the car and get it over with?" Maeve taunted, a smile behind her words. "You're already dead—what else could Balthazar possibly do? Oh…well I guess there is Hell. But other than that?"

Pushing Maeve's laughter out of my head, I focused on Allison. "Come on, pretty girl," I said, fear thrumming in my chest. "You can do this. You *have* to do this."

The gash bleeding through her blue jeans snagged on the broken window and she sobbed.

"Don't stop. I know it hurts. But you can't stop." We were so close. Another few feet and she'd be free. I kept my eyes on her, trying to figure out a way to distract her from the pain. "You know, one time I broke my leg," I blurted out.

She sniffled and looked up at me.

"I'd climbed this big tree on my dad's farm. I didn't tell anyone where I was going, so when the branch broke, I knew I was in trouble. I had to walk all the way home on that leg just to get there before it got dark."

"Why didn't you wait for somebody to look for you?"

"Coyotes. All I could think about was how I used to hear them howling at night. Our neighbor used to find his cattle torn to shreds."

She scooted a little farther out. "Didn't it hurt?"

The car groaned and tilted underneath us. Allison gripped the seat, her eyes wide.

"It hurt like hell, but it was a lot better than ending up like the cattle."

She squeezed her eyes shut and wiggled the rest of the

way through the window, into the pine needles and dirt on the side of the road. She crawled forward a few more feet and collapsed. Her cheek pressed against the wet pavement as she fought to catch her breath.

A loud *crack* split the silence, and the car lurched forward, its weight breaking the tall bone of a tree. Within seconds, it rolled off the side and into the chasm below, a chewed-up red spot swallowed by the dark.

Maeve's scream ripped through the mist that had started to fall, and in it, I heard her cry for revenge. I'd worry about that later. For now, I looked down at Allison.

I watched her breaths make foggy shapes as they puffed erratically into the night. Her lashes blinked away the tears that were running across her cheeks. No. This wasn't Allison anymore.

"Emma," I whispered as a beam of headlights curled around the bend in the road. "You need to flag down the car that's coming around the corner. You're going to have to get up."

"My leg…" She looked up, tears in her eyes. "Why can't you do it? Why aren't you helping me?"

Guilt tied my insides into knots, making it hard to look at the girl reaching up for my help. I couldn't give it to her no matter how badly I wanted to. Balthazar and his damned rules!

"I can't. I'm so sorry." I took a few steps back until she lowered her hand. "But you can do this. You're tough. Remember?"

Her gaze swung to the lights glistening on the pavement and she pushed herself to her knees. I took my chance. I let myself fade. Dissolve into the mist around me that was calling me home.

I watched Emma wave her arms at the slowing car. She

was safe. Alive. I closed my eyes, laughing with relief. I'd done it. I'd saved her. Except…

I looked up at the broken tree where Maeve had balanced only minutes ago. There was no way I could walk away now. Not when I'd led Maeve to her.

Damn it. This was bad on so many levels. I watched Emma collapse against the man from the car as he wrapped a jacket around her shivering shoulders. Warmth spread through my chest. Yeah…*bad* wasn't a strong enough word. Disaster was more like it. And I didn't care. She was worth it.

"I'll keep you safe. I swear it." I repeated the promise I'd made to her father, then closed my eyes and let the wind catch me and toss me into the night.

Chapter 1

Finn

Sometimes Emma made me feel so alive, I almost forgot I was dead.

Almost.

I sat on the floor across from her bed listening to her slow, steady breaths. I should have been more alert. I was supposed to be on watch. But it was so hard to concentrate on anything but her when I knew she was remembering.

Emma rolled over, pressing her face into the pillow. "Finn..."

I shut my eyes, trying to hold on to it. I wasn't stupid enough to think she'd remember this when she woke up, but damn it if hearing my name slip through her lips didn't sweep through me like wildfire. Scorching the places where blood used to run. Melting the hollow space where my heart used to beat.

I took a deep, unneeded breath and let the back of my

head thump against her overstuffed bookcase. This was never going to get easier. Two years of watching her through the invisible barrier of Balthazar's rules was really starting to suck. Especially when every time I blinked, another piece of Allison was breaking through the surface.

In the pale light of her lamp, I could see the neat row of cookbooks, nestled together like a family, holding all of the secrets Emma created in the kitchen. They smelled like flour and sugar and home. The next orderly row was packed with the worn-out novels she loved, and a new photography book her mom bought her last year. The last shelf belonged to the books her father had written, held in place by gold-framed pictures of him smiling and alive. Emma had so many words inside her. I was surprised they didn't fall out while she was sleeping. Thousands of words about mysteries and romance and life. Things I didn't know anything about.

Things that Allison had known *everything* about.

She whimpered from under the covers and I looked up. What was she remembering this time? What piece of the Inbetween and her time with me was she fighting? There was so much I didn't want her to remember. So much I *needed* her to remember. But that didn't matter. I was here to protect her. That's where it had to end.

I closed my eyes, trying to swallow my own crap lie. She mumbled something in her sleep and began to thrash under the sheets. I groaned and pushed myself up from my safe spot on the carpet, unable to sit there listening to her suffer anymore. I stopped a foot from the bed and knelt down.

"Shh…" I touched the edge of the mattress, forcing myself not to go any closer. "It's going to be okay." She was only a few inches away, but it felt like miles. Miles that left me wanting in so many ways that I ached. Hopefully my presence would be enough. There were times I swore she could feel me.

"What do you think you're doing?" a gravelly voice chided.

I looked up from the edge of Emma's bed just as Easton melted up from the polished hardwood floor beneath the window. Like an oil slick coming to life, he unfolded his long, shadowy legs until he was just an inkblot in front of the splash of lamplight on her wall. His violet eyes pinned me like a kid caught with his hand in the cookie jar.

Which I kind of was.

"Nothing," I lied.

"Yeah, looked like nothing." He strolled across the room accompanied by a wave of sulfur and smoke, the black serpent tattoo on his neck glinting.

"Jesus, Easton." I scrunched up my nose and climbed to my feet. "Don't they have a shower somewhere between here and the afterlife?"

"Screw you. You didn't just have to tow somebody's grandpa to Hell." He brushed something chalky and gray off his long coat, and a shudder worked its way down my spine. God only knows what—or who—it had belonged to. "Besides, I wasn't the one about to feel up a sleeping human."

"I wasn't—"

"Save it." He waved his hand dismissively. "We have work to do. I don't have time for your useless obsession with the human today."

"Will you please stop calling her that?"

"What?" Easton glanced up from Emma's vanity, where he'd been inspecting the various lotions, tubes, and bottles like he was on some alien planet. Then again, Easton had been dead for something like four hundred years and spent most of his time in Hell, so her stuff probably was sort of alien to him.

"'The human.' You make her sound like a freak. It's not like we're a different species, for God's sake. We were humans too, or don't you remember that far back?"

"*Were,*" he said, scowling at me over his shoulder. "Past tense."

Easton's clumsy fingers knocked over the bobblehead zombie on the vanity top and we both froze. Emma shot up from beneath the covers, gasping.

"Mom?" She shoved the tangled blond hair out of her face, her eyes trained on her rumpled reflection in the vanity mirror. "Was that you?"

"Not Mom. Just one of Hell's reapers, at your service." Easton leaned against the bookcase and grinned. "You're right, Finn. This is fun."

"Are you freaking insane?" I hissed.

He rolled his eyes. "Oh calm down, drama queen. It's not like she can hear us."

"You scared her."

"Are you kidding? She's scared of her own reflection. And that has nothing to do with me."

No. But the fact that Emma's life had been a horror movie waiting to happen these last two years had everything to do with me. I'd led a soul that hated my guts and was hell-bent on revenge right to her doorstep.

I turned my attention back to Emma. After she collected herself, she twisted her hair up into a messy ponytail and dug in her nightstand drawer for her journal.

"Dear diary…" Easton nodded at the journal. "What do you think she's going to write?"

I folded my arms across my chest. "Not my business."

He walked over to her bed and plopped down beside her. The mattress didn't creak or groan under his weight. The blankets didn't shift. He peeked over her shoulder at the book. A long tendril of honey-colored hair came loose from Emma's ponytail and fell across her eye. She tucked it behind her ear, but Easton blew on it so that it fell right back down. She swept it out of her face, looking frustrated, and Easton chuckled.

"Will you stop?" I said, feeling uncomfortable with how close he was to her. "This is so screwed up it's not even funny."

He raised a dark brow. "Oh? And what you're doing isn't?"

We could have gone back and forth like that for hours, but the call came. It always did. It started in my bones—a cold so cutting that it sliced through me like a machete. Easton's jaw clenched, his muscles taut and ready. He slowly closed his hand around the handle of his scythe, which burned black and softly smoked at his side. I flexed my fingers as the icy ribbons of death worked their way through each one of my limbs.

"Can you take this one for me?" I asked. "You're already going to be there, and I just got back—"

"No," Easton said. "Hell no. I have my own job to do. I can't keep covering for your sorry ass. Besides, do you have any idea how close you are to being caught? Don't push your luck, Finn. Just keep your nose down, collect your souls, and thank the Almighty that you don't have my job."

"I'm taking a risk every time I leave her. You know that."

"For the love of God. She'll be fine, Finn. It's just one reap."

"How do you know she'll be fine?"

He shrugged. "I don't. But that's the difference between you and me. I don't care."

With that, he vanished, consumed in a flash by the keening wails of the damned. The screams beckoned. Clawed at me from the inside out.

Rule One as a reaper: Death doesn't wait for anyone.

And it sure as hell wasn't waiting for me now.

• • •

By the time I seeped into form next to Easton, the pull was twining around my wrists, tugging, clouding every one of my thoughts. I shook my head and stared up at the lemon-yellow house engulfed in an angry tangle of flames that glowed in the dim predawn light. A few bikes and a shiny swing set slick with dew littered the lawn. A minivan sat devoid of life in the drive. I craned my neck to read the sticker on the bumper. *My child is an honor student at Rosewood Elementary.*

Seriously? Honor students and a minivan mom? I couldn't help but wonder what tragic scenario I was going to face this time as part of Balthazar's grand attempt to teach me a lesson.

"How many of these is he going to send me on?" I pressed the heels of my palms to my eyes and prayed for a different outcome than the one I felt hissing in my lifeless bones. "I get it, Balthazar."

Easton grunted. "Do you really? Where'd we just come from, Finn?"

"Good morning, boys." A voice, smooth as molasses, spoke up from behind us. We didn't have to turn around to know it was the final part of our region's trio. Anaya skipped over to my side.

"How many do you think are in there?" I asked.

She shrugged. "Only one way to find out."

I trailed after Anaya, Easton behind me, always the shade of gray between the dark and the light. Anaya stepped through a curtain of flames, but I stalled in the doorway. Something in my chest tightened. My throat closed up and a memory cemented my feet to the floor.

Flames lapped at the control board. Consumed the cockpit. Licked my skin with an orange serpent tongue. Water and panic all around me, and I couldn't drown. No. I was going to char. I was going to melt. I was going to burn.

"Let's go." Easton nudged me through the doorway. "I'm already getting another call, and I can't be in two places at once."

I forced myself to move through the house. Windows popped and shattered. The roof crackled like tinder on a campfire. Black billowing smoke consumed every inch of the 1,600-square-foot slice of soot-coated suburbia.

"Watch your step. This one's mine." Easton stared down at a man who had collapsed in the empty hall.

"Let me guess." I stepped over the man in plain white boxers and looked at Easton. "He's a liar? Did he take something that never should have belonged to him in the first place?" I scowled at the ceiling and threw my hands up in the air. "Come on, Balthazar. Deliver your little message so I can get on with my freaking day."

Anaya exchanged a weary glance with Easton, then stepped over the lifeless body and into a bedroom where a woman lay awaiting her reaping.

Easton knelt down and touched the man's temple. "He had an affair."

I stopped halfway down the hall and turned around, confused. "What?"

"He had an affair with another woman." He stood up and looked at the ceiling, then down to the beam lying on top of the man. "He was trying to save his wife when he died. Like saving her would make up for what he did."

Easton gave me a pointed look, and I groaned. Was this ever going to end? Was a death ever going to be just a death again? Knowing Balthazar and his obsessive need to get a damn point across, probably not.

I kept moving until a tug in my chest urged me toward a half-open bedroom door. Pink paper lanterns adorned the ceiling, waiting for the fire to consume them and turn them to ash. A little girl lay huddled under a yellow comforter waiting for me to do the same to her. A shadow lurked by her bed, waiting, hoping I'd be a no-show so the soul would go into limbo. Its smokelike fingers swirled around her tiny, trembling frame.

I glanced back at the fire creeping around the doorframe, licking at the walls, melting away the posy-pink wallpaper in an all-too-familiar dance. I couldn't waste any more time. I slid my scythe out of its holster and speared her flesh, gifting her with the mercy of death before the flames could get to her.

I watched her twitch and jerk until her soul quietly peeled away from her skin, leaving a too-small shell behind. The shadow hissed at me and seeped between the floorboards.

"Who are you?" her shimmering soul asked. She fidgeted nervously, her huge hazel eyes confused, accusing. "Are you an angel?"

It never got easier with kids. "Sort of."

"Where are your wings if you're an angel?"

A paper lantern lit up just above our heads.

"I said sort of, didn't I?" I fought past the smoke shrouding my vision to the hall where the next pull was coming from, and forced some patience into my voice. "Where's your brother's room?"

She trailed after me into the burning hall and I thanked the Almighty that Anaya and Easton had already finished with her parents.

"How did you know I have a brother?"

"I just know." I pushed into a bedroom with a KEEP OUT sign tacked to the front. Flames rolled out of the doorway and the heat sealed up the words in my throat. I shoved my hand behind me.

"Stay here."

"But—"

"I said stay here. Got it?" No way was I letting her see the charred remains of her brother. If I couldn't give her the life she deserved, couldn't give her Heaven, then damn it I'd at least spare her this memory.

She swallowed, not realizing the human function no longer applied to her, and nodded. When I emerged with her brother in tow, her eyes lit up. "Geez, Simon. I thought you were dead or something."

I grabbed both of their hands. "All right, guys. Let's go."

The little girl pulled her hand away, folded her arms across her chest, and frowned up at me. "We're not supposed to go with strangers."

Ignoring the inferno around us, I crouched down and stuck my hand out, folding her tiny vapor fingers into mine. "I'm Finn. I'm eighteen"—sort of—"and I like fishing and baseball. My favorite color is blue. My mom makes, *hands down*, the best peach cobbler you've ever tasted. Oh, and I used to fly airplanes."

She tentatively shook my hand. "What else?"

"Well…I'm afraid of spiders. Like pee-my-pants afraid of spiders. Even the little ones."

She exchanged a look with her brother.

I groaned. "Come on, guys. Even my best friend doesn't know some of this stuff. What else do you want here?"

"You really flew an airplane before?" the boy asked, speculative.

"Yep."

He shrugged. "I like him."

The little girl finally smiled. "Then I guess it's okay."

"Where are we going?" The little boy looked up at me with an anxious expression.

How to explain? I never knew what to say to kids to make them understand. I could have told him the truth, cold and simple like an instruction manual. They hadn't lived long enough to become who they were meant to be. Hadn't reached their potential. So I would take them to the Inbetween where they'd put in their time. Grow into a soul worthy of either Heaven, or a coveted second chance at life. And if they didn't grow into either of those…

A shadow melted out of the flames, lurking in the corner of the hall. Hungry. Desperate. I slipped my arm around both of them. They were kids. They wouldn't become one of them. I had to believe that.

I ruffled his hair and forced a smile. "How about a different question, pal."

"Okay. Why doesn't the fire feel hot?"

Half an hour, two souls delivered, and a gazillion unanswerable questions later, I found myself spilling onto my hands and knees on Emma's back lawn. The grass needles didn't bother to bend under the weight of my palms. The sunrise, just a pale echo of summer, edged over the horizon and poured through my translucent body, refusing to acknowledge my existence with a shadow. Like I needed them to remind me that I didn't belong here.

Easton loomed over me with something resembling sympathy in his eyes. "Nice landing."

"Shouldn't you be in Hell?"

"I could ask you the same."

Pushing past him, I made my way toward Emma's house. "Not today, Easton. Seriously, man. Just…not today, all right?"

"How long are you going to keep this up?" he asked. "She's not a kid anymore, you know."

"I know she's not." God, did I know it. My fingers tested the wall, dissolving through the brick of the house. I could feel Emma's nearness all the way down to my toes.

"You should let her go," he said. "I could understand it a few years ago, but now? Now it's past time for you to move on, and we both know it."

His words burned a path of rage through me, leaving charred remnants of dead nerve endings and hollow veins. "I do that and she's as good as dead. It won't take Maeve a week of tormenting her before she gets bored and kills her."

"I know." Easton looked resigned, as if he could accept the kind of life—or death—Emma would have without me here to protect her.

Of course he could. Death was his life. He reeked of Hell. Gambled with imps for fun. And he didn't love her. He didn't burn for her. He didn't break nearly every rule in the book and risk his soul for her on a daily basis.

I did.

"And if I'm sent to collect her again? What then?" I looked at him, needing him to understand. "You think I could do that again? Let her die? Rip her soul from her screaming flesh?"

"Better her than you."

"No!" I stepped into him, fuming. "*Not* better her than me. It's my fault she's in this position. Maeve never would've found her if it wasn't for me. Hell, I'm the whole reason Maeve wants to destroy her. How am I supposed to walk away and let her suffer for a mistake I made?"

"It wasn't your fault. You thought you were helping." He shook his head. "Hell, you *were* helping. She's alive, isn't she? Sure, she's got problems, but what seventeen-year-old kid doesn't? Haven't you ever read Judy Blume?"

I looked at Easton, his spiky sable hair blotting out the warm lavender sunrise. "*You've* read Judy Blume?"

"Screw you. You're the one haunting a high school student."

"I'm not *haunting* her. I'm protecting her."

"Look, my point is she's going to die someday, and there will be nothing you can do to stop it," he said. "She'll wrap her car around tree. She'll get cancer. If she's lucky, she'll grow so old her body will forget to wake up one morning."

"I realize that," I gritted out. "But I'll be damned if I'll let Maeve make her life hell until that happens, let alone be the reason she dies." The words held so much heat I could feel them scorching my mouth.

"This is—" Easton froze, whatever lecture he'd been prepared to deliver catching in his throat as he watched the kid from next door jog across the lawn. We watched him cast a careful look around, then tuck a leather sketchbook under his arm and shove Emma's bedroom window open.

"Looks like you've got competition," Easton said, watching him climb in. His scythe began to smoke on his hip. "I'll bet he even has one of those fancy pulses, too."

I rolled my eyes. I wasn't letting him get under my skin that easily. "Cash is just her friend. Besides, pulses are overrated."

"Yeah. Keep telling yourself that." He winked at me, then dove into the swirling black pit of screams that had opened beneath him. A Hell reaper's work was never done. And having that much darkness on his hands day in and day out didn't seem to bother him. Easton had been born for this job the same way Anaya and all her light had been born for hers. I couldn't think of anyone more fitting.

My scythe pulsed cold against my hip. I glanced up at Emma's window and frowned. Sometimes I wondered what job I was born for, because it sure as hell didn't feel like I was born for this.

Chapter 2

Emma

It was happening again. The dreams. The nightmares that felt more like memories than figments of my imagination. I pressed the pen to my journal and concentrated, trying to remember the fragments left behind. Flashes of a boy with soft green eyes. His lips in my hair. His hands on my waist. Panic and desire dueling in my veins like fire and ice. I'd been up for an hour already, and I could still hear his voice.

Please forgive me for this, pretty girl.

"Knock, knock."

Cash's voice wafted in with the breeze, stirring the sheer ivory curtains that hung over my blinds. I looked up from my journal to watch him climb through my window, his familiar sketchpad stashed under his arm. I snapped a mental picture and added it to the collage of memories that made up Cash and me.

"Please tell me your mom's already gone," he grumbled as he pulled a chair up next to my bed. "The last thing I need is her running off to tell my dad I'm over here trying to get in your pants."

"She's at Spin class." I looked at my alarm clock. It was too early for Cash to be awake, let alone at my house. "Trouble in paradise?"

He shrugged and pulled his pencil out from behind his ear, opening his sketchpad. "You could say that. What about you?" He nodded to the journal in my hands. "More dreams?"

I nodded and closed my eyes, trying to remember more of my dream. It was already fading. Damn it.

"Well, don't let me bother you." His lips quirked into a grin as he started to draw. His messy black spikes stood straight up on his head, flecks of red and gold paint glinting from the tips.

"What are you drawing?"

"You." His wrist moved fluidly, his pencil scratching against the paper as he studied the curve of my face.

I groaned and stuffed my face in my hands. "Seriously, Cash. I just woke up."

"Come on, it's for class," he said. "We're supposed to sketch someone in a natural pose. Someone who doesn't know we're drawing them."

I raised an eyebrow. "Seems a little stalkerish. Besides, I know you're drawing me, so that sort of defeats the purpose, doesn't it?"

"So pretend you don't know I'm here. Go back to whatever you were writing."

Not possible. I couldn't immerse myself in those kinds of memories while he was sitting here analyzing every one of my expressions. Cash knew me too well as it was. My horrible poker face was only going to make everything worse.

"Besides, the light is amazing in here right now. Don't move. Don't even blink. I swear, the way the sun is hitting you…" His inspiration must have stolen the rest of his words because he sank into a heavy silence, the hiss of his charcoal pencil speaking for him as it frantically worked at replicating my sleep-mussed state.

I peered around his sketchbook to see which T-shirt he was wearing today. This one said, *I'm only here because my flux capacitor is broken.* It was the same one he'd been wearing yesterday.

"You do realize kids in our generation are not going to get a reference to *Back to the Future*?" I asked.

"*You* just did," he said without looking up.

"Only because you've forced me to sit through it like three hundred times."

"Yeah, well, I don't wear them for anyone else. I wear them for me."

I sighed. So much for trying to distract him. "I never agreed to this, you know," I said fruitlessly. I knew he'd get what he wanted, even if what he wanted was my humiliation served on a silver platter. Or in this case, a leather sketchpad.

"I'll let you punch me if you let me finish," he said.

"Not good enough. You have to buy me coffee and a chocolate croissant *and* let me punch you."

"Hmm." Another graceful arc of the pencil branded more of me onto the page. "That's a pretty high price. Maybe we should make this a nude if I'm having to spring for croissants. Oh wait! I already did one of those last night."

He grinned down at the paper and waggled his eyebrows. The tiny silver piercing embedded in his right brow caught the sunlight. I clutched my journal to my chest and threw a pillow at him.

"You are so gross." I crawled out of bed to search for school clothes, then pulled open a drawer and grabbed a pair of jeans. "Who was it this time?"

He closed his sketchpad, tucked his pencil behind his ear, and wandered over to lean on my dresser. "Tinley. In my studio where my dad walked in, so as you can imagine, my house is a hostile environment right now." Cash snatched the journal out of my hand. "Are you ever going to let me see what you write in here?"

"Give that back!"

"Nope." He grinned. "I swear to God if I find hearts doodled around some guy's name in here, I'm gonna throw up."

I ripped it out of his hand and dropped it into the drawer. The only things in those journals were nightmares and disfigured memories of my dad. I didn't care about boys and Cash knew it. I didn't have the time, the patience, or the kind of emotional energy they demanded.

Cash peeked in another drawer and frowned. "Lace?" he said, distracted. "That's…disturbing. I feel like I just walked in on my dad having sex or something. Since when do you wear sexy underwear?"

I slammed the drawer shut on his fingers. "Quit snooping through my stuff!"

He shook his hand. "It's not like I haven't seen it all before."

"What's that supposed to mean?"

Cash walked over to the window and peeked out the blinds to see his house. "I like to do a monthly sweep of your room."

Horror made the room spin. "You go through my stuff?"

"No, not really. But I should. Just to make sure nothing weird is going on with you. Which I wouldn't have to do if you actually *talked* to me anymore."

"You're a real pain in the ass," I said. "You know that, right?"

"So I hear." He snapped the blinds shut and groaned. "Why hasn't he left yet?"

I stuffed my books and camera into my bag. "Probably because he's waiting to annihilate you."

"Hey." Cash leaned over and picked up the bobblehead zombie he got me for my birthday last year. "Nice way to treat Francisco." He brushed it off and placed it back next to my lip gloss and the fancy perfume Mom gave me that I never wore.

I gripped my bag, remembering the sound that had woken me up this morning. As if someone had knocked something over. "Sorry."

"I'll forgive you if you let me use your shower. I'd like to postpone my annihilation as long as possible, and want to smell good while doing it." He crossed over to my closet. "Do you still have any of your dad's old T-shirts around?"

I pulled Dad's Stanford sweatshirt from the back of my closet, stopping to run my fingers over the faded letters. It had been his favorite. So many memories swirled inside my head of him in that sweatshirt. "No shower and I better get this back," I said, tossing it to him. "And do you even realize what will happen if Mom comes home and finds you in our shower? I don't need that kind of drama."

I grabbed my clothes and headed for the hall. Cash followed me to the bathroom, where I slammed the door in his face. I heard what I guessed was his forehead thump against the door, and his muffled voice seeped through the wood. "Come on, Em. Don't throw me to the sharks."

I twisted on the hot water in the shower and spun around to grab my toothbrush. My hand froze, hovering above counter, shaking. On my mirror, the words *hello Allison* were written in smudged black eyeliner. I slapped my hand over my mouth to hold in my scream and stumbled back into the towel rack. Not again. I squeezed my eyes shut. Please not again.

Cash tapped on the door again. "Emma?"

I made my hands into a cup and breathed into them until my heart slowed.

"What's wrong?"

"Nothing," I said as soon as I could get the words out. Desperate, I grabbed the hand towel off the rack behind me and scrubbed at the mirror. I was not going back to Brookhaven again. No way was I spending my senior year in a mental institution. The condensation from the shower made it easy work, but my white towel had black splotches all over it by the time I was finished. Cash couldn't see this. Nobody could.

"She's crying out for attention," the doctor had said to Mom like I wasn't sitting right there. *"It's not uncommon for a young person to lash out like this after a traumatic experience."*

Cash tapped on the other side of the door with the toe of his shoe. "Are you okay?"

Taking a deep breath, I stashed the towel in the hamper and opened the door. He stumbled into the foggy bathroom, a tangle of arms and legs, before catching himself on the doorframe.

"I'm fine. But I really need to get in the shower." When he just stared at me I said, "We can hang out later, okay?"

I tried to close the door but Cash stuck his shoe in the doorway and pushed it open again.

"What's going on, Em?" His chocolate-colored eyes searched my face. "Every time I see you, you're writing in that stupid journal. You've been acting paranoid at school and you're sleeping with your light on again. Don't keep it all in like last time. Talk to me. I want to help."

I stared at his chest for a long moment before I said anything.

"Nothing's wrong." I forced a smile. He didn't look like he believed me. "Look, I just had a bad dream, okay? Everybody has them. I didn't give you crap when you had that nightmare about the clowns and Justin Bieber."

I expected him to laugh and defend himself by saying how drunk he'd been when he had that dream, but he didn't. He wasn't going to let this go.

"It's not just the dream and you know it," he said, his brows drawn together. "You're pulling away again. I can feel it."

I looked away, knowing he was right. Hating lying to him. "I said I'm fine. I've even been taking my pills. I don't know what else you want me to say."

"I want you to talk to me. I want you to stop feeding me the same bullshit you feed your mom. It doesn't work on me, Em. I know you."

How was I supposed to tell him I didn't know dreams from reality anymore? That I felt like someone or something was watching me. That I could feel them like a rush of warmth constantly running across my skin.

The answer was: I couldn't.

I closed my eyes, not wanting to look at him. "Cash, please."

He made a frustrated sound. "Fine. Then hurry up and let's

get something to eat. You'll feel better."

I rolled my eyes. "You just want me to cook you something."

"That, too." He put his hands on the doorframe so I couldn't shut him out. "Come on, Em. Don't make me go back home yet."

I sighed. Cash was like a stray dog. Mom fed him one peanut butter and jelly sandwich the day his mom left when we were six, and I hadn't been able to get rid of him since. He'd always be that sad boy sitting on my front porch with jelly on his cheek to me. "I'll bake you some scones after I get out of the shower, but Mom will ground me for an eternity if she finds you here. Sorry."

He frowned and raked his fingers through his black spikes. "Fine. *If* I survive the wrath of Dad, then I'll meet you out front in an hour. I'll take you to get your stupid coffee."

I waved him off but he stopped in the hall, his fingers tapping on the wall next to the last family picture we'd ever taken with my dad. "Who's Allison?" he asked.

I froze. "What?"

"Allison," he said. "You said it in your sleep the other night. You said, 'I'm not Allison.'"

Muffled memories that didn't belong to me clouded my mind and bled into the corners of my vision like ink. I blinked them away, wanting to scrub myself clean of them.

"Who is she?"

I shook my head and touched the doorknob, ready to put an end to the conversation. "Honestly, I don't know."

Chapter 3

Finn

Maeve was getting better at this. It made my insides crawl thinking she'd been this close while I was away. She'd been in Emma's bathroom, for God's sake. Ten feet from her bedroom. If she'd chosen to do something more than scare her, I wouldn't have been there to stop it.

I rubbed the back of my neck and stared at Emma across the sunny little kitchen. I had to figure something out. There had to be a better way than gambling with her life every time I got called out.

Rachel, Emma's mother, buzzed around the kitchen like a bumblebee in yellow and black workout clothes while Emma wiped flour from the counter and placed the milk back into the fridge. They were in the same room, but it felt like they were on opposite sides of the world. I wondered if it had been like this before her father died.

A timer dinged. Emma slipped on her oven mitts and pulled out a tray of pumpkin scones. Her mother plopped down onto a stool and started picking at one of the hot pastries. "I'm always starving after those Spin classes."

Emma slapped her hand away and started piling the scones into a brown paper sack. "These are for Cash."

"There's a whole tray!"

Emma sighed and tossed her one out of the bag. "You do know how to cook, you know. You certainly didn't live off cereal alone before I learned my way around a kitchen."

"Yes," her mother said. "But the stuff you bake always tastes better and I'm running late."

"For what?"

"I'm meeting Parker," her mother said, smiling. "He's driving me up to some little place near Owens Lake for brunch. They're supposed to have amazing frittatas."

Emma stared at the counter. "Don't you have to work?"

"I have an open house at three, but he promised to have me back in time."

Emma looked out the window. She was remembering again, which meant her pills weren't working. I wondered how long it would be before they started jamming a new prescription down her throat to make her forget. Maeve's stunt in the bathroom wasn't helping matters either. If I'd gotten there in time, I could have done something. At the very least cleaned it off the mirror before she could see it. I hated seeing her afraid. She deserved so much more than this.

I stood beside her and imagined what it might be like to talk to her. For her to know that I was standing there praying to the heavens for the ability to taste just one of those damned scones.

Standing close enough to feel her breath, I reached up and watched my fingers create silver sparks against her hair. Emma closed her eyes and the tension melted from her shoulders, like maybe she could feel what I was doing. I didn't think it was possible, but I did it anyway, hoping somehow, some way, I could make her feel safe. It would have to be enough.

She tucked a strand of her hair behind one ear and turned away. "I have to go to school," she said, grabbing her bag. "Are you going to be home for dinner?"

"No," Rachel set down her scone and wiped her hands on a napkin. "Parker's picking me up after the open house for some work banquet he wants to drag me to. I could have him come here if you want to meet him. He's been asking to meet you." She sounded hopeful.

"No. That's okay." Emma clenched her jaw and looked away.

Rachel picked up the little orange pill bottle that always sat in the same place on the counter. "You forgot your pill."

Emma flinched. "I already took one."

Her mother's blond brows pulled together. "Please, honey. Don't make me count them. You know...you know I'm just trying to help you."

Emma snatched the bottle from her mother's open palm, fingers trembling, and popped open the bottle. When she swallowed one, I wanted to pull the pill out of her throat. To tell her she wasn't crazy. To tell her the truth. But that wasn't an option. I was breaking enough rules just being here.

"Please don't be mad at me," Rachel pleaded.

Emma's brows scrunched together and she chewed on her bottom lip. She looked so much like Allison when she was mad it made me ache.

"You know what happened last time you got off your meds. Please don't put either of us through that again."

Emma sighed. "I took it, didn't I?"

Rachel nodded and stared down into her coffee cup. "Right. Sorry."

Emma gathered up the bag of scones in her arms. "Have fun on your date."

She darted out the door before her mom had time to say anything else, and headed across the green stretch of lawn between her house and Cash's studio, a little steel building next to his much-larger house. A steady stream of some kind of rock music that made my eyes twitch and my head hurt vibrated the metal walls. The door was propped open, and paint fumes drifted out into the open air. She shook her head and set the small paper sack of the pumpkin scones inside, then left without a word. He didn't notice her. He usually didn't when he was practically making love to one of canvases with a paintbrush.

"This…" Easton appeared beside me cocooned in a cloud of smoke. "This might be the most boring thing I've ever experienced."

I sighed.

"You seriously do this every day?" he asked. "Follow her around like this?"

"Yes." I climbed into Emma's worn-out Jeep Wrangler and settled into the tiny bench seat behind her.

He sank down beside me and grinned. "At least tell me you get to watch her shower?"

"I thought I asked you to stop following me around." Emma twisted the radio louder so I raised my voice. "Surely someone out there is in need of a lift to Hell."

"Nope." Easton propped his feet up on the empty passenger seat in front of him. "I'm on a break."

"Lucky me." I rolled my eyes. "How long are you going to do this?"

He shrugged and studied the gray felt ceiling. "I've been at it for two years, so yeah. As long as it takes for you to see reason."

"Great." I stared out the window at the cars passing by, the pine trees behind them melting into a bright green blur. A big truck with a Summerfield Peach Farm logo idled to a rumbling stop beside us at a traffic light, then surged forward again, taking part of me with it. I could almost feel the shuddering of the tractor beneath my thighs. Smell the bittersweet fragrance that a batch of ripe peaches lent to the breeze. When I closed my eyes, I could even see Pop. A crisp flannel shirt on Sunday morning. The white, crinkled laugh lines at the edges of his eyes. Proof that he did indeed smile. He always hated that the sun gave him away like that, like it made him look too soft.

"Hellooooo. Earth to Finn!" Easton snapped his fingers in front of my face.

I blinked away the memory then stuffed it back in its box, wondering how in the hell it had gotten out in the first place.

Easton nodded to the empty front seat, then to Emma trudging across the parking lot littered with kids. A light spattering of rain was dusting the windows, making it hard to see her as she disappeared like a needle in a haystack of high school students. "I don't want to worry you, but..." He hesitated. "I saw a redhead in the crowd with the kids. I know it's been a long time since I've seen Maeve—"

I hopped up and slid through the closed door, Easton right behind me. Cold metal sizzled through me, leaving a metallic-tasting tang on my tongue. As soon as the air hit me I felt it. Felt *her*.

No way in hell was I letting Maeve get past me again. Not after how close she'd gotten this morning.

"It might not have been her, Finn," Easton continued. "It was probably just a kid with red hair. What do I know?"

My skin prickled. My insides burned. "It's her."

A clap of thunder pulsed through the sky. Before the mirror incident this morning, it had been a couple of weeks since Maeve last came sniffing around Emma, but I never let my guard down. This was no exception. I pressed into the crush of students just as my scythe began to burn cold at my hip. The pull blasted through me like ice. I doubled over and clutched my side.

"Stop fighting it," Easton called out behind me. "I can watch her if you want."

"I can't," I gritted out, feeling bits and pieces of myself slip away like dust siphoned away by a gust of wind. I vaguely heard the school bell ring. Good. Even though it meant the shadows would get to the other soul before I would, I couldn't leave Emma now. I had to see her go inside before I took this reap.

I spotted Emma on the steps. Just a few more feet and she'd be through that door and safe. Well, safer than she'd be out here in the open. Maeve wouldn't risk messing with her in a room full of people.

But she wasn't taking those vital steps. The crowded courtyard had already mostly cleared. Emma stalled, one hand on the door, lost in conversation with another girl.

A giggle like glass echoed down from the rooftop.

Easton cursed.

High above where Emma stood, Maeve tiptoed along the gutter, balancing like a tightrope walker in a circus. She winked at me, then hopped on top of the giant metal bobcat sign that hung above the school entrance. I'm sure when they placed it there, they were thinking of team spirit and student morale. All I saw was a weapon with Maeve's finger on the trigger.

"Hey Finn!" Maeve hollered. Her bright red hair ruffled in the breeze, the sun glinting from the strands that had been blanched to a dull silver color. Her green cotton dress clung to her pale knees. Even from here, I could see the dark, hollow look settling into her eyes. The ashy color of her skin. The beginning of her transition into a shadow. "You think she'll go splat? I want to find out."

Maeve reached down and pulled at one of the cables. *Pop*. The big bobcat groaned as it tilted off-balance. Like a ballet dancer, she leaped and twirled, then reached down again. *Pop*. Souls only got stronger with age. And it seemed Maeve was intent on showing me just how strong she'd gotten.

"I've got to get Emma out of there."

Easton stilled. The grip that I hadn't even realized he had on my arm tightened. "And how exactly are you going to do that?"

The brunette girl talking to Emma waved and slipped through the glass doors. The last of the students vanished into the hallway.

A loud *snap* cracked through the air and my heart lurched. The big metal mascot banner tumbled loose from the brick wall and I ripped my arm from Easton's grasp.

Maeve wasn't just going to hurt Emma, she was going to *kill* her.

All I could see, think, or feel was Emma. Sprinting up the

steps, I sucked in a deep breath and filled my hollow lungs with air, forced the walls in my chest to hold it there. I willed my skin into existence without thought, only need. Emma looked up, horror registering on her face. I squeezed my eyes shut and barreled into her, knocking her over the railing, where we toppled onto a blanket of grass.

With a deafening crash, the sign behind us skidded across the concrete steps, splintering into sparks and blades. I lay there for a few seconds, stunned by the feel of Emma's solid warmth beneath me, the hectic swell of her lungs pumping against my chest. I was…touching her. Her sapphire-blue eyes stared back into mine. Our noses nearly touched. Her peppermint breath clung to my lips.

"You can see me," I said, breathless.

"Of course I can see you." Emma glanced over my shoulder, but she didn't make a move. "Your face is practically touching my face. It would be kind of hard *not* to see you."

I could barely answer. The impossibility of what was happening drowned me. Did she remember me? *God, please let her remember me.* I dug my fingers into the grass on either side of her face. "The sign…it fell."

"Yeah." Emma gulped and wriggled beneath me. "I can see that."

She didn't remember. I rolled off her, trying not to feel disappointed, just as Easton plowed through the bushes beside us like smoke. "Finn. I'm sorry man—" He looked back and forth between Emma and me and took a step back. "What did you do?"

I scrambled farther away from Emma and her warmth, shaking. "I…I…I didn't mean to."

"Do you think Balthazar is going to buy that?" Easton

snapped. "Because I sure as hell don't. Do you have any idea what this means for you?"

I staggered to my feet, refusing to break eye contact with Emma. Of course I knew. I just didn't care.

The school doors flung open. Students and faculty spilled out into the courtyard, their shouts echoing off the concrete building. Emma held my gaze for one last heart-stopping moment, then turned her attention to a teacher calling her name. Before she could look back, I let the air take hold of my skin until I faded into nothing.

"Emma!" A teacher with short gray curls stepped over a twisted hunk of metal that used to be the bobcat's snout. "Are you okay?"

"Yeah." She rubbed her knee and pushed herself up. "I wouldn't be if it—"

She looked back to where I'd been standing and her brows pulled together.

"You wouldn't be if what?" The teacher pushed up her glasses and looked right through where I was standing, invisible.

"Nothing." Emma touched her head, her face suddenly far too pale. "I think I hit my head or something."

The crowd swallowed her, taking her away from me. In the distance a fire engine's siren started to wail. Easton scowled and opened his mouth to rip me apart, but the words stayed stuck there. He grabbed his scythe. "He knows," he finally choked out.

I could already feel Balthazar's pull like fire eating its way through me cell by cell, overriding the call of the dead I'd ignored to save Emma.

Two strikes against me in a matter of a minute. I was so

screwed.

Easton gave in to the call, and without a word disappeared.

I held on a little longer and drifted toward the crowd. A fireman carrying a medic bag led Emma to a bench in the courtyard and checked her vital signs, while she warily looked into the crowd. She plucked a few blades of grass out of her hair and brushed her blue sweater off, her hands shaking.

I'd touched her.

She'd seen me. Talked to me.

But she hadn't remembered. I should have been thankful for that. If she ever remembered who I really was, what I'd done to her, to us… She'd hate me.

I braced my hands on my knees, unable to look away from her. My world was spinning. And it wasn't the hell I knew I was about to pay with Balthazar. It wasn't even the energy I'd spent touching her. It was knowing that everything had just changed. It was knowing there was no way I could go an eternity without that again. Balthazar's call turned to spikes in my skull, blocking my thoughts.

I would have given anything to have one more moment with her. To let her know I was there. That I'd always be there. But instead, I gave in to the wind. As usual, I belonged to death.

Chapter 9

Finn

The Inbetween. I couldn't make myself take another step closer. I'd spent too much time avoiding this place. Avoiding the memory of Allison and how badly I'd wanted her. Avoiding how that wanting had blinded me to the consequences of our relationship and doomed us both. Choosing to drop the souls off at the gates was easier than facing the memories that hid behind every shadow inside. Balthazar made sure I had plenty of reminders without this. But of course, that was my punishment. Every reap was connected to something I'd done, and I hated it. God only knew how much longer he was going to keep this up. After today…I had a feeling it wasn't ever going to end.

A gatekeeper in a gray hooded cloak raised a brow at me. "Are you coming in or not?"

I nodded and stepped through the gates, looking out over

the frozen horizon. Neither day nor night, light nor dark. Just a blanket of charcoal mist that I couldn't feel on my face, and a bouquet of stars butting against the glass floor beneath my feet. The swaying mass of silver wheat that always sat off in the distance tapered off into the rolling hills, where it was swallowed by shadows. There wasn't a single weeping willow, skyscraper, shipwreck, or double-decker bus, but their opaque shadows haunted the colorless terrain like ghosts of a land long forgotten.

Somewhere in the distance, the rush of waves washed over a shore that I'd never been able to find. Back when she'd only been Allison to me, Emma and I looked for hours once. Even after I'd been called away to a reap, Allison scoured the endless miles of nothing searching for the ghost of an ocean that didn't exist. I'd found her later lying on the glass floor staring up at a long, twisted shadow that rippled with far-away screams.

"I can't remember what this is," she whispered, sounding so small and lost. "I should know what it is, right?"

"It's a roller coaster," I told her, "or the shadow of one, anyway."

She just nodded, the quiet madness swirling in the depths of her ocean-blue eyes. "And I'm…"

I knelt down beside her and brushed the white-blond hair away from her neck. "You're Allison." I said. "You're my Allison."

I blinked away the memory when the throng of reapers gathering became too loud to ignore. A nervous energy bounced through the crowd like sparks—to be expected when the reapers from Heaven, the Inbetween, and Hell congregated in one place. I could feel those sparks in my chest, driving fear into my jittery limbs. We didn't get called in for a meeting like this too often, and it didn't take a genius to figure out this one was for me.

I stayed on the outskirts of the crowd, avoiding the stares and whispers that spread like a virus as I moved toward the gathering square. I wasn't just a reaper to them. To them I was the outcast who had broken an age-old rule and fallen in love with a charge, defied Balthazar in an unforgivable way, and gotten away with it. To them I'd spit in the face of God.

And now I'd done it again. They just didn't know it yet.

I searched for a safe, familiar face. Easton or Anaya, preferably, but at that point, I would have settled for Scout, a reaper who'd been recruited twenty years ago or so. Which meant he was still new. And stupid. His assigned territory bled into ours, so we crossed paths from time to time. He was the closest thing I had to a friend outside of Easton and Anaya, and while Scout might have been a lot of things, judgmental wasn't one of them.

Unable to locate the three of them, I was forced to face the reality of my situation. Balthazar was standing on the steps to the Great Hall, the only real building in the Inbetween, though none of us ever went in it. Shiny marble steps led up to the reflective structure, its walls like mirrors, so that it practically disappeared into the nothingness around it. Reapers milled around the dry stone fountain in the center of the meeting square, casting questioning glances my way. Balthazar pressed his lips together and narrowed his gaze on me.

That look said I was screwed.

"Ten minutes, people!" Balthazar's voice crashed through the crowd like a wave, echoing in myriad languages so there'd be no misunderstanding his message. "Get seated or I lose my patience. I don't think any of you want to find out what that's like."

Reapers scattered in a panic to find a place to sit. I shoved my hands in my pockets and hightailed it over to where I spotted Easton sitting down.

"Hey," I said, taking the seat beside him. He folded his arms across his chest and stared at the gold lectern at the top of the steps that awaited Balthazar's arrival. "You still pissed at me?"

"He warned you, Finn. He told you what would happen if you interfered in her life again."

"I told you, I didn't mean to," I whispered. "It…it just happened."

"You're an even bigger moron than I thought if you think he's going to buy that."

A dark gray fog rolled in, erecting walls of darkness around us, sealing us in. Not that we needed the reminder that we weren't allowed to mix with the souls. My little stunt with Allison had taken care of that.

I sank lower in my chair, hating that the reapers around us looked like they were about to witness an execution. Mine. "What do you want from me, Easton?"

His eyes, two violet slits, crushed me with their stare. "I want you to stop being too ignorant to worry about anything but that stupid human."

"Don't call her stupid."

"Fine," he hissed, leaning forward so that I couldn't escape the scent of brimstone and death wafting between us. "*You're* stupid. You're stupid and an asshole."

"What is your problem?" A few reapers with white jackets and eerily golden eyes raised their brows at us, so I lowered my voice. "This has nothing to do with you."

"Nothing to do with me? Who do you think he'll get to haul you off to Hell when he's done giving you second chances?"

I could only stare at him. Maybe it was because I was still a half-put-together puzzle without Emma. Maybe I was still high from touching her. Whatever the reason, I couldn't find the words to make any of this okay between us.

"You're my friend." His voice broke, something I'd never witnessed in over seventy years of reaping with Easton. "My *best* friend, you selfish bastard. And you're just going to…" He shook his head and pressed his lips together. "If you had any idea what Hell really was, we wouldn't be having this conversation."

I scrubbed my hands over my face, and looked through my fingers at Easton's black combat boots. I tried to imagine what he was telling me. The only Hell I'd ever known was living without Emma for fifteen years, not knowing what kind of life I'd sent her to. Was she happy? Was she safe? Was there someone who loved her as much as I did? I went so long without knowing. I finally spoke into the hollow of my palms, hoping Easton could hear me because I wasn't ready to look at him. "I'm sorry."

Easton shifted in his seat, leaned close enough to whisper. "Not as sorry as you'll be if you end up downstairs. You know your little fear of fire?"

I swallowed.

"They'll use it against you. You won't just burn. You'll melt. Slowly. And when you're nothing but a bubbling puddle of flesh and ash and blood, they'll reanimate you so they can do it all over again."

Easton's whispers burned me. I scooted an inch away from

him. From his heat.

He glanced down at the space between us and shook his head. "Do you even care what it would do to me to have to hand you over to them?" His bitter gaze held me hostage, searching for something. I wasn't sure what. "Of course you don't. All you'll ever care about is making sure your precious human is safe."

Easton stood up, knocking his chair over, but Scout caught it with the toe of his tennis shoe before it could hit the glass floor. "Are you two having another lovers' spat?"

He spun the chair around and sank into it backward, grinning up at Easton. For a moment, I thought Easton might grind Scout and his shiny blond curls into dust, but he just grumbled something under his breath and stormed off, leaving me suffocating in the rotting stench of death and decay he'd left in his wake.

"There's always so much more drama on your side of the border. Maybe I should ask for a transfer," Scout said as he winked at a pretty reaper from an East Coast territory. "But then, the east has its perks, too."

Scout looked the same as the day Easton had shown up to reap his soul. The same as the day he'd agreed to become one of us to buy his way out of Hell, forever frozen with the same tall athletic build, curly blond hair, and surfer boy tan skin that had gotten him girls when he was alive. And he was still using those looks to his advantage. Even in death.

We were all handpicked. Every one of us a soul that had crossed a moral line, just far enough to give Balthazar the leverage he needed to reel us in. I'd shot down at least three planes in my final hours. It may have been war, but to them, murder was murder.

I watched him undress the redheaded reaper with his eyes, trying not to feel annoyed. I'd known Scout for twenty years, and even in death he could only think about one thing. Though most of us weren't far off in age from Scout's nineteen years, when it came to girls, he seemed especially...enthusiastic. Balthazar told me once that younger souls were easier to transition. Better able to hold onto the power we were granted. I didn't know. I just knew there was something sad in seeing so many young faces representing the thing people feared the most. Death.

I turned my attention back to Scout, who had gotten the reaper girl's attention with a wide smile. "Do you ever think about anything else?"

"Sometimes. Just not today." He stood up and combed his fingers through his curls. "You mind if we talk about this later?"

I rolled my eyes and waved him off. "Just go."

I sank back, vaguely aware that Anaya had taken the seat on the other side of me.

"Hey, what happened to you?" She looked over at me. "I got dispatched to one of your reaps. Why didn't you take it?"

I watched Easton take a place alone on the far wall. Catching my eye, he dissolved into the shadow of a clock tower. "A complication."

She followed my gaze to where Easton stood. "What's his problem?"

"He says I'm a selfish bastard."

Anaya patted my hand and smiled. "Oh, Finn... Honey, that's because you are."

I couldn't help but laugh. At least the girl was honest. "Gee, thanks, Anaya."

"I didn't say that was a bad thing." She stared off into the distance. "That's what happens when you fall in love."

I searched for a scrap of sunlight in the heavy clouds overhead. "Have you ever been a selfish bastard?"

Anaya sighed and traced the toe of her sandal along the glass floor. Stars followed her, leaving wispy trails of blue-gold streaks across the dark black sky. Just when I didn't think she'd answer she said, "Yes. I loved someone once. I loved someone very much."

The trumpets sounded, preventing me from asking her more, and Balthazar took the lectern at the top of the stairs, overlooking the sea of chairs we sat in. His snow-white robe was snug over his broad shoulders. His blond hair brushed against his neck. Everything about him seemed youthful and new, except his eyes. The corners were creased with age and held too many years to fathom. Before he spoke, his eyes connected with mine, a look of disappointment clouding his gaze. It was so much like the look my pop used to give me that I ached inside.

He finally looked away, surveying the crowd. "It seems *some* of you don't remember the rules." He locked his fingers together behind his back, and all I could hear was the sound of ghostly waves washing up, receding, then starting all over again. No one even went through the motion of breathing.

"It's not difficult. There is no great secret to your afterlife. You collect the souls that pass for your assigned location." His silvery eyes flickered over me, then away. "When you are called to reap, you do not ignore that call, nor do you come back empty-handed."

The shocked whispers swirling around in the crowd grew louder and I shifted uncomfortably in my seat.

"You go *unseen* to the living. You do not *touch* the living.

You do not *associate* with the living." Balthazar slapped his palms down onto the gold lectern. The clap rippled through the mist. "Do I make myself clear?"

Anaya pinched my side. Like I needed her to drive home his point. I was breaking every rule imaginable. Everyone's time was being wasted because of me. I already knew this. And it didn't change anything. It didn't change the fact that Emma would be dead within a week if I did what they all wanted and walked away. But, okay. I could still do this. Balthazar didn't actually follow us around—I'd just have to be more careful about never going corporeal. I'd gone two years without touching her, after all. Today was impulse. Today was reckless. I couldn't let it happen again.

Anaya looked at me and rolled her eyes as if she could read my thoughts. I ignored her and hunched down farther in my seat.

"On a lighter note," Balthazar said. "I notice some of you are not keeping up with the current time period. I know to some of you who have been around for centuries, this may seem silly, but you are better able to transport your souls if they cooperate. They cooperate when they feel comfortable, and they feel comfortable with what they know. It only takes a second to envision a new look."

He frowned at a reaper wearing brown pantaloons, a white ruffled top, and a black hooded cloak. "Darius, you terrify even me. Do your homework." Smiling, he clapped his hands. "All right, everyone. Back to work. The dead won't collect themselves."

I looked at Anaya at the same time she looked at me. She wore a simple white sundress with a brown leather belt that carried her scythe. Gold gladiator sandals laced up her slender calves. They matched the gold band that wrapped around her biceps like a serpent.

"When was the last time you changed your style?" I asked.

She shrugged. "Doesn't matter. Some looks are timeless. Besides, I have an image of purity to uphold, Finn. We can't all run around looking like we just got off a shift at the Gap."

I looked down at my jeans, charcoal gray T-shirt, and canvas tennis shoes. I didn't need a mirror to know my hair was the same as the day I bit the dust: buzzed short around the back and sides, military style. The top had grown out on the trip overseas so that it curled just enough to remind me of the way I used to keep it as a kid. I ran my fingers through my hair and thought about it. "What's the Gap?"

Anaya stilled, a nervous smile on her face that she directed over my shoulder. I didn't have to turn around to know who it was.

"Anaya, lovely as always," Balthazar said. "Be a dear and give me a moment alone with Finn."

Anaya gave me a tight, worried smile then scurried away. She didn't make it far. A burst of white light consumed her with a gasp. The breeze around my ankles turned to fog, moved by Balthazar's force. The air crackled and hummed with a dangerous energy. In a flash, the other reapers were pulled away by the hungry fingers of death. I would've given anything for that hand to grab me in that moment.

Balthazar had Easton by the back of the neck and shoved him into the seat beside me. Easton's jaw clenched.

"Is there something either of you would like to tell me?"

I tried to catch Easton's gaze but he looked away. "No," I finally said.

Balthazar snapped his fingers and pain sizzled through

my insides. I groaned, gripping the sides of my chair. Easton grunted and lifted his chin.

"Did you touch her?" He glared at me. "I'm not an idiot, Finn. I felt you go corporeal, and I know you've been following her."

I chewed on the lifeless flesh on the inside of my cheek. Damn it…how much did he already know? When I didn't answer, Balthazar cursed under his breath.

"Has seventeen years of punishment not been enough to make you see reason?" he asked. "I give you reminders daily. What else do I have to do?"

"It was an accident."

The electricity drained from my limbs and I sagged into my seat. Balthazar turned away, pinching the bridge of his nose.

"Make me understand," he said. "Make me understand, because if you can't, then I am going to have to punish you. Do you understand what that will mean?"

I could've lied, but he would have found out. It was better to tell the truth this time. Balthazar made an impatient sound in the back of his throat.

"She'll die if I leave her alone," I said. "Maeve knows how I feel about her. She'll just keep torturing Emma until, one of these days, the 'accidents' she causes kills her. I can't let that happen. I don't see how *you* can let that happen."

"The problem with Maeve is no one's fault but your own. You know I have no jurisdiction over lost souls or those bound for the Shadow Land. You sealed Emma's fate the moment you pushed Allison through that porthole."

My body shuddered with the memory.

I slipped my fingers around Allison's trembling shoulders. Everyone was distracted. Even Balthazar had turned his attention to the last soul in line. It would have to be now. My chest screamed and ached with what I was about to do.

"Please forgive me for this, pretty girl."

I looked up at him, hopeless. "So I should just watch it happen?"

Balthazar's bottomless eyes looked me over. "I don't expect you to watch it happen. I can give you a transfer. But that's all I can offer you."

I closed my eyes and scrubbed my palms over my face. "No. I can stay away from her."

"Can you?" He raised a brow.

I pulled my hands away and stared at the ground. No. But I could be more careful. "Yes. Just don't send me away."

Balthazar studied me from a long moment. "She is not the girl from the Inbetween anymore. The girl you snuck into the shadows with. The girl you were willing to spite me and all of the Inbetween to save." He looked at me until I was forced to meet his gaze. "She's not Allison anymore."

"I know." I had to force the words out.

"I'm only going to say this once." Balthazar turned his eyes to a shadow in the distance that twisted and moved like a living thing. It looked like a willow tree caught up in a storm, but there was no way to tell. "There will be order among my flock. If you decide to disrupt that order again there will be consequences. I'm sure Easton could give you a glimpse of what those might be if I'm not being clear here."

Easton's shoulders tensed under his coat.

Balthazar leaned down until his icy whisper found my ear. "Do you need a glimpse, Finn?"

I shook my head. "You're clear."

Balthazar clamped his big palm onto my shoulder,

squeezing until I turned to smoke that drifted between his fingers. "Good. Next time there won't be a warning. Next time we'll be having this conversation in Hell."

My lungs lay dead and still in my chest as I watched him walk away. His threats wound around me like barbed wire, poking and prodding me, making me terrified to move. I looked at Easton. It wasn't fair that I'd dragged him into this. I understood that. It didn't mean I knew what to say.

He leaned up and gripped the metal chair in front of him, staring at the space between his arms rather than at me. "Are you going to stop now?"

I opened my mouth wanting to tell him *yes*, but the words wouldn't come. It wasn't that simple. Not with Emma. "She saved me when I didn't think there was anything in me worth saving. I can't just stand by and watch her crumble. She's broken, Easton."

Easton glared at me. "She's broken because of *you*. You broke her when you played with fate and sent her here. You broke her when you should have left her alone two years ago. She could've died and gone to Heaven if you hadn't gotten her out of that car."

I closed my eyes and ground my teeth together until pain bloomed like sunlight. He was right. And I didn't want to hear how right he was. I'd ruined everything for her because I was selfish. Because I couldn't stand the thought of an eternity without her. Because I didn't want her to move on when I couldn't go with her. Even if I did have the chance to know her again, she would never forgive me for what I'd done.

I felt sick.

"And you're going to keep breaking her until there is nothing left to break if you don't figure out a way to let her go."

I looked away. She made me feel alive again. She made me feel things that should have stayed buried with my body at the bottom of the ocean. God…I'd been dead for so long, I didn't know how to give that up. "What if I can't?"

Easton grunted and clutched his scythe, which glowed red between his fingers. Just before he let himself be pulled away by the call of the damned, he whispered, "Then I think you better get used to the idea of Hell."

Chapter 5

Emma

I shut my blinds and let my eyes adjust to the dimness of my room, then flipped on my camera. I felt so unfocused. Rattled even. And by a stupid boy, no less. One I could have sworn I'd seen before, but when I tried to pin down the memory in my head, it floated just out of my grasp like a dream. The way he looked at me, though… It was like he knew me. Like he wanted to consume me. And the way that look sent shivers down my spine made me want to let him.

I shook my head to discard the cute guy's face from my mind and focused on the digital camera in my hands. It didn't matter how he looked at me. Once he found out I was the crazy chick who had spent half of junior year in a mental institution, he wouldn't look at me like that again. And even if he did…it didn't matter. It didn't change anything. I was stupid for even thinking about it.

My phone buzzed beside me and I jumped, dropping the camera on the bed. I stared at the screen, not wanting to answer it, but sighed and picked it up anyway.

"Hey, Mom." I put it on speaker and set the cell phone in my lap.

"I just got off the phone with your principal. Are you okay?" She sounded frantic. "You should have waited for me to pick you up."

"You're thirty minutes away. Besides, I'm fine," I said. "I'm not even hurt. Promise."

She sighed and the sound of two car doors slamming shut sounded in the background.

"I'm coming home," she said. "I can have someone else cover the open house."

"Why?" I picked up my camera and turned it over in my hands. "So you can watch me do my homework? I can do that without you here."

She sighed. "You're *sure* you're okay?"

"Yes!"

"Okay…I'll be home right after the open house then. Don't leave the house until I get home. Got it?"

"Yes. Got it."

"Love you."

I told her I loved her, too, then leaned back against my pillows and clicked through the pictures I'd taken at last week's pep rally until the images blurred together. The boy's green eyes stayed superimposed on the backs of my lids, offering a glimpse each time I had to blink.

My bedroom window slid open and a gust of cool air swirled into the room. Cash. He must have heard already. Crap.

"What are you doing here? Don't you have calculus this

hour?" I asked, refocusing on the camera.

He ignored my question and turned on the lamp by my bed. "Are you okay?"

I closed my eyes. "How did you find out?"

"Are you kidding? I got three texts before I even got to school. Not to mention the mess they're still dealing with out front."

I considered watering down the truth. If I told him everything, he was just going to worry. But if I didn't tell him, he would just find out from the gossip queens at school, and then he'd be pissed. He was a pain in the ass when he was pissed.

I let my head thump against the bed frame and stared at the ceiling. "The sign fell while I was standing under it. Somebody knocked me out of the way before it landed. End of story. It's not a big deal."

He leaned on my desk, his brows pulled together. "Don't tell me it's not a big deal. You could have died."

Like I needed him to remind me. We both knew this wasn't the first time I'd had a close call like this. And whether he wanted to admit or not, we both knew it wouldn't be the last. Thinking about all of the times I'd only been a second ahead or behind being the victim of a major "accident" made me want to swathe myself in Bubble Wrap and never leave my room. "I'm fine."

Cash folded his arms across his chest. I could hear the worry in his quiet sigh, could feel his eyes on me, looking for scratches, bruises, anything that might drive me over the edge. "Do you need to go to the hospital? Just to make sure—"

"The paramedics already checked me out at school. I have a scratch on my knee, that's it." I looked over at him. "How did you get out?"

"You act like it requires blueprints and some big escape plan to get out of that place." He sat a little paper sack and a foam coffee cup on the table. "I just left."

"You're going to get detention again," I said. "And your dad is going to flip out."

He shrugged. "That's okay. You can make it up to me. We can order pizza for lunch and watch really bad daytime television."

I slumped farther into the bed, wanting to do just that. Hide in my hole and refuse to face the rest of the world. But I couldn't. Not when Mom was forcing me to take this stupid yearbook class.

You're not involved in anything, Emma. You need a dose of normal. How about more school activities?

"You know I can't," I said. "If I don't get the senior pictures for yearbook ready by Mr. Hall's deadline, he's going to fail me. Missing today is already going to screw me. I'm going to have to work on it from home."

Cash frowned. "You wouldn't even be worrying about this if it wasn't for your mom. It's total bullshit for her to make you take yearbook our senior year. You're not supposed to be taking pictures of the memories—you're supposed to be making them with us."

"I know." I sighed, then turned back to my camera, hoping he'd drop the drama. I clicked through a picture of our mascot doing a cartwheel. The cheerleaders spurring on the crowd that sat in shiny silver bleachers. Two football players in blue and white face paint. Half of them were ruined, marked up by a random white spot that kept appearing on the prints. "Have you met the new guy yet?"

I wished I could stop thinking about him. Yeah, he'd saved my life, but did that require that every thought be devoted to the guy? Couldn't I just bake him a pie or something? I blinked and there he was again. Green eyes wide, amazed and nervous all at the same time. Something in my chest fluttered.

You'd be dead if it weren't for him.

Part of me couldn't help but think it would be *over* if it weren't for him. I didn't know whether to be angry or grateful.

"What new guy?" Cash asked.

"The one I sort of met in the quad today," I said. "He saved me from being squished."

"You mean the *someone* who knocked you out of the way?" He looked like he was fighting a smile. "So he's a guy?"

"Yeah, I think he must be new. I've never seen him before." I think.

"I don't think I've met him. What did he look like?"

I shrugged, feeling my face flush. "I don't know." I bit my lip, stalling. "About your height. Kind of short brown hair, green eyes…" I averted my eyes. "Cute."

"Do you like him?" Cash finally broke into a full-on grin. "Of course you do! He saved you. Chicks love that crap. Does this mean you're actually going to go on a real date now?"

"Can we talk about something else? Please?"

"You're no fun."

I laughed. "If I'm not fun, why do you keep coming back?"

"I ask myself that every day." I punched him in the arm and he chuckled. "Hey, you're coming to the senior bonfire thing tonight, right? Maybe your new *boyfriend* will be there."

"No way. I'm not going to that." I frowned. "And he's not my boyfriend."

Cash groaned and fiddled with the beaded hemp bracelet

I'd made him while he was at summer camp, like, four years ago. I couldn't fathom why he still wore the stupid thing. The guys at school gave him hell for it.

"You have to. You're the yearbook photographer. You owe it to your fellow seniors to document these memories," he said.

"I seriously doubt they want me documenting their booze binges and beer-goggle hookups."

"You can Photoshop the beer bottles out. And as for the embarrassing hookups…you wouldn't deny me that kind of entertainment, would you?" He grinned. "Think of all the blackmail opportunities."

"I have a better idea." I held out my camera. "Why don't you take this and document all the debauchery you want."

"Me? I don't know how to work that thing." He nudged my camera away. "I create art with my hands, not machinery."

I sighed and let the camera fall into my lap. "You should probably go to school. I'm not going to be a lot of fun today. I've got to figure out a way to fix these stupid pictures."

He picked up my camera and turned it over in his hands. "What's wrong with them?"

"They're ruined." I moved over so he could sit next to me on the bed. "Well, some of them anyway. I think my camera is busted."

"What's wrong with them?" His eyebrows drew together as he studied the pictures. "The spots?"

"Yeah. There." I pointed to the unusually large ball of translucent white light at the corner of the screen. I grabbed the stack of pictures I'd printed last week and picked out the few that had the spot. "These, too."

Cash held a photo up to the light. "You know what these look like, don't you?"

"No. Enlighten me."

"Orbs," he said. "My aunt is really into this stuff. She went on a haunted tour at an old abandoned tuberculosis hospital in Kentucky last year. Got all kinds of pictures like these."

I snatched one of the pictures and studied the spot. "What are they supposed to be?"

"I don't know." He tossed the picture back onto my bed and laced his fingers behind his head. "Ghosts, I guess."

I swallowed the odd sensation in my throat. My stomach fluttered.

Dad.

Could it be him? If it wasn't him…no, it had to be him. I didn't want to think about what else it could be.

I gave my head a little shake and stomped out the feeling of hope. I couldn't start thinking like that. I wanted to look at this as some kind of proof. But I couldn't. Thinking like that would just land me back in Brookhaven Psychiatric Hospital listening to the real crazy people scream themselves to sleep at night. I closed my eyes against the shiver rolling down my spine and when I opened them again, I did my best to seem indifferent.

"I haven't exactly been to any haunted hospitals lately," I said. "These were taken all over the place. School, my house, by the lake even. Explain it now, Professor Paranormal."

Cash leaned forward and gave me a crooked smile. "Maybe it's not the places that have a ghost attached to them. Maybe it's you."

Maybe it's me… Uneasiness and excitement bubbled in my stomach. I jumped off the bed and headed for the hall. "Hang on a minute. I'll be right back."

If it was me, there would be more orbs. There would have

to be. I dug through the top of Mom's closet and pulled down the big photo box that said "Emma" in purple scrapbook letters. She used to always put every photo in a scrapbook, but since Dad died, she hadn't kept up. Most of the pictures didn't even make it into an album now.

I dropped the box on my bed and dumped the pictures into a four-by-six-glossy pile of Emma. Cash picked up a few and laughed.

"Holy shit, I completely forgot how nerdy we used to be." He flashed a picture at me. "Dude, check out your sunglasses in this one."

I grabbed the picture and looked at it. Nerdy sunglasses, check. Orb, no. I threw it back in the box and pulled out a few more. All from before Dad died, none with orbs.

"What are we doing?" Cash asked.

"Looking for…" I switched to a more recent pile and stopped. I'd found one.

A glowing white orb hovered over my shoulder in a picture of me at last year's neighborhood block party. I handed it to Cash and found another. And another. I sat down, trying not to hyperventilate. Goose bumps rose across my skin as I stared at all the orbs that lay across my bed at that moment. What were they? *Who* were they?

Something inside me told me I should know.

"They're in, like, half of them," I whispered. "But there aren't any in the pictures from before."

"What?"

"Orbs." I tossed a few more pictures into his lap. "Look at them."

Cash stared at the pictures in his lap. "So, you think all of these are ghosts? You think you're being haunted by a poltergeist or something?"

I allowed myself to think the thoughts I'd kept locked up tight for the past two years. Like someone wanted me dead. Like someone else wanted me alive. Sometimes everything went cold, like ice under my skin. Other times a sensation so warm and safe swept over me that I could hardly believe it was real. It was when I felt both, like today at the school, that everything seemed to go wrong. In those moments, I almost believed I was crazy. It felt like there was this invisible battle being fought around me and I was continuously caught in the crosshairs.

And it had all started the day my father died.

"I don't know what I believe," I said. It had only taken my saying how I felt once for them to lock me up and double my therapy sessions. I wasn't stupid enough to say it again.

"Hey," Cash leaned over and rested his elbow on my knee. "It's just the camera, okay? Your camera is busted. That's it."

"Then explain the other pictures. The ones Mom took. And there aren't any in the pictures before my dad died. None."

"Fine. It's not the camera. But Em…you can't do this. Not again. If you start talking like this again, they're going to put you back in Brookhaven. So, I'm asking you to drop it. Please."

It wasn't in my head. I had to prove that to him. I bit my lip. "Or I could get a Ouija board?"

When he didn't say anything I peeked at him.

"Emma…" He pinched the bridge of his nose.

"What if there *is* some sprit following me around?" I sat up on my knees and tugged his hand away from his face so he'd have to look at me. "If there is, they'd probably talk to us, right?"

"A *spirit*. Seriously?" Cash shook his head. "Maybe we

should wait until I'm drunk to have this conversation."

My throat ached, but I had to get the words out. "What if it's Dad?"

He grabbed my hand and folded it between his warm fingers. I could smell Red Hots on his breath and the leftover paint on his hands. The only sound was the rattle and swish of the washing machine on the other side of the house.

"It's not your dad," he whispered.

I blinked back a tear. "How do you know?"

"Because your dad was a good guy." Cash squeezed my hand. "He was too good not to go to Heaven. If there's a God, and I know you believe there is, he wouldn't let your dad wander around down here all alone."

"Then what if it's something else? Someone else?" My voice trembled like glass ready to shatter. "What if it's whatever has been trying to hurt me the past two years?"

"Those were accidents," Cash said gently. "When you got home from Brookhaven, you said you understood that."

I'd said whatever they wanted me to say to get out of that place.

Cash let go of my hand and folded his hands in his lap. He had that worried look on his face. It was the same look he had when he visited me at Brookhaven. When I told him about the memories that didn't belong to me. When I told him I knew I was going to die. God, I hated the way he was looking at me.

"I'm not crazy," I whispered. "I just want to try it."

He sighed and his shoulders slumped. "I know you're not crazy, but I don't want you to give your mom any more ammunition. I can't lose you like that again."

I nodded, but the emotions crawling around inside me made me want to scream. Cash was my person. He was supposed to be the one who believed me when the rest of the world thought I was nuts. But maybe I was. Maybe he was right to say the words that came next. The words I didn't want to hear. The words he didn't want to have to say.

"Did you take your pill today?"

I picked up my remote and turned on the TV so I'd have somewhere else to look. So that there would be something but this god-awful silence between us and the resentment brewing in my gut.

"Stop it." Cash grabbed the remote from me and pointed it over his shoulder to turn it off.

"Stop what?" I grabbed my pillow and tucked it against my chest so he wouldn't see me shaking. "It was a stupid idea. We're done talking about it."

His dark eyes burned into me. "Don't do this." He stared down at me, jaw clenched. "Don't shut me out."

"You don't want to hear what I have to say," I said.

"It's not that! I just—"

"You just what?"

Cash stopped and looked at me like he knew he wasn't going to get anywhere. He was right. He shook his head and slipped off the bed the way I wanted to slip out of my skin. He was going to be able to walk out my door and leave all this behind. But I couldn't. Not when it was my life. Not when it was going to be my death.

"It's happening all over again, isn't it?"

I felt like I was being analyzed under a microscope. Diagnosed all over again. I wanted to scream at him to stop looking at me like that. I squeezed the pillow tighter. "I'm fine. Just go home. Please."

Cash sighed. "If you're so fine, come with me to the

bonfire."

"You don't need me there."

"I *do* need you there." He hesitated for a moment, then kicked the side of my bed and stuffed his hands into his pockets. "Who else will talk me out of making a complete ass of myself?"

This. *This* was why I loved Cash. Why he was the one stable thing in my life while the rest of the world spun out of control around me. He always knew what to say to ease the pressure, make me smile, make me forget why we were fighting in the first place.

"You'll do that whether I'm there or not, and we both know it."

Cash smiled, but I could tell he wasn't ready to let the rest go. He was waiting for me to snap again. I wanted to be mad at him for it, but if I was being honest, I was waiting for it, too.

"Besides," I said. "You'll ditch me as soon as you find somebody to take home."

"I won't." He balanced an empty Dixie cup from my nightstand on top of my head like a little red top hat. "I'd never leave you alone. Promise."

"You don't have to babysit me. I'm not going to do something stupid."

He knelt down in front of me. "I don't want to babysit you. I want you to come have fun with me and forget about all of this crap for a little while."

I slapped the cup off of my head. "Fine. I'll meet you there."

"Why don't you just ride with me?"

He knew I'd bail if I didn't go with him. Any other day, I wouldn't have been caught dead at one of these stupid bonfires.

Especially after what happened today. God, I really wanted to bail, but the look on his face made my chest feel tight. I couldn't let him think I was shutting him out. Besides, I was still about a gazillion pictures short for the yearbook.

He lingered in front of my window, waiting.

I pulled at a thread on my shirt, already feeling the fear wind like vines around my throat, and said, "Pick me up at seven."

Chapter 6

Finn

I missed the feel of rain. It poured from the gray October sky in buckets, in such a hurry to get to the ground that it rushed right through me. If I were alive, I'd be drenched. Instead, I stood frustratingly dry, staring at the soft light coming from Emma's window as the dimming sky turned everything around me into shadows.

When I was alone like this, it was too easy for my mind to wander into territory that made what was in front of me that much harder to deal with. I closed my eyes and gave in, letting images of Allison swirl around in my head. It was useless to try to stop the memories of her. They always won, no matter how hard I tried to block them out.

Allison leaned her head against my shoulder. "I wish I could have known you while we were both alive."

"Oh yeah?"

"Yeah. Mama and Daddy would have loved you." She laced her fingers through mine. *"Daddy never liked my other boyfriends."*

I laughed and pressed a kiss into her hair. "I don't want to hear about your other boyfriends."

"Jealous?" I could hear the smile behind her words.

I pulled her into my lap and tucked her hair behind her ear. Our skin turned to sparks when it touched. I brushed my lips against hers and said, "Very."

Allison kissed me back, then pulled away, her breath cool against my face. "Don't ever leave me, Finn." When I didn't respond she frowned. "Say it. Say you won't ever leave."

"I won't ever leave you."

My chest ached with the memory and I cursed myself for letting it out. It only made being this close to Emma harder. I wanted to touch her like that again. I wanted to keep my promise. I wanted—

"Why are you standing out here in the rain?"

I didn't turn around. Out of the corner of my eye, I could see Maeve's brilliant red hair flowing like a halo around her head. Instead, I stared at Emma's window, waiting for the right moment to go back in.

"She's changing." I folded my arms across my chest. After seventeen years of Maeve taunting and harassing me, and me not being able to do anything about it, I was exhausted. I was in no way, shape, or form in the mood for this.

"And?"

"And I'm giving her some privacy. I doubt she'd want me to see her without her clothes on. Some girls are funny that way."

Maeve laughed, maybe to be cruel, maybe just to make

fun of the idiot standing in the rain. Hell, maybe she just truly thought it was funny. Either way I couldn't stand the sound of it. "What do you want from me?"

"Who said I want anything from you?" She tiptoed around me, lithe as a ballet dancer, fingers laced behind her back. I couldn't help but notice the inky black veins inching their way up her pale neck, and the streak of gray weaving its way through her red hair. The darkness was eating her from the inside out.

"So you're just here to torture me some more then?"

"I'm waiting you out." Maeve stared though glittery hazel eyes at Emma's window with an unsettling amount of hate and want. "I figure you'll get called out eventually."

"Don't count on it."

Maeve stood in front of me to get my attention and placed a hand on her hip. "Hey, shouldn't you be writhing in pain somewhere right now?" She smiled. "Did you think Balthazar wouldn't see your little stunt today at the school? That was clever going corporeal like that to save her. Clever, but stupid."

"I wouldn't have had to it if it weren't for you."

"Why not do it again?" she asked. "Go on. Go talk to her. Make her fall in *love* with you all over again. Think of how happy you could be!"

"Maeve…"

"To hell with that, think of how happy *I'll* be when Balthazar turns you to dust for it." She laughed. "Or even better, how much she'll despise you when she finds out what you did."

I would have given anything in that moment to have the ability to annihilate a lost soul. To haul her off to Hell myself. But I didn't. Unless it was a soul exiting a body, it was out of

Balthazar's jurisdiction, which meant I couldn't do a damn thing about Maeve. To Balthazar, one lost soul wasn't a good enough reason to bring down the Almighty's wrath. All I could do was watch her try and try again, and hope to God I—or Easton and Anaya, if I was desperate—got there in time to stop her. And she knew it.

The porch light flickered on, signaling the approaching darkness. I closed my eyes and remembered the look in Emma's wide eyes as she stared back at me, seeing me for the first time in two years. The rush of heat, that hopeful desire inside me bursting into flames as I realized the impossible was possible.

Behind us, laughter bounced through Cash's little studio, and the walls pulsed with music, drowning out the ping of raindrops on the metal roof. He had a girl in there. He usually did.

Maeve stared at the building. "Don't you miss it? Being alive? Having a body?"

"Go away."

Maeve paused, examining me like a lion about to devour its prey. After all these years, she was still painfully good at finding my weaknesses. "I do. I miss being touched." She grinned. "I miss boys."

My fingers moved down to my waist. My wrist brushed the scythe there.

"Have you seen the kid next door?"

I didn't answer.

Maeve touched her lips and sighed. "I'll bet he's a good kisser. But I'm sure Emma knows all about that, right? Can you imagine it? His mouth on her lips?" She giggled. "If she hasn't gone there yet, I'd bet money she thinks about it. Hell, she probably *dreams* about it. I know I would."

"Please leave," I said, exhausted. "I can't do this right now."

"I'll tell you what. I'll make you a deal."

"I don't make deals with…" I gave her a sidelong glance. "With whatever it is you are now."

"Don't give me that crap, Finn. You and I are the same, and you know it."

"No. We're not. I came here to protect her; you came here to hurt her. Trust me—we're not even in the vicinity of being the same."

That seemed to strike a chord. I could feel the heat of her anger scorching me. "It was my turn! That body…" She pointed a shaky finger toward the house. "That *life* belonged to me. And you stole it! *She* stole it!"

"She didn't do anything. I did. You want to hurt someone?" I turned to face her. "Hurt me."

She smoothed out her hair, a ripple of flaming silk under her milk-white fingers. "I intend to. But since you can't feel physical pain, emotional will have to do."

She smiled, but it wasn't pleasant. It was like a snake shedding its skin. Her brows furrowed, the dark wheels in her head grinding into motion, and then she darted away so quickly she faded into a blur of green and red. Everything seemed to move in slow motion. Maeve's pale hand reaching out, ready to dissolve through burgundy brick. Emma's slender silhouette behind the window. Everything went red. Common sense fled my mind. I didn't even realize I'd moved until I looked down and Maeve's wide eyes were staring up at me. The only thing separating the blade of my scythe and her pale neck was a thread of fresh air.

She giggled like I'd told a joke. "It won't do anything to me and you know it."

I cocked my head to the side. "Well, we could always try it and see what happens." I moved the blade at her collarbone. Raindrops fell through us both, undeterred.

"Go ahead." Maeve smiled and inched her neck up closer. "It's embarrassing, isn't it? All those empty threats. You really are hilarious, Finn." She pushed off the wall and swirled through me like vapor.

I holstered my scythe. "You can't keep this up forever."

"Sure I can. I've got loads of time thanks to you."

It was a lie and she knew it. It's why she was so desperate to hurt Emma while she could. The darkness was ready to swallow her whole. She didn't have long before the shadows took her completely.

I ran my hands through my hair and gripped the back of my head. My fingers twitched, aching to grab my scythe again. "When are you going to get it? I won't let my guard down. Ever."

She stared at me for a long moment, no doubt seeing the anger harden my face from the inside out. "Tell you what, Romeo. You give up now and I won't make it painful for her. Then you two could float off into the sunset together. What do you think?"

What did I think? I didn't know what I thought anymore. I knew I'd do anything for her. I knew I'd give anything for this barrier between us to disappear so we could be together again. But giving into Maeve, giving up my position and letting Emma die, then whisking her away before another reaper could take her... It wasn't going to happen. What kind of afterlife would that be? Sure, we'd be together, but we'd also be lost. Wandering the earth, just waiting for the shadows to descend. I wouldn't do that to her. I wouldn't do that to us. "I think you're completely insane if you think I would help you kill my reason for existing."

"God, I don't get you! What's even more annoying is that I don't get her! She's wasting it away! She sits in that hole of a room with her stupid journal, or takes pictures of things she refuses to actually experience. Riveting stuff there." She stopped to roll her eyes. "I swear it's the saddest, most boring waste of life I've ever seen." She finished with a sigh, plopping down into the wet grass.

A spike of cold lashed at my hip. A call. Of course I'd get one now. I blinked up at the sky. What the hell was I supposed to do now? I couldn't leave like this. Not with Maeve a few feet away and a whole night of high school partying on the horizon. "What would you say to a truce? Just for the night."

She laughed. "Why in God's name would I do that?"

I spotted Cash jogging across the lawn, his jacket pulled up over his head to protect him from the rain, and the tightness in my chest eased. He stomped onto the lit-up porch and beat on Emma's door. At least she wouldn't be alone. Cold seared my insides and I knew I couldn't ignore the call any longer.

"You know what?" I smiled at her, and then watched Cash's disappear into the house. "I think she'll be fine. I'll see you later."

Maeve's face hardened into a cold expression. "Fine?" She glanced at the house and darkness pulsed beneath her pale skin. "Don't count on it."

I opened my mouth but the words didn't come. The cold inside was too much. Pulling. Clawing. I shut my eyes against the pain and when I opened them again, I was gone.

Chapter 7

Emma

I slid my camera strap over my head as I followed Cash up the winding hiking trail toward the party. The crackling hiss of a bonfire and the tawny glow that suffused the trees led the way. I glanced around at the melting shadows that dripped from the dying hemlocks and sturdy pines. Under the safe blanket of daylight, the mountains here were beautiful. But here in the dark, all I saw was a thousand ways to die.

I needed to get my head checked. Again. I wasn't the girl who went traipsing through the forest at night without a care in the world. I was the girl who barely escaped falling signs, loose power lines, and bottles of pesticide that just happen to fall into pots of stew. It made my head hurt and my pulse pound just thinking of all the near misses.

A soft rumble of thunder rolled across the sky on the other side of the mountain, blotting out the echoes of music and laughter from the party. I jumped and looked up at the dark smudge of clouds wandering over the moon.

"Are you sure this is safe?" I jogged to catch up. "If it rains, there could be mudslides, or flooding, or—"

Cash wrapped his arm around my shoulder and laughed. "Will you stop worrying? Nothing's going to happen. Besides, I checked the weather before I left the house. It's all headed west of here. We're good."

I nodded, still not feeling safe, and dug through my pocket for my tube of peppermint ChapStick. Cash led me into the clearing before I had a chance to finish sliding it across my lips, waved at somebody, and nudged me to do the same. I lifted my hand, not really sure who I was supposed to be greeting, but mostly surprised that they'd gotten the bonfire lit in the first place. Everything was still slick and shiny from the rain.

I tucked the ChapStick back into my pocket, brushed off the wet leaves sticking to my jeans, and glanced at Cash. He looked ethereal bathed in the glow of the bonfire. The few piercings he had reflected the flames, his skin bronzed like a fine caramel glaze. Royal-blue paint shimmered from his left cheek when it lifted with a smile. He laughed at something someone shouted at him and grabbed a beer bottle out of the dirty blue-and-white cooler.

"I guess that means I'm driving us home." I scanned the crowd for something to photograph that I could actually put in the yearbook. So far my material was pretty limited.

Cash popped the top. "Guess so."

"I thought you didn't wear those for anybody else." I pointed to his T-shirt that said, *F.B.I. (female body inspector)*.

He flashed me a lopsided grin. "Trust me. This shirt is absolutely for me."

I laughed, wondering if there could possibly be someone else like Cash out there. I doubted it. Cash was sarcasm and seduction wrapped up with a gooey artistic center. He didn't need a T-shirt to get any girl he wanted. All he had to do was look at them. The bad part was that he knew it.

"All right, you've got me here." I poked Cash in the chest. "Don't even think about ditching me."

"I told you I wouldn't. Now come on." Cash grabbed me by the elbow and steered me into a crowd. He took a swig of his beer and motioned to a couple making out near the tree line.

"There. Get a shot of that."

I snapped a photo. "Why?"

"Because when he finds out that she has an overprotective big brother who's an offensive lineman for Cal, it's going to be pretty friggin' hilarious," he said.

"Oh yeah?" I raised a brow as I checked the flash on my camera. "How do you know?"

Cash frowned and rubbed his jaw. "Don't ask."

I spent the next half hour snapping shots of people, begging them to at least pretend to be sober. Around shot twenty-two, I looked up and realized Cash was missing. I shouldn't have been surprised. This always happened. He'd come stumbling back eventually, smelling like strawberry lip gloss and beer, and apologize for ditching me. I sighed and went back to taking pictures. If I had to be there, I was going to load my camera up with enough images to get Mr. Hall off my back. Seventy-three shots later, I had practically nothing that would be suitable for school publication. At least Cash would have his blackmail.

I searched for Cash and came up empty. I finally grabbed Ronnie Simmons by the arm before he could whiz by toward the cooler.

"Hey! Emily, right?" he slurred.

I sighed. "It's Emma. Have you seen Cash?" I took one last look around the clearing. "I'm ready to leave and we rode together."

Ronnie chuckled and put his hand on my back. "Out here."

I let him guide me into the trees, refusing to let fear get the best of me. Other than the fact that he never remembered my name, Ronnie was a decent guy. I was more afraid of what Cash was doing out here in the woods. He could be so stupid when he was drunk.

Once the sounds of the party were just an echo behind us, Ronnie stopped and nodded behind us to a heavily twisted batch of trees that surrounded what looked like an old, well-used fire pit. "Good luck getting his attention."

I could barely make out the swaying shadow in the distance, so I pulled my camera up to my eye and zoomed in on where he was pointing. For the millionth time that night, I heard the words, "Get a shot of that!"

Cash and Tinley Rhineheart were a tangle of limbs and lips. He pressed her against the tree, only breaking away long enough to whisper something in her ear. She giggled and they were kissing again.

Without understanding why the stupid thing was even there, I swallowed the lump in my throat and snapped the picture. Part of me wondered if I'd ever get to a point in my life where I'd allow a guy to lead me off like that and kiss me until I couldn't breathe. The other part of me said it was ridiculous to want to give those breaths away when something out there was so intent on stealing them. I forced the thoughts out of my head. Who needed to live when you had a best friend who did enough of it for the both of you?

I turned around and headed the direction Ronnie had gone, feeling so out of place in the world around me that I couldn't catch my breath. I swiped the back of my hand across my cheek, finding warm wetness there, and scowled at the tears on the back of my wrist. *Stupid.* Why was I crying? I didn't want that life. I didn't. I couldn't.

"Ronnie?" I felt suffocated by the darkness around me. "Ronnie!"

He was gone. He'd left me in the dark alone. In the woods. Fear made my throat close up, but I swallowed through it. This didn't have to be a big deal. I just needed to get back on the trail we were on. I pulled my cell phone out to use the screen as a flashlight. Wait…were we even on a trail? Why hadn't I paid attention? God, this was going to suck.

I spun around, trying to ignore the panic in my chest. It was okay. I could find my way back. I could just follow the sounds of the party. We hadn't gone that far out. I heard the sound of water rushing through the dark. The bonfire had been set up next to a stream. I headed in the direction of voices and water, trying to fit the two sounds together to pinpoint one location. I was going to kill Cash for this. If he was just going to ditch me every time we came to one of these things why drag me along? It not like I wanted to—

Something cold swept over the back of my neck. I whirled around and stared into the thick, consuming dark. Whatever it was slithered over my skin again, and a twig snapped somewhere off in the dark distance.

"Is somebody out there? Cash?"

No one answered. A set of fingers brushed over the back of my shoulder and fear exploded in my chest. I spun around, eyes wide.

"Cash!" I held my camera so tight my knuckles turned white. "Ronnie! This isn't funny, you guys."

Someone tugged on my ponytail and I yelped. Cold exploded across my skin, under my skin, and everywhere inside. I tripped and caught myself on a tree trunk, scraping my palms. My pulse pounded so hard I could feel it in my neck. I couldn't seem to form a thought, let alone an escape.

Think, Emma! I balled my hands into fists and spun around, ready to scream.

I squeezed my eyes shut and held the sound in my throat. I couldn't scream. What would I say? Someone I couldn't see pulled my hair? I had a bad *feeling*? Every person at this party already thought I was crazy.

I couldn't go back to Brookhaven. I couldn't.

I opened my eyes, determined to find the party. Someone laughed in the distance, so I started forward. I was so close to the water I could smell it. I'd just follow the stream back. Yellow eyes glinted at me from the trees. Nighttime creatures hummed and slithered and chirped from places that only belonged to the murky palette of midnight. I'd almost convinced myself that no one had been there when something iridescent moved through the trees. It flickered like a flame for only a second before being snuffed out by the dark.

I took a step back, ready to bolt, but stopped. Something moved through the underbrush, along the trail. Footsteps. Something bigger than an animal. Footsteps with so much purpose they could only be human.

Oh, thank God. "Hey!" I called out, rushing toward the sound. "I'm kind of lost. Can you show me how to get back to the party?"

The footsteps stopped, but no one answered. The cold returned, crackling along my skin like frost, and I shivered. Something was about to happen. Oh my God it was already happening…

I took a second step back. A third. I didn't let myself blink. My heel felt the earth crumble beneath my shoe, and I stopped to glance over my shoulder. It was pitch black, a seemingly endless crevice. I could hear water trickling, rushing, splashing through the maze of riverbanks below. How far down was it? I didn't want to find out.

A wave of cool breath whispered across my face. My skin prickled. My eyes widened, staring at…nothing. No one. Yet that breath—

Something hard knocked me off-balance and I fell backward, off the edge. My hands flew out in front of me, grabbing for something, anything, and one closed around an exposed root three feet from the ledge. My back slammed into the mud wall behind me, and I swung like a pendulum above the water below while I tried to find something else to grab onto.

Rain sprinkled from the sky and spattered my face. So much for that storm moving west. The root I had a hold of was secured in the mud wall, but the rain was making it slick and my fingers were already starting to slip. One, two, three fingers came loose. My hand started to cramp. *No, no, no, no, no! Please no!* Not yet. Please not yet. Darkness started to swallow my vision. A fresh batch of panic tightened my chest.

"Emma!" A male voice that sounded familiar permeated the haze. "Hold on. I'll get something to pull you up."

Hold on. Right. Just… One of my hands slipped free of the root I was holding and my heart slammed into my ribs so hard

I lost my breath. I yelped and reached out, grabbing onto more half-exposed roots in the dirt wall to catch myself. Numb from shock, I pressed the side of my face into the mud wall. "I'm going to fall!"

"No, you're not," the male voice answered. "I won't let that happen. Here."

He swung a big branch over the side and I looked up at the shadow of a boy holding on to the other side. "Grab it."

I nodded and adjusted my hold to the branch. "Please don't break," I whispered.

"You're going to have to help me out a little."

He pulled on the branch, and at the same time, I jammed my feet into the mud wall to climb up. Once I was up over the edge, I spilled onto my hands and knees. My fingertips tingled. My brain felt numb from fear. I dug my nails into the soil and gasped for air.

"It's okay. Shh." Someone settled beside me and my insides buzzed with awareness. "She'll never hurt you again, I swear it. I don't care what I have to do," he whispered as if he were mainly talking to himself.

I wiped my face on my sleeve and looked up. It was the boy from the quad. He sat with his elbows resting on his knees, his head in his hands. Wait a minute—she? He'd said *she*. I scrambled onto my knees, eyes darting, suspecting every shadow.

"Is she gone?" I choked out. "Where is she?"

His green eyes connected with mine and ignited with an emotion I couldn't comprehend. He nodded and sat up, leaning a few inches closer to me. He held out his palm the way you would to a frightened animal. I wondered if that's what I looked like just then, eyes wide, flinching from his touch.

I knew that's how I felt. Like a deer that someone had just grazed with a bullet.

"She's gone," he said.

I wrapped my arms around my knees, rocking until my tailbone went numb and I couldn't feel the ground beneath me anymore. *I should be doing something right now. I should call the cops or something.* I thought about the last time I'd called for help. Paranoid schizophrenic. That's what they'd called me.

"Was she real?" I asked. "Someone was there, right?"

The boy leaned back, a wary look spreading out over his face as he scratched the back of his head. "Yeah."

I rubbed my scraped palms. I didn't understand. It had never happened like this before. All of the other times they had been accidents. Like the sign at school, or the woman whose steering wheel locked and she almost hit me on my bike. This was purposeful. This was someone trying to hurt me. Mystery guy held up my camera like an offering, then sat it in front of my feet.

"I think your strap broke when I was pulling you up," he said. "Sorry."

I stared at the cleanly sliced strap, at his long tan fingers tapping against his knee.

"How did you know I was here?" I finally asked. "Are you stalking me or something?"

He laughed. It was a nervous, broken harmony of sound that did funny things to my insides. He picked up a twig and scratched something into the dirt between his thighs. "Just good timing, I guess."

I wanted to laugh, but it wasn't there. I wasn't sure *what* was inside me. The only thing I could feel was that prickling cold crawling under my skin. I scratched my arms until they felt raw, wanting it out.

"Hey, are you okay?"

I looked up and for maybe the first time really saw the boy sitting across from me. He had a sad look on his face. Not the kind that showed how he was feeling at that second, but the kind that's branded there after seeing things that can never be unseen. His light-brown hair was cropped close around his scalp, the longer pieces on top stained gold from the sun. His jaw was strong, classic looking. He looked like he belonged somewhere else, a place where it was normal for boys to look like James Dean and rescue damsels in distress.

He looked like he belonged at this bonfire about as much as I did.

I nodded and closed my eyes, trying to puzzle out the weird fluttery sensation that invaded my stomach when I looked at him. "Thank you," I said. "I...I didn't say thank you before."

He looked at me for half a second, then back down to the dirt. His lips tipped up into a lopsided smile that looked incredibly underused. "Anytime, Emma."

"How do you know my name?" I hadn't told him at school. He hadn't given me the chance.

"It's...it's complicated."

"Can't be that complicated. It's actually a pretty simple question." I stood up, hoping my shaky legs would support me. My heart started a slow and steady pound. Someone had pushed me. And this guy was the only person around. It was too convenient. I didn't believe in convenient. I peered into the darkness, hearing only crickets. How far had I wandered from the party?

"Look, I have to go," I said.

He looked up at me with those kryptonite eyes, confused.

"Where are you—" He clutched his hip and his words choked off into a groan. His face paled.

"Hey are you okay?" I reached out and he jerked back from my touch.

"I'm…fine. Maybe…you should…find Cash…now."

I realized he was shimmering. Every second that passed, his face twisted with more pain and he grew a little more iridescent. I backed away, and for reasons I couldn't place right then, grabbed my camera and snapped a picture of him.

He glared at me in disbelief. "Wh-why did you do that?"

I shrugged, playing nonchalant when really I was terrified. "Why not? I need pictures for the yearbook."

He groaned again and for a split second, he flickered out of existence. "Emma…*go*."

Hands shaking, I lifted the camera up to look at the display. He wasn't there. I blinked, hoping the image would change, but it didn't. He…he wasn't there. Just an out-of-focus white cylinder of smoke where a cute boy with amazing green eyes should have been standing.

An orb.

"Please. I don't want you to see this." He gripped his knees.

I stared at him, everything blank within me, and realized I wasn't breathing. With a crash, the reality of what was happening fell down around me. I inhaled a deep, shuddering gasp of air and my knees nearly gave out. Something in me said to stay. Something in me said to run. And every inch of me wanted to touch him. To grab hold of him and not let him disappear again. He was my proof. If he disappeared, so did any hope I had of convincing myself I wasn't crazy.

"Go find Cash," he choked out. "Don't leave his side. Go home and don't stop until you get there. Do you hear me?"

I nodded dumbly, gripping my camera. A gust of wind rushed between us, and in one blinding flash, he was gone. There wasn't any denying it. He was…he was…

"Oh, God." I stumbled back, unable to breathe. Fear pulsed through my veins until everything went fuzzy. My head spun with so many thoughts, I couldn't keep track of them. But the one that stood out from the rest was his voice.

Go home and don't stop until you get there.

He sounded afraid. And if *he* was afraid, then something told me I should be, too.

I didn't think about it anymore. I turned around, refusing to think about the things that lurked in the shadows around me, and ran.

Chapter 8

Finn

My feet hit the sand and I stumbled. It was soft and grainy, a bright white under the moonlight and the stark black night. The pull was so strong, my head throbbed and my thoughts slammed together inside my skull.

It had been too close. I'd almost lost her. Maeve had… she'd *pushed* her. Sent her over the edge of a freaking ravine! The panic was still so fresh in my chest, it burned. I leaned over and gripped my knees until the world decided to stay in one place. If that soul I'd peeled off US 395 had asked one more question, I would have lost her.

She had seen me. Talked to me. She'd taken a freaking picture of me. I groaned, wanting to bury myself in the sand and burrow my way to China. If I'd thought it was actually possible to hide from Balthazar, I might have tried it.

Behind me, a girl screamed, the sound shrill and filled with terror. It was all I needed to hear to know I was in the right place. I stood up and made my way down the beach. White frothy waves washed up onto the sand, then receded back into the darkness. I made sure not to touch them, staying a few feet out of the water's reach to avoid it grabbing me and pulling me into a memory I didn't have the time or energy to relive right now. Not after what had just happened with Emma.

"He's not breathing!" In the darkness, the girl looked like a shadow beating on another shadow's chest. "Oh God, Brett. He's not breathing."

"Move!" The other kid shoved her out of the way and pressed his mouth against a boy's blue lips. There wasn't a breath in his chest except for the artificial one his friend was forcing in. He was already gone. Waiting for me. I cocked my head to the side and watched it all unfold. What was Balthazar up to this time?

"Come on, Justin," the boy gritted his teeth and wiped a tear from his cheek.

Damn it. I did *not* want to know his name. Names were personal. There was no room in my head for personal. The glow from the bonfire made it easier to make out their faces now that I was closer. The lifeless boy in the sand was still, his glassy blue eyes fixed on the starry sky. His skin looked like ash, an awful, final color against his vibrant orange swim trunks.

As bad as he looked, he probably looked a hell of a lot better than I must have looked after I'd died. At least this kid was still in one piece.

I shuddered and focused. The girl sobbed over his body, but the boy she called Brett kept shoving her away so he could pump on the lifeless chest that was beyond any kind of help he could offer. I couldn't watch this anymore.

With one swift motion, I gave him death, swinging the scythe over my head to bring down enough force to get a good hold on the soul. He was ready. I only had to pull once and he came stumbling out onto the wet sand, falling to his knees. A faint shimmer made his blond hair glisten and his blue eyes glow. Slowly, he turned his head to the side and watched his friend try to work the life back into him.

"Brett," his voice wasn't anything more than a cracked whisper. "Stop. Just…stop."

Sheathing my scythe, I stood next to him. "He can't hear you. You're dead." It seemed obvious, but some of them didn't get it. God…my job sucked.

He looked up and glared at me, a cold hate in his eyes. It was obvious that Justin wasn't one that needed reminding. "Yeah," he said. "I got that."

"He said he could swim." The girl shuddered, wrapping her arms around her knees. Her wet brown hair hung in ropes around her face. "I thought you guys said he could swim."

"I thought he could…" Brett's voice trailed off into a pained whisper as his palms stopped pumping and came to a rest against Justin's chest. "Try the cell again."

A phone call wasn't going to help this kid. I looked at him, then back to the girl, still trying to figure out the riddle Balthazar always wove in.

Her fingers trembled around a little glowing screen. "I still don't have any service."

Brett stood up and snatched the phone from the girl, wiping more tears onto his arm. "Then I'm going up to the car. We need to call for help." When she started to stand with him, he pinned her with a wet stare and shook his head. "Don't you dare think about leaving him."

She nodded and sank back into her imprint in the sand, tears making a mess of her pretty face.

"Could you swim?" I asked.

Justin stood up and started to brush the sand off his knees. His fingers passed right through and he stopped, shaking his head. "No," he said, softly. "Not very good anyway."

"Then why did you tell them you could?"

Justin didn't respond. Instead, he watched the girl with willowy arms, who was sobbing again. "Because when the girl you've been in love with since the fifth grade asks you to go for a midnight swim with her, where she's going to be wet, and in a bikini, you do it." He sank down into the sand beside her. "I…I never even told her how I felt about her."

And there it was, like a slap in face. One stupid mistake had cost him everything. Separated them forever before they even had a chance. One stupid mistake had cost *me* everything. Balthazar was never going to let me forget it. How many mistakes was I going to make before I got it right? By this point, I didn't know what was right anymore. What was wrong. If Balthazar was trying to make me doubt myself, it was working. I hated him for it.

"Point taken," I said to the sky, then looked back to Justin.

His pain was too familiar. I didn't like it. It was almost as if it were leaking out of him and crawling across the beach to find a way into me.

"Tell her now," I finally said. "You won't get another chance. So do it now."

I'd at least give the kid that. It wasn't much, but maybe it would give him some peace. Peace wasn't really in my job description, so I wasn't sure if I was doing him a favor or hurting him more.

He didn't look back at me. Just nodded and started to reach out to touch her but stopped, close enough for a breeze to hum between his fingertips and her hair. "I'm sorry, Brenna," he said. "I'm sorry I never told you I liked you when we were kids. I'm sorry I never told you I loved you when we were more than kids."

He buried his face in his hands, his shoulders tense, his back all shuddering bones and ashen skin. "I'm sorry I invited Brett to come tonight. That was stupid. If I hadn't invited him, maybe I would have been brave enough to kiss you. I wouldn't have been able to stop kissing you. I wouldn't have gone into the water. You wouldn't be sitting here looking at me like I'm something that's going to give you nightmares for the rest of your life."

I stared into the clear, warm night, listening to the words bleed from his lips. Trying to shake how uncomfortable they made me feel. I might have told Allison how I felt in our very last moment together, but it didn't do any good. Now she was another girl. Another girl who didn't remember me. She didn't know how I felt. She was never going to know.

Whether I liked it or not, Justin's words had started something inside me. The steady sting of longing burned its way through me like a fuse. Before I could stop it, the pain inside me exploded to life. I'd never get to tell Emma these things. And I wanted to. I didn't realize until this moment how badly I wanted to tell her I was sorry. Sorry for choosing this life for her when she could have had something so much better. She could've had what she always deserved—Heaven. Somewhere in the distance, sirens started to wail. Brenna cried harder until she gave in and lay across Justin's cold chest.

"Please don't be gone," she cried. "Not yet."

Justin made a choked sound and I closed my eyes as if I could block it all out. A few shadows slithered up from the rocks, drawn in by the scent of desperation and death. I reached out and wrapped my fingers around his arm to pull him up.

"Time to go."

His eyes turned into burning blue orbs. His hands shook in front of him. "Where?" He looked back at Brenna again. "Where are you taking me?"

God I hated this part. There was no explanation that would make him feel better. Not one that didn't include a lie. One by one, faces flashed behind my closed lids. Faces with black holes for eyes, and darkness flowing through their veins where blood used to be. Allison's face, dark and desperate, was the last one to appear. It lingered for an unbearable moment before I blinked it away.

That wouldn't happen to this kid. He'd move on. He'd be saved for something better. Once I swallowed the lie, I took him by the arm and stepped into the twilight that swirled in front of us. I needed to get this over with. This kid, his words, they started fires inside me I didn't know how to put out.

I was so damn tired of burning.

"Hey man," he said, panicked. "You didn't answer me. Where are we going? Heaven? Hell?"

I didn't know what to say. So I just said, "Somewhere in between."

Chapter 9

Emma

I barreled into my bedroom and pulled the plastic shopping bag out of my jacket. My hands wouldn't stop shaking. My head wouldn't stop spinning. He'd disappeared. Vanished like smoke swept away by a gust of wind. What did that mean? What the hell was he?

Besides a guy who had saved my life *twice* now.

This couldn't wait another minute. Whatever—whoever? —was doing this was going to ruin my life. I refused to let it.

I tore into the bag and slid the purple and black Ouija board box out onto my bed, then paused to smooth the blanket around it. Like it mattered. If anybody found out I was doing this, I'd have a whole new bed to worry about at Brookhaven, complete with a roommate on so many downers she looked asleep even when she awake.

My cell phone rang and I jumped. I squeezed my hand into

a fist to stop the shaking before I answered it.

"Where the hell did you go?" Cash slurred on the other line.

"I…I came home," I said. "I parked the Bronco in your driveway. Sorry I took off."

"I don't care about the Bronco. Are you okay?" he asked. A girl laughed in the background and he shushed her. "You don't sound okay."

"I'm fine." I tried not to look at the board in front of me. "I just don't feel good."

"I'm coming over." He pulled away sounding muffled. "Hey Tinley, I need to go home."

"No!" I gripped the phone tighter. "Don't. Mom's home, and she's still up. I'll just see you tomorrow."

He grunted something I couldn't hear, then finally said, "Fine. But call me tomorrow."

"Hey," I said before he could hang up. "Don't drive home, okay?"

Cash laughed. "Yes, Mother."

I pressed the end button and dropped the phone.

I could do this. I *had* to do this. Nervous energy coursed though me. Consuming me. I ripped the lid off the box and set the board on my bed. It didn't look like anything to be afraid of. It was just a board. I touched the letters and sat the pointer gingerly on top.

Chapter 10

Finn

I pressed my palms against the brick wall outside Emma's room and tried to muster up the courage to do what I'd decided to do back on the beach. If only a wall was all that separated us. Sometimes it felt more like an ocean of lava. Especially when there were things inside me, ripping me apart, needing to be let free. And damn it, I wanted to let it all free. I wanted to walk in there and tell her things that had been locked up in me for the last two years.

I leaned my forehead against the brick. No. I couldn't think like that. Thoughts like that were going to get me in trouble. Again.

The energy of another reaper sparked against my skin. I spun around. Along the side of the house, a glow sliced through the shadows. Anaya. A streak of moonlight caught her hair and tangled with her braids, making them shine.

I half expected her to blow around the house with the force of an atom bomb, ready to rip into me for being here. But she didn't. She wasn't even watching me. She was watching… Cash.

He waved to the car that had just dropped him off and stumbled around the house, tripping through the shadows. Anaya's eyes followed him, almost longingly, until he climbed through his bedroom window and closed the blinds.

I stepped out of the shadows. "Anaya?"

She jerked her gaze from Cash's window and blinked, as if she was waking up from a dream. "What?"

"Everything okay?" I asked hesitantly, watching the way her eyes flitted to Cash's house again.

"Y-yes." She sounded flustered. "Why wouldn't it be? I was just…"

I waited, hoping with everything in me that I was wrong about what I'd just seen.

She scowled at me. "Don't give me that look, Finn. You're the one lurking around the human girl's house in the middle of the night."

"I'd hardly call it lurking."

"Then what *are* you doing here?" She folded her arms across her chest. "I'm not stupid. You're up to something."

I glanced back at Emma's house. At the flickering glow from the candles in her window. "I'm trying to remind myself why it's a bad idea to go in there and talk to her. Why it's a bad idea to go in there and do *more* than talk to her."

"I'm not going to stand here and lecture you. I'm not Easton, and you don't need a babysitter. You already know why it's a bad idea."

I knew it was a bad idea. But now that I'd gotten a taste

of what touching and talking to Emma felt like, I didn't know how much longer I could do this. Stay away from her. Pretend everything inside me wasn't burning with the need for her to really know me. I closed my eyes, feeling the weight of my decision warm all of the hollow places inside. When I opened my eyes again, Anaya was shaking her head.

"You're going to do it anyway, aren't you?"

"Probably, but you were never here." I said. "And if you were never here, then I didn't see you looking at Cash like you wanted to doodle his name in your diary."

"I wasn't—"

I raised a brow and she stopped. She looked over her shoulder at Cash's house and bit her lip. "His name is Cash?"

"Yeah," I said. "And I don't have to tell you why it's a bad idea. Right?"

Anaya glanced down to the scythe beginning to glitter and glow in her leather belt. She wrapped her fingers around it and nodded. "Right."

"Anaya? Tell me you'll watch out for her. If something ever happens…if I'm ever not there and you are, just don't leave her alone."

Her lips lifted into a small smile. "You know I will."

"Thank you."

I waited for the burst of light to consume Anaya and deposit her on the other side before I sprinted across the yard. Emma had seen me in the woods. Talked to me like I was real. Maybe I could make this work. She didn't have to know everything. Just enough. I stopped myself a breath away from her bedroom wall.

It's now or never, Finn.

I exhaled and slipped through the cold brick until the

warmth of Emma's room surrounded me. I don't know what I'd been expecting to find, but Emma huddled over a little plastic board on her bed wasn't it. And the hope in her eyes… It was hope that she wasn't crazy. Hope that the little board in front of her could prove it. She deserved so much more than this. She *was* so much more than this. She was determined and loyal and beautiful and everything I wanted to be. She took care of the people around her. She took care of me once. She took care of me when she should have hated me.

I sat down on the bed across from her and balled my fingers into fists. I hated this. Hated that she was resorting to something so ridiculous because of what I had done. What I had caused. That what I'd done had hurt her this badly.

Emma pulled her long blond hair over her shoulder and took a deep breath. Two of her fingers rested on top of the pointer. "Is there someone here?" she asked, eyes closed. "Please. Please talk to me if you're here."

Screw Balthazar and his threats. If I didn't go corporeal, he'd never know.

I laid my fingers beside hers and moved the pointer to the word *yes*.

Chapter 11

Emma

I froze, afraid to move my fingers. Afraid to breathe. My eyes stayed glued to the word under the wooden pointer.

Yes.

"Oh my God." I jerked my hand away from the board and clutched it to my chest. My heart thumped until I could feel it in my palm like a pulse. I didn't know what to do next. All I knew about Ouija boards was what I'd seen on lame YouTube videos, and that didn't seem like much help to me now that someone—or something—was actually answering.

"Who are you?" I finally asked. When I realized my hands were still clasped to my chest, I dropped one down to the pointer, but it slid out from under my fingertips before I could touch it. "F," I whispered, saying the letters out loud. "I. N."

The pointer paused then slid around in a circle before coming back to N.

In that moment, the board was the only object that existed in the world. The mountains around my house could have come crashing down. The stars could have fallen from the sky. I don't think I would have noticed any of it. This was one of those moments when everything changed. The kind of moment when reality becomes something else. When it didn't move anymore, I looked around the room, expecting to find something. Finding nothing.

"Finn," I breathed. "Your name is Finn?"

The pointer slid to *yes* and I sat up on my knees, my breaths rushing in and out of my lungs. That name…

"Say it again."

I laughed at the shadow of a boy with green eyes and pressed my hands against his chest. "What?"

"My name. The way you say it…you say it like it matters. Like it still means something."

I kissed the corner of his mouth and whispered, "Finn."

I blinked the vision away. My heart thudded painfully in my chest. The green eyes, that voice… *Oh God.* I couldn't catch my breath. It was him. He was the one at the school. In the forest. In my head. My dreams. I stared at the board. *Finn.*

"Can I see you?" I bit my lip, not letting myself think about what I was really asking for. I just knew I wanted it. Everything inside me wanted it. "Like I saw you earlier tonight?"

Nothing happened. No sparks of magic. No phantom light transforming into the boy I'd seen with jungle-green eyes. The pointer didn't even budge. Disappointment twisted in my chest. This couldn't be it. This couldn't be all there was. I needed answers. I needed to know why he was here. I needed way too much for this to be it.

That memory was still inside me. His lips, his hands, the

way I felt like I was going to explode if he kept touching me. *Finn.* What the hell did this mean? Was it even real? Or did I just want it so badly that my screwed-up brain had created it all?

"Finn?" I called in a shaky voice, staring at the pointer, willing it to move. Willing it to prove I wasn't as crazy as the doctors thought.

It didn't.

So I was crazy, then. I squeezed my hands into fists so hard my nails left little crescent imprints in my palm, pushed myself off the bed, and stomped down the hall into the kitchen. Pills. I needed pills. I flipped on the light and one of the bulbs popped and went out, turning the kitchen a shade dimmer. I grabbed the little orange pill bottle off the counter. I'd already taken one today, but clearly I needed more clarity. I needed to get this memory…no. This *hallucination* out of my head.

"Don't take those," the now-familiar voice said.

I squeezed the cap until my fingers went numb and turned around. He was there, standing in my kitchen like he belonged there. Like he'd always been there.

Finn looked at the bottle in my hands. "You're not crazy, Emma. You don't need those."

The pill bottle clattered to the tile floor. I jumped back, heart thundering in my chest, lungs eating up all of the air around me until I felt dizzy. It all clicked together. The guy in my dreams, the guy who had saved my life twice…he was here. Standing in front of me. How was this even possible?

"What are you?" I closed my eyes and pictured the agonized look on his face just before he'd dissolved and disappeared into the night like a ghost.

"I'm not…alive."

A breath shuddered out of me and I opened my eyes, half-expecting him to be gone. But he still stood by the gray granite counter looking uncertain. Looking like a dream. "What does that mean?"

"It means I'm dead. I'm a soul."

Dead. The word floated around in my head, not feeling real. Dead was what my dad was. Dead was a cold, rotting body in the ground. I looked at Finn. At the warm color of his lips. The worried look in his vibrant green eyes. I couldn't make the word fit with him.

Finn took a step closer. I backed away, but he followed.

"I'm not lying," he whispered.

I stared at his chest so I wouldn't have to look at his face. It didn't move. It. Didn't. Move. The only breaths I could hear were my own. Fear started a slow, steady burn in my chest. My heart felt like it was in my throat, raw and achy. A few minutes ago, all I wanted was this. Now I didn't know how to feel. God…I couldn't…I couldn't…

I took a deep breath and threw open the cabinets in front of me. Then I grabbed a mixing bowl and plopped it onto the counter along with my favorite muffin tin. I needed something to do with my hands. Something to do with my mind, because I felt very close to losing it.

"Say something," Finn said behind me. "Tell me what you're thinking."

I spun around, keeping my back pressed against the counter.

"I…" I bit my lip and exhaled a shaky breath. "I don't know what to think. I don't even know where to start."

He hooked his thumbs into the front pockets of his jeans, dragging them lower around his waist. "How about you tell me what you want to know, and I'll talk."

Before I could form a question, another memory knocked the breath out of me and clouded my thoughts.

The sky looked cold. A dull pewter color that blended with the swaying silver wheat surrounding me. Finn stepped over me, blocking the sky. He hooked his thumbs into his jeans and grinned down at me.

My stomach fluttered and my knees forgot to support me. I sagged against the counter. "I know you. I want to know how I know you."

Finn grabbed the back of his neck and groaned. "Can we talk about something else first? Anything else."

"Are you doing this?" I gripped the wire whisk in my hand so tight my palms felt numb. "Are you showing me these things? The dreams?"

I waited for him to tell me what a wackjob I was. That I was imagining things. God, I actually *wanted* him to tell me I was crazy. Because nobody was going to believe the alternative. The alternative would mean I'd spent a summer in a psych ward for nothing.

"I'm not showing you anything," he said. "I'm just a soul, Emma. I don't have the ability to make you see things."

Then it was all real. I didn't know what to say. I had so many questions, but I couldn't stop my head from spinning. I pulled flour and sugar out of the cupboard and set them on the counter so I wouldn't have to look at him. I couldn't think straight when I was looking at him.

Finn pulled out a stool and sat. His gaze swept over the mess cluttering the counter. "What are you doing?"

"Making blueberry muffins," I said. It sounded normal. I needed normal.

"Now?" His brow arched.

I tucked my hair behind my ear and felt my cheeks heat. "I…I bake when I'm nervous. It helps calm me down. Helps me think."

His lips lifted into a small smile. "My mom used to do that when she couldn't sleep. We'd wake up and find enough pies to feed a small country. She'd stay up all night baking and only keep one for us. She always gave the rest away."

"You said she used to." I chewed on my bottom lip and played with the whisk handle. "Why doesn't she now?"

Finn's gaze dropped to the cluttered counter but I could tell he was seeing something else. Something I couldn't see. He finally broke the silence and said, "She died."

"I'm so sorry." I didn't know what to be more sorry about. The fact that his mom was dead, or that he was. It was too crazy to even think about.

"Don't be. Everybody dies," he said, a hard edge to his voice. He watched me measure out flour and dump it in the bowl, my hands shaking so hard that most of it ended up on the counter instead. "Am I making you nervous?"

"Yes." I set down the flour. "But maybe I wouldn't be so nervous if you would stop sitting there like this is normal. Because it's not. This…this is so monumentally *not normal*."

Finn nodded, his eyes consuming me with every blink. The fan I'd set up in the kitchen earlier rotated, blowing a few strands of hair into my face, where they caught on my eyelashes. I couldn't help but notice that Finn's hair didn't budge.

Unable to process the image, I pulled the mixing bowl against my stomach and started dumping in the rest of the ingredients. At least it was something to keep my mind off how completely unhinged I felt. Something to take my mind off the fact that I was standing here having a conversation with a ghost. If that's even what he was. I watched the flecks of flour and blueberry swirl and fade into the batter. If only life was as simple as this.

Finn was standing beside me. I whirled around and my breath caught in my throat. I hadn't even heard him get up. "What are you doing?" I said, my voice shaking almost as much as my knees.

"I thought you wanted answers."

I closed my eyes letting the low timber of his voice melt me. "I do."

"Then touch me."

"That's okay." I pressed into the counter behind me, cursing myself for backing myself into a corner. "You say you're dead. I believe you."

Finn's gaze shifted to my mouth then back up to my eyes. "Touch me anyway."

Chapter 12

Finn

Emma didn't say anything right away. I watched her bite her bottom lip, no doubt contemplating whether this was a good idea.

She raised her hand uncertainly. "Don't move. I'll scream if you move. My mom has a gun and lives by the 'shoot first ask questions later' motto, just so you know."

I smiled. "Wouldn't hurt me anyway."

Her fingers brushed my chest. Dove deeper until her palm was stirring the space in between my lungs. Warmth whispered through me. I closed my eyes and suppressed a groan. This feeling. *This* was what I'd been missing.

Emma jerked her hand back. "You — You're breathing."

I looked down at my chest, pumping like I'd run a marathon. "Yeah."

"You weren't breathing a minute ago. D-d-do you need to

breathe if you're…"

I watched the steady rise and fall of my chest. "No, but sometimes I can't help it."

It took about five seconds for the color to drain from Emma's face and two more for her to register this as a nightmare rather than reality. She made a choking sound in the back of her throat and edged around me, backing away. Her back hit the refrigerator and she froze.

"I would never hurt you. Don't be scared."

"Oh my God…you…you're a ghost. I'm talking to a ghost. I really am crazy."

"You're not crazy. I swear." She looked up at me, eyes flooded with moisture and hope. "I've been protecting you for two years. Since your dad's accident. You just couldn't see me before."

"My dad?" Her voice broke. "You know my dad?"

"No," I said. "Not exactly. I only met him once."

"But you said—"

"I met him when he crossed." I lowered my voice as if it might make the words easier to hear. "I met him when he died." I couldn't stop the disappointment from washing over me. Even with me talking to her, she didn't remember me from that day.

"Can I talk to him, too?" She sounded hopeful. "I can get the board. Maybe if you helped—"

"You can't talk to him," I cut her off. "He's not here. He's somewhere so much better than this." And she could have been with him if it wasn't for me.

Emma sank down onto the floor and I followed her. A tear wore a track through the flour on her cheek. I could almost feel her fracturing inside all over again.

"Did he say anything?" she finally whispered. "When he died?"

"He was worried about you," I said. "He wanted to make sure you were okay. That's all that mattered to him."

"Was he afraid?"

"For himself?" I raised a brow. "No. And he shouldn't have been. Some of us would give anything to get to go where he went."

Emma wiped the tear from her cheek, quickly, like she didn't want me to see it. So I pretended I didn't.

"So, he's in Heaven?" she asked. "There really is a Heaven?"

"Yeah." I leaned my head against the refrigerator beside hers. "And a Hell. And an Inbetween. And other places you really don't want to know about."

She sat up and looked at me. "Which one do you go to… when you're not here?"

I looked away. "I go to a lot of places. But I guess if you were going to pin me to one, then the Inbetween."

"What's that?"

I tried to figure out a good way to explain it to her. There wasn't one. "It's…it's exactly what it sounds like. It's kind of like a sorting ground for souls in between Heaven and Hell. It's where I met you…"

I stopped, floundering for the right words. Who was I kidding? There weren't any right words. I'd loved her. And I'd pushed her into a life where we could never be together. I'd unleashed an evil soul on her for something she didn't even choose. Would she have chosen it if I'd have given her the chance? No. She never would have chosen to sacrifice someone else for herself.

"What do you mean where you *met* me?"

"I knew you when you were a girl named Allison," I said carefully.

"Allison? Like the name on my mirror?" Fear ignited like a flame behind her eyes and her entire body tensed. "Like the girl in my dreams?"

"You haven't always been Emma. You had another life before this one. That girl might have died, but you share the same soul."

"What, like reincarnation?" she said. "You're saying I was reincarnated?"

"Yes."

Emma stared at her hands, letting her flour-coated palms slip across each other. I wanted to reach out and wrap my fingers around hers to steady them. Instead, I scooted back an inch to give her some space. Space to accept this. To accept me.

"The dreams," she whispered. "The voices. It's all real?"

I sighed. "Yes."

Emma took a deep breath. Another. "I don't understand why you're… Why *are* you here?"

Tell her. The words were right there, but I…I couldn't. She would hate me. And even if she didn't, she might do something stupid like try to sacrifice herself for Maeve. Because that's the kind of person she was. Someone who would die to right a wrong. I couldn't let that happen. Not when it was my mistake. Not after everything I'd done to keep her alive.

"I made a promise to your dad to keep you safe," I finally said. It wasn't a complete lie. "I don't intend to break that promise."

Emma squeezed her eyes shut and shook her head. "Protect me from what? From who?"

I took a deep breath and closed my eyes. I didn't want to see her reaction. "A soul named Maeve followed me here. She used me to find you two years ago. She knows who you are. And she wants to hurt you."

When she didn't say anything, I rested my hand between us on the tile. "Your accidents... They aren't accidents."

She seemed very far away in that moment. "So, you're saying this soul has been trying to hurt me? All of the accidents—it's been her every time? B-because she thinks I'm this Allison girl?"

"Yes."

"But...I didn't do anything to her!"

"It's not about you," I said, feeling the guilt flare to life inside of me all over again. "It's about me. She wants to hurt me. So she's trying to hurt you."

"Why would her hurting me hurt you?" Emma looked at me expectantly. "You barely even know me."

A thousand memories of this girl bombarded me. Each one making my chest swell and ache. I looked at her out of the corner of my eye. "I know you better than you think."

"You mean you knew *Allison*."

Knew, loved, pined for... "Yes. And I cared about her very much. Which is why Maeve targeted *you*."

"Why?" Emma sounded horrified. "What did you do to her to make her hate you so much?"

I looked at the floor. I couldn't look at her. Not when I was lying like this. "Some people just don't know anything other than hate."

Emma twisted the bottom of her shirt around her fist. "Why are you letting me see you now? Why let me think I was crazy for two years? Why...why leave me in a freaking mental institution for three months doubting my own sanity when you had the ability to tell me what was going on the whole time?"

"I wasn't allowed to let you see me before."

She cocked her head to side. "Then why are you allowed to now?"

I thought about the hell Balthazar would put me through if he found out about the minuscule moment we were sharing now and shook my head. "I'm still not allowed to."

"So that means you could get into trouble for this. You're breaking some kind of cosmic rule here, right? Because you think I'm Allison?"

I nodded.

"Y-you have the wrong girl." Emma stood, knees wobbly, eyes full of fear. "There's been some kind of mistake. I'm not that girl you knew. I-I-I'm just not her. I can't be."

I stepped into Emma, feeling her warmth draw me in. She looked up, eyes wide, her peppermint breath fanning across my face.

"What are you doing?" she gasped, unable to catch her breath.

I ran an iridescent finger down her arm to her wrist, watched it scatter like stars across her skin. Her breath hitched in her throat. Her heart beat so hard the sound rippled through me like a shock wave. When her eyes met mine, the amount of want in them nearly brought me to my knees. Even through the fear and anger she had to be feeling, I knew she felt what I felt. The connection. The warmth. The *rightness* of this moment.

"Tell me you feel it," I whispered.

"I-I—"

"Do you?"

She released the breath she'd been holding. "Yes."

I let my thumbs brush down her arms and she gasped. Fireworks ignited across the places that I touched. Emma's eyes opened. Glistening with wonder. Wide with fear.

"Trust me," I said. "You're that girl."

Chapter 13

Emma

I didn't want to be that girl, but Finn made me feel like I was. I'd never had a guy look at me the way he was looking at me. Like the world would shatter if I didn't exist. I cradled my hot chocolate in my mug and glanced at the clock. Two in the morning. I needed to go to sleep, but I didn't want to wake up and realize all of this was just another dream.

Finn sat on my bed. "What's wrong?"

"Nothing," I ran my fingertip along the warm lip of the mug. "This is just a lot to take in. When I woke up today, I didn't exactly think I'd meet a dead guy and find out I had a whole life before this one."

"Can I ask you something?"

I looked up at Finn's curious expression and nodded. I think I would have told him anything. Anything to get to keep looking at him. He was one of the most beautiful things I'd ever seen. It made me wish he'd actually show up in a picture.

"What did you expect to happen when you pulled out that board?"

I shrugged. "I don't know. Not this."

"Are you disappointed?"

The fear in his voice made my gaze drift up to meet his. Was I disappointed to find out there was someone trying to kill me? Yeah. Was I disappointed in meeting him? Finally having someone make sense of my life and tell me the truth?

"Of course not." I paused. "You know, I don't even know your last name."

"Carter. My name is Finn Carter." He smiled and watched me settle back into my pillows and take a sip of hot chocolate. "Do you have any idea how torturous it is to watch you drink that?"

I licked some marshmallow cream off of my bottom lip and lowered my cup. I expected him to look at the cup like he'd give anything for a taste, but his gaze never left my mouth. "How long has it been since you've tasted…anything?"

He laughed. "Are you trying to ask me how long I've been dead?"

"Yes."

He sat back against my headboard, so close I could feel the warm electricity coming off his skin. "Too long."

"What do you miss the most about being alive?"

He shifted on the bed and tilted his head back to stare at the ceiling. My gaze slid from the curve of his chin, down the smooth, tan column of his neck. He finally said, "Mom's Christmas dinner for sure. She made the best cobbler. And the jokes Dad used to tell to make us forget the heat while we were working the crops." He stopped and swallowed hard. "I miss too much. That's why it's easier not to remember."

My throat felt tight listening to him talk about all the things he didn't get to have anymore. "I'm sorry."

"You were always good at that." He slid me a glance and grinned. "Making me remember."

"Is that a bad thing?"

He shook his head. "No. Remembering is what keeps you human, I think."

"You seem pretty human to me." I set my mug on my nightstand and yawned. As much as I hated it, sleep was pulling me under. My eyelids felt like they had lead weights attached to them. "Do you care if I go to sleep?"

Finn folded his arms behind his head. "As long as you don't snore."

I laughed into my pillow and burrowed under the blankets. I reached out to turn off the lamp and darkness blanketed the room.

"Hey, Finn?" I ran my hand over my pillow, glad the light was off so he couldn't see how red my face was.

"Yeah?"

"When you said you've been watching me the last two years…" I paused, listening to him waiting beside me. "Does that mean *all* the time?"

There was only silence for a moment but then he said, "What do you mean? Have I—"

"Have you seen me…you know…without any clothes on?"

"N-no. Of course I haven't. Why would I—"

He sounded horrified and I couldn't help but laugh. "Okay, okay. I believe you."

He laughed a little, sounding relieved. "I really haven't. I swear."

"I know," I whispered. "Hey...don't leave, okay?"

I couldn't really see him, just a faint shimmer in the dark, but I heard him shift closer to me. "I'll stay as long as I can."

"Promise?"

"Always."

Chapter 14

Emma

I trudged into my kitchen early the next morning, tempted to crawl back into bed after only getting around three hours of sleep. But I really didn't feel like hearing my mom yell at me for the mess in the kitchen.

When I'd woken up, Finn was gone. All I had left was the memory of his touch, his fingers creating magic as they danced across my skin. His touch felt like warm electric current, nothing more than a breath, but a breath that left me wanting so much more. The nightmares about random souls trying to kill me I'd had last night weren't helping matters either. But at least it sort of made some sense now.

I looked around the kitchen. At the mess I still had left to clean. I groaned and started tossing dirty dishes in the sink. I grabbed the bowl of crusted-over muffin batter that I never got around to baking and dumped the goop into the garbage can.

Part of me still held out hope that it had just been a dream. A figment of my imagination. The other part needed someone to slap some sense into it, because that part of me was panicked he might never come back. Somewhere inside my skull, a headache started to form.

"It looks like a bakery exploded in here," Cash said from the hall.

I shrieked and nearly dropped the metal mixing bowl I was holding. "You scared the crap out of me! What are you even doing up this early on a Saturday?"

Cash slid onto a barstool. "Dad made me get up and clean the gutters," he said. "You look really tired. Need some help with this?"

"Yes, actually. That would be awesome. My mom's going to freak out on me when she wakes up."

"Well, I *have* been told that I'm made of awesome." Cash picked up one of the leftover cupcakes I'd baked the day before for my mom's open house.

"Who told you that?"

"I tell myself every day in the mirror." He grinned and shoved half of the cupcake in his mouth, then grabbed a clean spoon off the counter and stared into it. "You are made of awesome. You are the master of your own universe. You have a really huge—"

"Enough!" I laughed.

"What? I was going to say, really huge *cupcake*." He waggled his eyebrows and licked the frosting off his bottom lip.

I slapped him with my dishrag. "I thought you were going to help clean this up?"

"What does it look like I'm doing?" he asked and worked at getting the rest of another cupcake in his mouth.

"It looks like you're stuffing your face," I said, and went back to the dishes.

After he swallowed, he licked his lips and wiped the crumbs off of the counter. "So what's up? Did you have a bad night or something?"

Warmth stirred my hair, swirling down the neck of my sweater. I looked behind me and yelped. Finn was standing so close the hairs on my arm started to rise. The metal mixing bowl clattered to the floor and I dove to grab it. "Damn it!"

"Don't worry. He can't see me unless I want him to," Finn said. "Just act like I'm not here."

Right. Like it was that easy.

Cash picked up the bowl before I could and helped me wipe up the floor. "You're jumpier than normal. Seriously, what's going on with you today?"

"Nothing." *Nothing besides the fact that I'm seeing dead people.*

"Nothing always means something with girls," he said.

I focused on the boy who knew more of my secrets than my mother. Then my gaze flitted to the ghost of a boy standing behind him. Finn's brows were drawn together. The look in his eyes sent warm tremors racing through my insides.

I couldn't tell Cash this.

"I don't know," I said, drying my hands. "I just don't want to talk about this right now. Is that okay?"

Cash nodded and backed away, wiping the flour on his hands on the *That's What She Said* T-shirt he was wearing. "I can give you some space if you want."

"Yeah." I averted my gaze, unwilling to look at either of them. Instead I stared into the darkness outside the kitchen window. "That would probably be best."

"All right. Are we still on for movie night?"

I blinked, letting his words sink in. "Movie night?"

"You. Me. *Lethal Weapon*. We've been planning this for two weeks."

I nodded. Good. This was good. Maybe that's exactly what I needed. Normal. Cash. Popcorn. Stupid movies. "Yeah. I'll see you tonight."

"Cool. Later." Cash grabbed another cupcake and disappeared through the front door. I spun around looking for Finn the instant the door closed.

"Look, you can't—" I realized no one was there and the words died inside the hollow of my mouth. Somewhere deep in my chest, something started to ache. Finn was gone.

Chapter 15

Finn

"He's doing this on purpose," I said to Easton.

My brain was starting to feel like a patchwork quilt of death. Images of bodies stitched together in bloody little square-shaped memories were branded onto my retinas. Ever since the meeting, I'd barely had time to stop my head from spinning between reaps, let alone check on Emma as much as I'd like. I had a feeling that was the point, but was it punishment or a diversion? It felt like both.

It didn't help that I couldn't get last night with Emma out of my head. I didn't *want* to get it out of my head. Talking to her until she fell asleep. Watching her crooked grin as she drifted off… She'd looked just like Allison in that moment. It had taken everything in me not to go corporeal and touch her.

Easton peered into the dark alley in front of us. His violet eyes swirled with death. A rat scurried between my legs before it disappeared into a knocked-over metal trash can. Deep in the shadows, someone was whimpering. "Of course he's doing it on purpose," he said, pulling his scythe out. "What did you do this time?"

I'd let her see me. Touch me. I'd told her everything. Well, almost everything. That I'd barely managed to keep myself from going corporeal was the only reason the flesh wasn't being filleted from my body at this very moment.

Revealing myself to her was probably one of the worst decisions I'd made since pushing Allison through the portal, but it felt…amazing. Seeing her rattled and sleep-deprived in the kitchen this morning didn't, though. If we were going to do this, I'd have to let her get her sleep. The thought stopped me. *Was* I going to keep doing this?

When Easton raised a brow, waiting, I finally just said, "The usual."

"Well if it's your *usual,* then you're lucky a marathon of reaps is all he's done."

Easton slipped between the two crumbled brick buildings and I followed close behind. We were going to have to move fast. This kind of dark was a world all its own, where things crept and crawled and died in the night. The shadows were going to be hard to spot here.

Easton stopped a few feet from two ruined bodies, lying in bloody heaps on the pavement. The faces were black and blue and swollen beyond recognition, their limbs folded and bent into odd angles. They'd been beaten to death. I pressed the back of my wrist against my mouth and backed away a step.

Easton looked at me over his shoulder and raised a brow. "What's the matter, sweetheart? Squeamish?"

"I just don't see many like this." I stepped up to get a better look and frowned. My reaps were generally people who still needed to grow up. Ones who were straddling a moral line. Not grown men part of a drug deal gone wrong. "They're older. Way older than my usual reaps. Weird."

Easton frowned and stepped into a dark puddle of blood that glistened in the green glow of the streetlamp. "That's because they're supposed to both be mine."

I couldn't hide my relief. "Thank God."

But something was wrong. The pull was there again, burning and insistent. Forcing my feet toward the dead guy in the blue Windbreaker. "What's going on?"

Easton looked at the dead man and back to me, his dark eyebrows drawn together like he was trying to figure out a puzzle. "You have to take him."

"What? But he's not mine."

He tipped his head back and groaned into the night. "Don't you get it? Balthazar's making good on his promise. Did you honestly think an unusually busy day at the office was going to be your only slap on the wrist?"

I shook my head almost mechanically, not wanting to believe it. No way did he know what I'd done last night. I hadn't gone corporeal. I'd made sure of it.

"He warned you," he said. "Now it's time for you to get that glimpse he promised. And if we're all wearing our *honesty hats* here, I think this might be just what you need. Maybe if you see what he's threatening you with, you'll stop being such a dumbass."

My chest throbbed with something like fear, but it was nothing compared to the clawing need to take the soul in front of me. A hollow hiss crept out of the darkness. Against the brick, a shadow slithered up the wall and then vanished, camouflaged by the night.

"Come on." Easton nudged my shoulder. "Just follow my lead."

I stepped forward and slid my scythe from its holster. All I could see when I stared down into the man's cracked-open face was flames. Searing, painful, nightmare-inducing flames. I didn't want to do this. Son of a bitch I did *not* want to do this! Out of nowhere, a cold whisper circled my ear.

Get to work, Finn, or I might decide to make your stay more…permanent.

Balthazar's voice sent a shiver racing down my spine. Closing my eyes, I swung out and listened to the whistle of metal fly through the air before it plunged into the man's soft flesh. Easton and I yanked at the same time and the souls came up, side by side, with dazed looks on their faces.

They looked gray, no shimmer, not an ounce of light left in them. The one with shaggy black hair swallowed and looked behind them at the shells of their former selves. "Holy sh—"

Easton laughed and slapped him on the shoulder. "Trust me, friend. There's nothing holy about where you're going. And just a tip." He leaned in close and balanced his arm on the soul's shoulder. "Don't say *holy* down there. They don't like it."

"Down there?" The soul backed away from Easton until he was standing in a pile of empty flesh. "What are you talking about?"

"Oh, please. Tell me you're brighter than that." Easton pointed to the silent guy in the blue Windbreaker. "Look. Your buddy over here already has it all figured out. Don't ya, big guy?"

He nodded, staring blankly at the blood-splattered pavement. "Hell." He looked up at his friend. "We're going to

Hell, Caleb."

"Ding, ding, ding!" Easton smiled. "We have a winner."

At the sound of his words, a loud *crack* split the pavement, and screams echoed from the pit. A black, oil-like substance bubbled up from the crevice and started a slow and steady swirl, picking up screams and tossing them into the night. I stepped back and clenched my jaw. I'd seen the freak show that was Easton's departure for the underworld lots of times, but this time it was different.

This time they expected me to go with him.

"Anybody feel like a swim?" Easton slid his scythe back into his belt. Before either of them could say a word, he had the dark-haired guy by the arm. Easton gave me a two-finger salute and stepped off the ledge and into the black vortex of screams, dragging the flailing soul named Caleb behind him.

My soul tried to back away but I grabbed him by the wrist and shook my head. "Don't make this worse than it has to be."

I didn't think after that. I just wanted to get this god-awful night over with. I wanted to get back to Emma and make sure I hadn't driven her off the deep end. Squeezing his wrist, I stepped off into the darkness.

Hitting the ground sent a shock wave of heat up through the soles of my feet. Ash fluttered down out of the sky like dirty snow, and barbed wire stretched down the path on either side of us, held up by intricate iron fence posts that were topped with skulls. The sharp metal thorns dripped with something red. Up ahead, an enormous structure of jagged ash-covered stone erupted from the ground, the entrance blocked by two flaming gates.

When Easton stopped just short of the gates to talk to someone cloaked in black, I turned in a slow circle, not wanting to see, but needing to. An island of misfit playground equipment sat solemnly on the other side of the fence. I couldn't stop staring at one of the rusted swing sets. It looked just like the one Henry and I used to play on after church on Sundays when we were little. One of the swings glided back and forth with no one in it. Next to it, a merry-go-round with chipped red and yellow paint turned slowly. A boy laughed. I wiped the ash out of my eyes and moved closer to the fence.

"Finn!" the voice squealed. "Push me higher!"

A young boy stood on the other side of the fence, the right side of his face charred. Embers glowed through the hollow hole in his cheek, exposing a row of little white teeth. On the good side of his face, one bright-green eye peered back at me.

"Henry?" I whispered. My little brother shouldn't be here. Couldn't be.

"You're going to burn, Finn," he said. The embers sparked a flame at the bottom of his blue button-down shirt and sped their way up the right side of Henry's chest, but he didn't cry. He watched me until the orange flames swallowed him.

"Henry!" I gripped the barbed fence, but strong hands pulled me back.

"What are you doing?" Easton spun me around to face him. I swallowed and looked past him at the two souls we'd reaped looking at me like I'd lost my mind. "Who's Henry?"

"My brother. He…" I glanced over my shoulder, but nothing was there anymore. Only rock and ash and the sound of a girl screaming like her guts were being ripped out.

"They're using your memories," Easton let me go. "Suck it up and get back to work."

All of this and we weren't even inside the gates of Hell. I blinked up at the sky, trying to shake away the image of Henry burning as I trudged back to the souls.

"Let's go," Easton said. The flaming gates swung open and I barreled through into the darkness. Heat seared my skin. Memories burned the inside of my skull. I blinked away the drop of sweat that trickled down into my eye.

Wait.

Touching my fingers to my forehead, I stopped. I was sweating. "How…?"

"Once you cross through the gates, you're flesh. It doesn't matter what you are. Alive. Dead. Something else. They want you to be able to feel the pain."

"I-I don't understand," I stammered. "This…it's impossible."

"Don't say that," Easton said. "They'll just take it as a challenge."

He jerked his chin to motion for me to follow, so I did, letting the flames at my back drive me forward. It was dark in the cave and things hissed and growled from the corners.

We came to another set of smaller gates and Easton rapped his scythe on the bars. "Special delivery!"

When the soul beside him started to cry, Easton rolled his eyes. "Seriously, man? Did you honestly think a drug dealer and a rapist would end up anywhere else? You really should consider the occupational hazards that go along with a career before you commit yourself."

Easton brushed the ash off his jacket like he was talking about the guy's 401(k). I didn't know how he could be so calm in a place like this.

Out of the corner of my eye, a girl with soft blond hair bled into my vision. I gritted my teeth and turned my head. Emma stared back at me with empty pits for eyes. Black spider-webbed veins popped up from her pale white skin.

"What's wrong?" she whispered. "You still love me, don't you, Finn?"

A sick feeling churned in my stomach.

"You did this to me," she sobbed. "Look at me. Look at me!"

It's not real. It's not real.

The gates creaked and swung open. Two hooded figures stepped out and sized up the souls in tow. Long, curved, dark claws poked out of their draping sleeves. Red eyes glowed from the empty black spaces where faces should have been.

Easton shoved his soul at one of them and nodded for me to do the same. I couldn't shove him like that. Instead, I patted him on the back and gave him a gentle push. He squeezed his eyes shut and said, "Shit…just tell me when it's all over."

The demon under the cloak laughed and clutched him around the throat. "That's the best part. *It's never going to be over.*"

Chapter 16

Emma

I stopped pacing to check the clock for the hundredth time. Checked the lock on the door. Made sure there was nothing in my room that could possibly impale or crush me at a moment's notice. Where the hell was Finn? He said he was here to protect me, but I hadn't seen him since the kitchen incident this morning. Cash was still giving me space, so I'd spent the whole day alone. Terrified. How was I supposed to deal with knowing some evil soul wanted to hurt me? What if he didn't show up in time when something happened again?

He may have promised Dad he'd keep me safe, but Finn couldn't be around 24-7. I couldn't just sit around waiting to be a victim now that I knew what was going on. I had to figure out how to protect myself. But how was I supposed to fight something I couldn't see coming?

I grabbed my laptop. There had to be a way to fight this on

my own. Or at the very least, a way to help protect myself until help arrived. I didn't really know where to start, so I Googled *how to ward off an evil spirit* and cringed at the thought of anyone looking at my history. That thought alone was enough for me to turn on my private browsing. I clicked on the first site that looked halfway legitimate and read an article called "Eighteen Ways to Rid Your Home of Evil Spirits."

It said you could do things like hang horseshoes above your doors and burn candles. I shook my head. Yeah, I'm sure Mom would go for me hanging horseshoes all over our house. I read on about psychic mediums and exorcists. These might have been one of the better options, but Mom would have me committed for sure if she found out I had someone over trying to cleanse our home of unwanted spirits. There had to be something. I scrolled down and stopped.

Smudge your home with sage. Open all of the windows in your home and light a bundle of dried sage. Sage is thought to clear away negative energy and spirits. Catch the ashes with a plate held underneath the bundle and walk around your home to cleanse it with the smoke.

That one seemed easy enough. Something we kept in the kitchen and it wouldn't get me committed. Most of the rest seemed flat-out ridiculous. But really, what didn't at this point? I clicked on another site, reading incantation chants and prayers, saving them to study later. A few were short enough to memorize on the spot, so I did. Cash would have said this was stupid. Mom would have said it was crazy. But it was all I had. It was all I knew how to do.

Cash poked his head through my window and I slammed my laptop shut. "Is your mom in bed yet?"

Relief washed over me as I glanced at the clock again. It

was after nine and she was still on her date. I wondered if she was going to come home at all. I pushed the thought of her with anybody who wasn't Dad out of my head, nodded, and waved him in.

"Good." He grinned, tossed a duffel bag through my window, and crawled in after it.

I stared at the bag. "What happened?"

He plopped down onto my bed and dug a DVD out. "Nothing."

"An overnight bag doesn't mean *nothing*."

He shrugged and fiddled with the DVD case. "Captain Asshat lost a case. I don't feel like dealing with his crap tonight. That's all."

That was all he needed to say. It was all he'd needed to say for the last eleven years. By this point, my room belonged to Cash almost as much as it belonged to me. I sighed and slid his bag under my bed so Mom wouldn't see it if she came in.

"You're not taking my good pillow again." I yanked my pillow out from under Cash's head and loaded the DVD player. With everything that had happened the night before, I didn't think I'd be able to watch most of it, but it was still nice to have the distraction and Cash right where I needed him. I lay down next to him and stuffed my pillow behind my head.

The movie started and cheesy cop lines and eighties hair lit up the screen, but I couldn't concentrate on it. All I could think about was Finn.

"You ready to tell me what's wrong?" Cash elbowed me in the side. "You've had thirteen and a half hours of space to mull it over. Not that I've been counting."

I shook my head. I didn't think I'd ever be ready. Maybe this was something that would always have to be just for me. I didn't want to ruin the time I spent with Cash trying to convince him of things even I didn't understand.

"I do have a present for you, though." I reached over Cash and pulled a little green photo album out of my nightstand drawer. I dropped it in his lap and smiled when he picked it up and started to flip through the pictures. "I printed them today. I can't use most of them for the yearbook, so you get to keep them. All the blackmail your evil little heart could desire."

"Are these from the bonfire?"

All of them except the picture of Finn. "Yep."

"Will I be disappointed?" he asked.

"I doubt it."

"You…" Cash stopped to laugh at a picture. "Are beyond awesome. You know that, right?"

I shrugged.

"Seriously. You have a future as a card-carrying member of the paparazzi."

The word "future" dimmed my mood, but I didn't let it show on my face. Ever since Dad died, I'd been waiting for the other shoe to drop. That fate would get me, too. And now that Finn had confirmed there was a psychotic ghost out there intent on making my life a living hell, I had to wonder what kind of future was in store for me.

Cash flipped through a few pictures, chuckling, then raised his brows and turned the album around to show me the picture of him and Tinley kissing.

"What?" I asked. "You said you wanted entertainment. Just think of the blackmail opportunities."

Cash grinned and slid the picture out of its sleeve. He folded it up and shoved it in his back pocket. "Nice try, but that one's going straight to the incinerator."

"Don't you want to keep it so you have something to show the grandkids? I can print you an eight-by-ten if you want."

Cash shook his head. "Nah, I give this one another week. Maybe two."

I studied the side of Cash's face as he flipped through the pictures, stopping at every other one to laugh to himself. Everyone thought he was perfect. Nobody knew what I knew. He was damaged, just like me. Maybe not in the same way, but when he was a sad little six-year-old on my front porch, something inside him broke. I wondered if he'd ever find a girl who could fix it.

"When are you going to stop doing this?" I asked.

"Doing what?" Cash squinted at a picture.

"Treating girls like they're disposable," I said. "You know they're not all like—"

His eyes snapped up, a flash of anger flared behind them, before he managed to cover it up. "Like Mom?"

"I didn't mean it like that."

He blew out a sigh and shook his head, dropping the album onto my comforter. "I know. Look at my dad, though," he said, staring at the ceiling, clasping his hands over his stomach. "He's miserable. He's been miserable for eleven years because of a *woman*. He's probably going to be miserable for the rest of his life. What have I ever seen that would make me want that?"

"It's not always like that."

He laughed at me. "How would you know? As far as I know, you've never even kissed a guy."

I winced and put some space between us. I knew he wasn't trying to hurt me on purpose, but reminding me about how I'd been stuck in a mental institution while he was screwing half of the girls in Lone Pine didn't make it sting any less.

Cash got quiet, probably realizing what he'd said. He sighed and raked his fingers through his hair. "Em, I'm sorry. That was a chickenshit thing for me to say."

"It's fine." I bit my lip, thinking about the board last night. And Finn. Seriously, what guy would want to date me? I was a walking freak show. The only guy who had ever looked at me like I was something more than crazy or a friend was dead. "I know I'm screwed up."

"It's not fine," he said. "You just wait. You're going to get a clean slate when we go to college next year. Guys will be beating down your dorm door. I'll have to kick all of their asses of course, but at least the opportunity will be there."

My bedroom door swung open and Cash jumped up. Mom stood in the doorway, dark circles framing her blue eyes. "What's going on in here? You know you are not allowed to have boys in here after nine."

I sat up and sighed. "He's not *a boy*. He's Cash."

"Boys?" Cash raised a brow. "Do you even talk to any besides me? Bet she had to brush the dust off that rule."

I rolled my eyes. "Shut up."

Mom sighed and pinched the bridge of her nose like she was fending off a headache. "Go home, Cash. You are more than welcome to come back during visiting hours, but if I catch you in here again this late, I'm having a conversation with your father."

Cash looked out the window toward his house. "I…I guess I'll see ya tomorrow, Em."

I nodded, trying not to smile. That was code for, *I'll wait outside until your mom goes to bed before I sneak back in and get us both grounded.*

"Sorry," I said once I was alone with Mom. "We were just watching a movie. It's not a big deal."

Mom leaned against the doorframe looking exhausted and every bit her age. Without her usual caffeine buzz, it was easier to read her. She was worried. And mad. "Honey, you're not nine anymore. You can't be with that boy all hours of the night. What would the neighbors say if they saw him crawling though your window in the middle of the night?"

I sighed and began braiding a strand of hair that hung over my shoulder. "He *is* the neighbors, Mom."

She threw her hands up in the air. "I'm not in the mood for this tonight. I've got an early meeting tomorrow."

"You've got an early meeting or you've got another date?"

The words came out more bitter than I'd expected, but there it was. She stared out into the empty hall. It seemed so much emptier without Dad here. Everything felt emptier. I just wished she wasn't in such a hurry to fill that emptiness with someone else.

"It's been two years," she said softly. "I can't be alone forever just because you want me to be."

"That's not what I want."

She turned around, her eyes glistening. "Then what *do* you want? Because I'm trying to find a way to be happy. I don't understand why you can't try to find that, too."

I stared at the floor. "I do want you to be happy. I just…I miss him."

She sighed, and a few seconds later I felt her palm smoothing the hair over the back of my head. She kissed my forehead. "I miss him, too, but he's not coming back. It's awful and it's not fair, and there's nothing I can do to fix that. You're not going to be happy until you can learn to let go. Until you stop wishing you'd died along with him."

Sometimes the truth was a lot harder to hear than a lie. And hearing the truth from my mom was like pouring lemon juice on an open wound. When I didn't say anything else, she stood up, shaking her head. "Good night, Emma."

"'Night, Mom."

She shut off my light and darkness swallowed the room. I curled into a ball on my side to compress the pain in my chest. I lay there thinking about Dad. Thinking about Finn, and praying with everything in me that he'd come back. I lay there hurting until Cash crawled in beside me.

"You want me to sleep on the floor in case she comes back?"

"No."

His arm brushed mine and it felt like ice. I scooted over to make room and felt him slip under the comforter.

"Hey," he whispered.

"What?"

"You did the Ouija board thing, didn't you?"

I pressed my face into my pillow. "Why?"

He chuckled and his shoulder blades knocked into mine. "Because the box is sticking out from under your bed, Einstein."

I cringed. "Yeah. I tried it."

"Well," he turned over on his side to look at me but I kept my face buried in the cool safety of my pillow. "What happened?"

"Nothing," I lied. "Nothing happened."

Cash didn't say anything. He snuggled down into the blankets and pressed his back against mine. I soaked in his heat and fought off sleep. I would have given anything not to dream, but I knew that wasn't going to happen. I could already feel it pulling me under.

Chapter 17

Emma

Sunday morning, I tapped on my laptop waiting for the search results to tell me who Finn Carter really was. The first name that popped up was an actress. The second was some kid's Facebook page in New Jersey. I glanced up at Cash still sleeping in my bed, the covers wrapped around him like a cocoon, and wondered where Finn was. Seriously, where did a dead guy go for a whole day and night? After scrolling through a few pages of search results, I finally reached a point in the list that caught my eye and frowned.

World War II Deaths: Find your ancestors now at Ancestry. com/military

I clicked on the link and scrolled down to *Finn Carter, born 1924.* Clicked on that. But it only led me to a reference to an old newspaper clipping that I didn't have access to here. I frowned at the screen. The library. They had a record there of all kinds of old newspapers. I scribbled down the information in a notebook and ripped out the page. Cash groaned as I folded it into a neat little square and stuffed it into my back pocket.

"Are you going to sleep all day or what?"

Cash sat up and combed his fingers through his messy black hair. He squinted at the alarm clock and then at me. "Why? Do you have somewhere you need to be?"

"Actually, yeah." I jerked the blankets off of him and grabbed his bag out from under my bed. "So move it. Besides, if Mom comes home and finds you in here, I'm dead."

Cash stood up, pulled his T-shirt over his head and dug in his bag for a clean one. I couldn't help but look. This must have been how Cash got the girls at school to fall for his crap. Make them laugh with a funny T-shirt, then peel it off and make them drool. His chest was a hard sheet smoothed out by tan skin. The muscles in his stomach stood out as he stretched the new T-shirt over his head. Most girls would have been entranced. All I could think about was what Finn might look like with his shirt off. My face felt warm, so I looked away and fumbled for one of the tubes of peppermint ChapStick that littered my vanity.

"Where are you going, anyway?" He mumbled through the fabric over his face. "I could go with you if you want. The only plan I had for today was sleeping in and since you've already screwed that up…" His head popped through the other side of the T-shirt and he grinned.

"I'm going to the library," I said, sliding on the lip balm.

"The library?" Cash sat on my bed and dug through his bag. "It's Sunday. Why in God's name would you want to go there?"

When he pulled out a pair of jeans and grabbed the waistband of his sweats, I tossed the tube back onto the vanity and held my hand up. "Keep it in its cage, Casanova. And not everyone thinks the library is a waste of time. Some people actually *like* books."

Cash rolled his eyes. "I always knew there was something wrong with you. Now turn around so I don't ruin you for other men."

I slapped my hands over my eyes and turned around, listening to him shimmy in and out of his clothes. When he was done, I grabbed my backpack and slid the window open for him. I hated sending Cash back home when his dad was there, but I didn't really have a choice. If there was information about Finn out there, I was going to find it.

• • •

"Emma!" Ms. Godfrey, the librarian, said in a loud whisper as she opened the locked library doors. I don't think I'd ever heard the woman speak louder than that. "It's been so long."

I smiled, thankful I could always count on Ms. Godfrey to be here on a Sunday and let me in outside of business hours, even though I'd avoided the place for the last two years. I followed her in and looked around at the stacks and shelves I used to hide in when I was a kid. There were so many memories of Dad here. "Yeah, it has."

"You know, your father's books are still one of our most popular series," she said, correctly interpreting my silence. "I had to order extra copies because we couldn't keep them on the shelf."

My lips felt numb from the fake smile. My gaze drifted to the local author section, where they still had Dad's picture up.

He smiled back at me, his dark hair rumpled like he'd meant for it to look that way.

I looked away. "That's really great, Ms. Godfrey. I'm sure he'd be happy to hear that."

She pushed her glasses up her nose and touched my shoulder, giving me the sympathetic look that everyone around here had mastered over the last two years. "What brings you here on a Sunday, honey? Are you working on something for school?"

I pulled the folded paper out of my back pocket. "Yeah, actually. I need to find an old newspaper article for a report I'm doing for history."

I handed her the paper and she gave it a quick once-over before handing it back. "You'll have to check the archives by year." She pointed me to the back of the library and patted my shoulder. "Let me know if you need any help."

"I will." I forced one more smile, then made my way to the tables where the newspaper viewers sat.

After two hours of searching and coming up empty, Finn Carter was starting to look like nothing more than figment of my imagination. I was about to give up, but then there it was. There *he* was. Finn Carter 1924-1942. I glanced around the empty library to make sure no one was looking, then clicked the highlighted name. An old South Carolina newspaper article lit up the screen. An obituary. Something in me sank, ached, but I read on anyway.

A fighter pilot, Second Lt. Finn S. Carter, has officially been reported dead as of early Monday morning, according to his father, John S. Carter of Charleston, SC. He had previously been missing since June 6, 1942 over the Pacific Ocean where he lost radio signal somewhere near the Midway Atoll.

Lt. Carter enlisted in May 1941 and won his wings in April 1942 in Dothan, Alabama. He had been overseas a little over a month when he died. He attended Charleston High School, and worked on his family's peach farm. He is survived by a father, a mother, Susan Carter, and one younger brother, Henry Carter.

I clutched the edge of the desk and leaned in close when I saw the picture. A very alive Second Lt. Finn Carter stared back at me in black and white. His uniform was pressed. His smile was wide and bright and young. Way too young to be dead. He looked like he was ready to take on the world. I reached up and touched the screen. For once, I wasn't shaking. For once, I had the proof that what I thought was reality and not a hallucination.

A laugh slipped from between my lips and I slapped my hand over my mouth to stop it. This was real. He was real. And if he was real... My giddiness over finding the article faded. If he was real, he was really dead. The sweet, funny, beautiful ghost of a boy who had been in my house less than twenty-four hours ago had really rotted at the bottom of the ocean somewhere. I shoved myself away from the desk feeling nauseated.

The feeling stayed with me all the way to my Jeep. I wrapped my hands around the steering wheel and stared out the windshield. How long could Finn keep this protecting thing up? It was obvious he was supposed to be somewhere else or he wouldn't keep disappearing. He said he was breaking rules to be here with me. How long before whoever made those rules stopped him?

I needed my journals. Needed to go over Maeve's attacks. Now that I knew what they were, maybe if I could figure out a pattern. Then I could be better prepared. Predict her moves before she made them, and have the sage and incantations ready for when she did. It was a long shot, but it was all I had.

By the time I made it into my room, my brain was humming with all of the information I needed to gather. I climbed into bed and stared at the pile of journals I'd dumped onto the comforter. There were so many. So many dreams. So many memories. I picked up the first one and peeled back the cover, running my fingers over the page. This was the first book. The one they'd given me at Brookhaven that documented what they had called delusional paranoia. I felt sick just looking at it, but I shook off the feeling and read.

I told Mom I went running because it was the first sunny day we'd had in a week. I really went running because I didn't want to think about Dad. The faster I ran, the farther away the accident felt, so I ran until I hit Church Street. I would have gone farther but that's where it happened. I remember the whisper.

"Move."

And then the power line was flying at me and I was running across the road as fast as my legs would go to get out of the way. Everything felt cold and I didn't understand why because a few minutes earlier I'd been sweating. Once I reached the grass, I just watched the power line squirm across the road. It was right where I'd been standing. All I could think was that I should have been dead.

Knowing now that Maeve had caused it, knowing that whisper had been Finn and not just a broken part of my brain, it was like I was seeing it in a different light. I placed my palm over the words, hating the memory. It had happened two months after the car accident, and was the first of many accidents. I read over a few more entries that the doctors had made me record. There wasn't any pattern, no regular time frame. The only thing they had in common was the fact that I knew they weren't accidents.

I opened another journal and stopped when I reached the first entry I'd made about the car accident. The one I'd survived. The one Dad hadn't. Why had they made me write this down? Was having this all recorded for eternity really supposed to help me?

I could still hear Dad. I could still remember the moment right before it happened.

"I want to quit," I said, staring out the window. Raindrops splattered against the windshield so hard you could barely hear the Journey song on the radio.

"Why?" Dad asked.

"Because I don't…" I thought about the other cheerleaders. They lived for it. I lived for the moment practice was over. "I don't feel like me."

Dad sighed and patted my hand on the console. "Then you don't have to do it."

I looked at him, hopeful. "I don't?"

Dad laughed. It was the last one. The last smile. "No, you don't have to do anything that doesn't make you hap—"

He never got to finish because the world shattered and went black after that. The next thing I remembered was lying in the back of the ambulance and wondering why my dad wasn't there.

"What's wrong?"

I jumped at the sound of Finn's voice and slammed my journal shut. "You came back," I breathed.

He stepped closer to the bed, eying the leather-bound journal half-covered in my sheets. "What were you doing? You look sick."

"Homework." I pulled my hair over my shoulder. "Where have you been? You just disappeared yesterday."

Finn walked over to the wall and ran a shimmering finger over a glass-framed print on my wall. "I was at work."

I took a breath and exhaled slowly, pushing the memory of Dad as far away as I could, trying to focus on Finn.

"Work? Dead people have jobs?"

He smiled. "Yeah. Some of us do."

I watched him as he made a point not to watch me. "What's your job?"

"I…just a messenger. I deliver things to where they are supposed to go."

"What kinds of things?"

"What kind of homework are you working on?"

I chose to ignore his question the same way he'd ignored mine and chewed nervously on my bottom lip as Finn examined the black-and-white prints on my wall. He was completely engrossed, his gaze sweeping across the landscapes that I'd captured at their most beautiful moments before trapping them behind glass for as long as the frames would hold. These pictures were the only good things to come out of Mom's insistence that I take yearbook.

"Where were you from?" I asked, inching to the edge of the bed. I'd seen it, but I needed to hear it from him. "You know, when you were alive."

"Charleston." He glanced over his shoulder at me. "South Carolina."

"Did you have family there? A job?"

He paused. "Why do you want to know all of this?"

"I just feel like I should know something about you," I said.

"I mean, two years of following me around? You probably know everything about me. Probably even know what color my underwear are right now."

He rolled his eyes and grinned. "I have no clue what color your underwear are."

"I still want to know." I didn't just want to know. I needed to know more about him than the fact that he was dead. I needed to put a name to this feeling eating me from the inside out. I needed to understand how someone who wasn't even alive could make me feel like this.

"I worked on my dad's farm," he finally said, so quiet I could barely hear him. "He taught me to fly. To dust the crops." He laughed to himself and stared at a blank spot on the wall. "My brother was always so jealous of that. He'd hide my boots, so I couldn't leave him behind."

"So are you my guardian angel?" I finally asked the question that had been eating at me all day. He didn't turn around. Instead he moved on to the next print, the one I'd taken at Lone Pine Lake a couple months ago.

"No. I'm not an angel. I already told you. I'm a soul. I used to be person. And now I'm just…lost." He trailed off. "Lost and terribly invested in a human that I couldn't leave now, even if I wanted to."

"Do you ever want to? Leave, I mean?"

Finn finally turned around to face me, his outline shimmering with a silvery dust. It was like he was wrapped in the Milky Way, cloaked in a translucent blanket of stars. "No. I have never thought of leaving you for even a second."

I didn't say anything. Instead I leaned forward and traced the jagged outline of Mount Whitney with my fingertip.

"This one's my favorite," I whispered. "I'd forgotten I set

the timer. I didn't even realize till later that I'd taken it. I'm usually not in my photos." I looked at myself staring across the horizon, the lake reflecting a mirrored image of the setting sun behind the pine-dotted crags that etched the rocky terrain. Beside me was a shimmery light, a spectacular sunburst of color against the plain gray horizon. I'd always thought it was just a reflection of the sun off the camera lens. Now I knew better.

"I remember." Finn touched the shimmery shape beside me and smiled.

I looked back and forth from the picture to Finn, trying to fit the two images together, until my fingers found their way to the glass. At least I could touch this.

"Tell me something about you," he said.

"You already know everything about me."

"No, I don't," he said. "I don't know what goes on inside your head. I don't even know what you want to do after high school."

I glanced at Finn, at the floor, at the pictures. I felt like he was asking me to crack myself open and show him my insides with that one simple question. "I'd like to own a bakery someday. The kind where people can come in and sit at little iron tables and soak in the smell of bread when it's cold outside."

The second I allowed myself to think it, the pain started. Dull. Achy. The kind that always accompanies something you want but can never have.

"Why do you say that like you'll never have it?" he asked.

"Because I won't," I admitted, twisting my toe into the floor. "I've barely made it though the past two years alive. Why should I expect to have a future to plan for?"

"Hey." Finn moved so close to me I could feel his warmth on my skin. "You'll have those things. You'll have everything you've ever dreamed about wanting. Do you hear me? I'm not going to let anything happen to you. Haven't I proved that to you by now?"

I shook my head. "No. I can't keep relying on you. What happens when you can't be there? I need to know how to protect myself."

"I…" He looked tortured. Guilty. And for a moment I hated myself for making him feel that way. "This is all my fault. I'm sorry. You have no idea how sorry I am."

"Don't be sorry. Just tell me what to do."

"I wish I knew. Now that you know…maybe you'd have some kind of chance even if I wasn't here."

He didn't sound like he believed the words coming out of his own mouth.

I held my breath as he reached his hand up to my face. I leaned in, expecting to feel the cold, breathy vapor of his touch, but the sensation never came. By the time I let myself breathe again, he'd already dropped his hand and backed away.

"What's wrong?" I stepped into him, wanting, needing him to touch me. I was so raw inside from that memory of Dad that I needed this more than I wanted to admit.

"Emma…don't."

He said it but he didn't back away. He just stared at my lips and his chest started to move with unneeded breaths. I stepped closer. So close I could feel his warmth crackling between us like static electricity. "Please?"

The silence between us seemed unending, an ocean of unspoken words stretching on for miles between us. I stared up into bottomless green eyes that seemed to be searching my face. Ever so slowly, I reached for his cheek. Silvery blue sparks ignited in the paper-thin space between my fingertips and his skin.

Before I could touch him, he tripped over his own feet trying to back away from me. "I-I can't touch you," he stuttered. "I'm sorry."

"I know you can touch me." I didn't mean for it to sound like an accusation but it did. "You've done it before. At the school. I *felt* you that day. You felt…real. Why not now?"

Finn stabbed his fingers through his hair. "You think I don't *want* to touch you? Do you think I wouldn't give anything…"

"Then do it!" A lump swelled in my throat and I pressed my lips together. Why did I need this so badly? I felt like I was going to break apart if he didn't give me this. "You don't get to say you *want* to touch me, then run away. If you can't, then you have to tell me why. Why—"

"Because he'll know!"

"Who?"

He groaned and touched his hip. "I have to go."

My heart lurched in my chest. "You can't! Look, I'm sorry. I shouldn't have—"

I didn't finish. It wouldn't have done any good. Finn had disappeared. Again.

Chapter 18

Finn

The next afternoon, I seeped into Emma's house on a gust of cold wind and tried my best to brush the smell of death from my clothes. I went to the kitchen and checked the time on the stove. 3:27. Within minutes, she'd walk through that door and drive this god-awful worry out of my head. I'd been out on reaps all day. A shooting victim. A kid hit by a car. The list went on and on. I didn't even know if she was okay. If she even knew that I wasn't there to protect her. I paced around the living room, into the kitchen, and back again. I was about to invade the bedrooms when the front door opened. I braced my hands on the walls on either side of the hall, feeling relieved as I watched her walk in.

"Mom!" Emma tossed her book bag on the counter and pulled open the fridge. "You home?"

She pulled out a bottle of orange juice and twisted it open.

I stood still, silent, wanting to watch her for just a moment. Her hair was piled on top of her head like an artfully tangled ball of gold thread. Loose wispy pieces framed her face. She took a drink of the juice, licked a droplet from her lips, and shoved the sleeves of her white cardigan up to her elbows. "Mom!"

"She's not here," I said from the hall.

Emma yelped and grabbed her chest. "You gotta stop doing that."

"Sorry."

She smiled and leaned on the counter. "You're back."

I grinned back as I walked into the kitchen. God, that smile of hers was infectious. "I always come back."

"I thought you were mad at me." Emma put the cap back on her orange juice and stuck it in the fridge. "You know. For the touching thing."

"I had to go to work." I looked away. "And I wasn't mad. I just…you have no idea what that does to me. Watching you practically beg me for something I *can't* give you."

"So you can't touch me but you can touch that?" She motioned to the banana I was twirling on the counter.

I stared at the counter and frowned, thinking about Balthazar and his threats. She didn't need to know that. It would just make her feel guilty for my being here. My voice came out rougher than I wanted it to when I said, "This is different."

"How?"

Emma placed her hand over mine. My skin scattered like a school of twinkling fish before pulling back together. I watched the colors of our skin meld then separate, feeling a jolt of connection race up my arm. This was the problem. When I was with Emma…nothing else mattered. The lines disappeared. I could barely remember the rules I was supposed to be following. It was taking everything in me not to force my skin into existence and lace my fingers through hers for real. I could barely keep myself together like this, knowing she wanted me to touch her. I pulled my hand away.

"The universe has boundaries. Touching a human, like *really* touching, is one of those boundaries. If I gave in and crossed that boundary, it would send off a signal. I wouldn't be able to hide it. I may have the ability, but I'm not supposed to use it."

No. Instead I had to be tortured with wanting something I'd never be allowed to have. Emma looked at me, worry creating creases between her eyebrows. I needed to lighten things up. She was going through enough without all this.

I picked up the banana and twirled it around my fingers like a six-shooter. "That time I pulled you up with the stick? I never touched you directly. The stick was just like this banana—they're not going to get me in trouble. The universe doesn't care if I mess with fruit or dead tree limbs or inanimate objects. I haven't checked on vegetables, though. I might get zapped out of existence if I try messing with something as dangerous as a bell pepper."

Emma leaned forward on the counter and grinned up at me. "I better keep the celery in the fridge, then. I wouldn't want you to be tempted with something so off-limits."

I laughed, but only because it's what she expected me to do. Really, it was hard to laugh at anything at this point. I'd had three days with Emma now. Three days of talking and laughing and getting her to look at me like I was something other than a dead guy. I didn't want to let this go. Being in the same room with Emma and her knowing I was there. Being in the same room with her and knowing she *wanted* me there. It felt like my own personal Heaven.

I was just waiting for Balthazar to take it all away.

"Finn."

I didn't realize how close Emma had gotten until I caught an intoxicating whiff of her scent. Oranges and some kind of flowery lotion. I couldn't help but wonder if she tasted as good as she smelled.

"You okay?"

I forced a smile onto my face and nodded. "Yeah. Of course."

She pulled her sleeves down around her hands and balled them in her fists, looking doubtful. She bit her bottom lip, studying me before a smile lit up her face.

"What are you thinking about?"

She stood up. "I'm thinking we should do something fun. It doesn't always have to be gloom and doom you know."

I raised a brow. "You do know I'm dead, right?"

"Come on. Humor me."

"What did you have in mind?" I could think of a few things I would have done if I was alive. I imagined what it might be like to take Emma by the hand and pull her down onto the sofa with me. To kiss her until neither of us could breathe. To feel her laughter against the hollow of my neck.

"You want to watch a movie?" She followed my gaze to the living room.

I shook the fantasy out of my head, embarrassed. "Um… yeah. Whatever you want."

"Do you even like movies?" she asked. "What do you even like to do?"

I shrugged, thinking back to a time I'd forced myself to forget. I thought about Pop's old records. The scratchy, haunting voices that rippled through the living room at night when he and Mama thought Henry and I were asleep. We'd get up sometimes and sneak into the hall to watch them dance. Pop would catch us giggling and wink at us, then press his finger to his lips. Then he'd dip Mama back and make her laugh in a way I'd never heard a girl laugh before. "I used to like music."

"Really? I'll be right back!" Emma darted down the hall.

I groaned. "You don't have to drag your music thingy out here. I'm fine, really. We can watch the movie." God, I didn't think I could take the screeching sounds that Emma called music today. Not after all that death. I just wanted—

Emma marched down the hall carrying a big brown case. She lugged it into the living room and set it on the table, then popped open the lid. A record player. She glanced up at me with those heavenly blue eyes and smiled.

I gaped at her. "How do you…"

Emma started digging old records out of a drawer across the room. "It was Dad's," she said, flipping through a stack of records. "Well, his father's anyway. Dad liked to listen to these after Granddad died."

She finally settled on one and crawled across the carpeted floor with it tucked under her arm. She hid it from me as she placed the needle on the vinyl disc and sat back smiling. "I always loved this one."

The needle gave life to the music, and Billie Holiday's butterscotch-rich voice wafted into the air around me. I swayed, unable to stop myself. I remembered the smell of flour and sugar on Mama's hands, the cadence of Henry's laughter as it mixed with mine.

Emma sat on her legs and hummed along to "The Very Thought of You," her eyes closed, completely unaware of the world around her. Her eyelashes were soft as feathers against her face, her humming a soft vibration in her throat. The ceiling fan ruffled the gold threads of hair around her temples. A hair tickled her cheek and her nose twitched.

I could feel the thought coming before it even formed. It started in that sad, hollow space in my chest, then worked its way up my aching throat. I could feel it behind my lips, fighting to be heard. Burning me up inside. But I couldn't say that to her. I didn't have a right to. So instead I let it run loose in my head. Three words that wouldn't stop.

I love you.

I couldn't stay still any longer. I crossed the room until I was standing over her, this girl I loved. She stopped swaying and looked up at me. I reached out my hand. "Dance with me."

Emma just looked uncertainly at my outstretched fingers and chewed on her lip. "But if you touch me, you'll…"

"Then we won't touch. Just dance."

Emma stood, pulled her hands out of her sleeves, and stared at her feet, looking lost. I stepped closer, so close I could see my shimmer reaching out toward her skin, like metal to a magnet. I never needed to breathe, but now, in this moment, I couldn't stop my lungs from pumping.

We moved together wordlessly. A step to the right. A smooth glide to the left. My shimmer sparked and hummed with energy the closer she got. I wanted to do like I'd seen Pop do with Mama, tip her back and make her laugh like a girl in love. I didn't. Instead, I settled for leaning in as close as I could, letting my unnatural breaths coat her neck. She shivered.

"Hey, at least it won't hurt if I step on your foot," I said.

Emma chuckled and reached her hands up as if she meant to place them on my shoulders, then stopped herself and dropped them back down to her sides. "I never know what to do with my hands."

"Well…" I leaned back and adjusted, so that my hand was out waiting. "If we were doing this for real, you'd put your left hand here." She hesitantly raised her hand and placed it in front of mine so that our palms nearly touched. "And in a *very* desirable world, my hand would go right…here." I placed my hand near her waist and she shivered, accidentally arching into my touch. My chest swelled with want and in an instant, my fingers scattered into a thousand iridescent particles, swimming around her like silver smoke. I pulled my hand back, watched my fingers take shape again, and wiggled them at her.

Emma released a pent-up breath and laughed. "Wow."

I shrugged and kept moving. In the background, Billie crooned and somehow managed to put exactly how I was feeling into words.

"The mere idea of you. The longing here for you. You'll never know, how slow the moments go, till I'm near to you," I sang softly into Emma's hair. Billie sounded way better of course, but the words felt too right in my mouth not to say out loud.

"You've done this before," Emma said. "I can tell."

"What?"

"Danced with a girl." Without actually touching me, she went through the motion of running her palms over my chest. I ached for her to close that space, but she never did.

I tried, unsuccessfully, to steady my voice. "Just once. School dance."

Emma smiled and did a little twirl. "What was her name?"

I couldn't think. Didn't really want to think about anything that didn't begin and end with Emma, but a flash of a girl in pink satin swaying nervously in my arms shook me. I smiled. "She wore a pink dress. I remember that. And I was so nervous I thought I might throw up."

Emma giggled. I didn't think I'd ever get tired of hearing her laugh.

"Did you love her?" she asked quietly. We stopped moving. Silence swallowed us. Then the crackling hiss of the record sounded and a new tune began.

"No," I said. "No, I didn't love her."

"Have you…" Emma took a step back and tucked her hair behind her ear. She wouldn't look at me. "Have you ever loved anyone…like that?"

I may not have been able to say the words, but I couldn't stop myself from moving toward her. Emma looked up at me, the question still lingering in her eyes. With an overwhelming burst of resolve, I let the words free. "Just you."

Her eyes widened and glistened with moisture. I didn't even think she was breathing. I wasn't breathing, either. The moment was too big to let even a breath ruin it.

"Emma…" I couldn't finish. I felt raw and needy. Alive. I leaned down, my lips just a whisper away from hers. I could feel the air clawing at me, trying to pull me from this moment, threatening to turn me to vapor if I closed the last bit of space between us, if I didn't get my emotions under control. I didn't want to let it. I—

The front door opened.

With a gasp, I let go, tumbling into vapor. Emma stared through me looking frantic. Reaching out.

Her mom tossed her keys on the counter, then walked into the living room. "What are you doing with that?" Rachel asked, looking right through me.

Emma shook her head like she was coming out of a daze and balled her hands into fists at her sides. "Um, just…listening to music. What else would I be doing with it?"

Rachel looked at the record player and her eyes dimmed and watered, obviously reliving memories all her own. She closed them and took a deep breath. "That's an antique," she said and walked out of the room. "Put it away."

Emma closed the lid to the record player and sighed. "You better come back," she whispered into the empty air, then gathered the record player in her arms and carted it out of the room.

I stared out the window, watching leaves twirl and dance through the air as they rained down from the trees. Somewhere in the back of my mind, Billie sang on. I could still smell Emma all over me. They say the dead can't sleep, can't dream. But as I stood there lost with wanting, I couldn't help but wonder when I was going to wake up.

When my scythe started to pulse with cold, I didn't even try to fight it. I needed to get out of there. Away from Emma's smell and the feel of her warmth. I needed to leave before I gave in and did something I couldn't take back.

Chapter 19

Emma

"Who is he?" Mom leaned on the counter, studying my face intently.

I finished dumping the rest of the lettuce into the big wooden salad bowl. "What are you talking about?"

"Just tell me it's not Cash." She held her hands up in surrender. "I don't think I could take that."

I rolled my eyes and laughed. "It's not Cash. It's not anybody."

"Well, I'll tell you one thing, it doesn't take ten minutes to make a bag salad for one," she said, grinning. "And it definitely doesn't require that much smiling."

Heat blossomed across my cheeks and I tossed the tongs in the bowl. Stupid salad. Stupid *me* for standing here daydreaming about a guy who didn't even have a heartbeat! I closed my eyes and pressed my palms to the counter so that I could feel grounded, and not like I was about to float off into space. It was useless. Anytime I closed my eyes, Finn was there. Smiling. Laughing. Almost kissing me. My heart hammered out a happy rhythm just thinking about him.

Everything else in my life might have been in shreds, but in that moment, with Mom in the kitchen and Finn in my heart, I felt happy. I felt like I wanted to be alive. Whatever that took. Whatever it meant. I wanted more of what I had with Finn. I wanted more time with Cash. More time with my mom. For the first time in a long time I felt like I had something to look forward to. And there was no way I was letting anyone take it from me.

Mom laughed at my smile and tucked a strawberry-blond wave behind her ear. "That's exactly how I looked the day your dad kissed me for the first time."

I breathed through the tight feeling in my chest, wishing she'd go on. She never talked about Dad anymore. And she had no idea how much I needed her to. Anything to bridge this always-widening gap between me and the memory of him. "How did it happen?"

She looked up at me surprised. "I've never told you?"

I shook my head and bit the inside of my cheek.

"Well, it was a disaster." She laughed and touched her lips. "It was supposed to be our second date, but I got sick. So I called and canceled because I didn't want to infect him."

I smiled, trying to picture it.

"But your Dad...he wouldn't give up that easily. He drove over to my dorm anyway and brought me soup and a movie. He said he didn't care if he got germs as long as they were mine."

"So, he kissed you then?"

"No." She stirred the spaghetti sauce I had on the stove, then turned back to me. "No, first I spilled hot soup on him. And *then* he kissed me."

I laughed and rinsed a pan that smelled like oregano and garlic. I tried to picture what my dad would have been like back then but I couldn't. All I could picture was Finn with his lips so close to mine it made my chest hurt in a way I'd never felt before.

"Do you feel that way about the new guy?" I asked, scrubbing the pan a little harder.

She sighed. "I'm not looking for a replacement for your dad. I'm just looking for someone to have a life with. To be happy with."

"You didn't answer the question."

She was quiet for a moment but finally said, "Yes. Parker makes me very happy. It's different than with your dad, but nice."

I thought about how happy Dad had made us. How he'd make us pancakes on Saturday mornings and tell cheesy knock-knock jokes while we ate.

"Knock knock," he said and stuffed a giant bite of banana pancake into his mouth. I couldn't wait to answer.

"Who's there, Daddy?"

"Cows go." He set his fork down and smiled at Mom, who beamed back at him.

"Cows go who?" I asked.

"Cows don't go who, Emma. They go moo."

The doorbell rang, shattering the memory, and I set the pan in the sink. "Is that him?"

"Yes." She sighed and darted over to the mirror on the wall to check her hair. "Be nice, Emma. He's really excited about meeting you."

I dried my hands on a dish towel. He might have been excited about meeting me, but I couldn't say I felt the same. How was I supposed to be excited when the conversation with Mom had left memories of my dad swirling around in my head like a dream? A dream I didn't want to wake up from. Mom reached over and pulled the rubber band out of my hair, so that it tumbled down in waves over my shoulders. "Be nice," she said again.

Of all the things Finn had saved me from, why couldn't he save me from this? My fingers settled on the doorknob, stalling, and the doorbell rang again.

"Emma! Answer it!" Mom called from the kitchen.

I sighed and pulled the door open to find my mom's new boyfriend on the other side, surrounded by trick-or-treaters. He grinned and stepped back to let a miniature Spider-Man and a princess rush up to the door. "Trick or treat!"

I'd almost forgotten it was Halloween. It was hard to remember holidays when your life felt like Halloween every day. I missed the days when Cash and I used to dress up and terrorize the neighborhood. Well, Cash terrorized. I usually just helped him take the blame in exchange for half of his candy. Mom pointed to a bag of candy on top of the fridge and I grabbed it.

"Here you go, guys." I dumped a handful of mini Kit Kats into their sacks, then watched them run around Parker to get to the next house. I gave him a hesitant smile and set the bag of candy outside so I wouldn't have to keep answering the door.

"You must be Emma. Wow, it's nice to finally meet you." He stuck out his hand and I mechanically shook it, not really knowing what to say. All I could think was, *If Dad wasn't dead,*

I wouldn't be meeting you.

I pulled my hand away and stepped aside so he could come in. "Um…yeah. Nice to meet you, too."

He was cute. I'd at least give her that. He had the kind of crew-cut brown hair and burly build that made me wonder if he was a cop, and the kind of wide, puppy-dog eyes that made me wonder if he had the hardness to back up such a title. And I had never seen Mom so googly-eyed over a guy since Dad. It made me uncomfortable to be in the same room with them looking at each other like this. It felt like I was choosing sides, and this wasn't the side I was ready to be on.

"It smells amazing in here," Parker said, smiling. "Is someone baking bread? You never told me you cooked, Rachel."

I snorted and chewed on a carrot from the salad. "That's because she can't."

Mom gasped. "Emma!"

"What? You can't."

Parker chuckled. "Well, it smells like she's a good cook."

Mom finally gave in and laughed, too. "Emma's the cook around here. She's pretty amazing when she gets into a kitchen."

Parker looked between us, then to the stove. "While this smells great, would you like to join us for dinner, Emma? I'm sure your mom wouldn't mind."

I forced myself to smile. "That's okay. Thanks, though."

He nodded. "Next time, then."

Mom smiled and kissed him on the cheek. I wanted to throw up. I wanted to throw up because he was nice. And she was happy. And everything seemed perfect. But it wasn't. It wasn't ever going to be perfect again. Not without Dad. I leaned my head against the wall.

"Well, we're off," Mom said. "Are you sure you'll be all right?"

I watched her sling her purse over her shoulder and take Parker's hand. "Yeah. I'll be fine."

She stopped at the door and pointed at me. "No boys. And that includes Cash. If you let him over here, he'll eat all the Halloween candy before those poor kids have a chance."

I laughed. "I set it on the front porch. That's probably going to happen regardless."

I waved them both off, then watched Parker's Honda zip out of the driveway through the kitchen window above the sink. I didn't know how to feel. Relieved, maybe? At least he was nice. And he seemed to make Mom happy. As much as I hated this reality, that's exactly what it was. Reality. And I had to find a way to deal with it.

I sighed and leaned on the sink, the smell of the food cooking making me a little hungry. The only sound in the house was the whir of air through the heating vents and the bubbling of spaghetti sauce on the stove. It was too much quiet. I needed something to drown out the thoughts. Music. I whirled around to grab the little kitchen radio Mom kept on the counter and froze.

All four of the kitchen chairs were stacked on top of one another, reaching all the way to the ceiling. The oak legs were jammed into the backs of each chair, making an eerie tower. I hadn't even heard them move. My muscles coiled into tight knots and I pressed myself against the cabinets. A cold burst of air swirled into my lungs with my next breath. I touched my throat and shook my head. Maeve. She was here. How did she do that so fast…

Something crashed against the wall in the living room and I grabbed on to the counter behind me. She was here. And Finn wasn't. My brain pulsed with fear, making everything fuzzy.

Think, Emma. Think!

Sage. The website had said burning sage would clear a home of unwanted spirits. It was sage, wasn't it? I darted for the refrigerator and dug through the clear drawer we kept herbs in. Behind me, it sounded like something was sliding along the wall. I didn't get a chance to turn around to see what it was. A picture frame crashed into the refrigerator next to my face and I screamed. My heart pounded out a deafening rhythm in my chest. I could feel it behind my ears as I fell to my knees and fumbled through the drawer. Rosemary, oregano, thyme…

Sage! I peeled open the package and pulled the little green leaves out. There wasn't much left, and it wasn't dry, but it would work. It *had* to work. If it didn't…no. No thinking like that. I grabbed a lighter from the drawer by the sink, bundled the sage, and watched the blue and orange flame char the ends. They smoked softly, but when I pulled the flame away, nothing. It wouldn't light.

The lights flickered and one of Mom's decorative plates slammed into the microwave next to my head, breaking into a hundred paisley pieces.

"Damn it!" I hunched down and sparked the lighter again. "Please light," I whispered through the panic thick in my throat.

Nothing. No flames. No smoke.

No, no, no! This could not be happening. "Light, damn you!" I screamed and rolled my thumb across the lighter switch. The metal burned my skin, but I ignored it, holding the flame under the leaves until I couldn't stand it anymore.

The flame snaked around the leaves. They shriveled, turning black, and smoke finally swirled up into the air. Shaking, I waved it around, choking on the smell.

"Get out," I said, holding the leaves up in the air. *Please work. Please work.* The pots on the stove started to vibrate and rattle. A wooden spoon I'd left in the spaghetti sauce started to spin circles in the pot. I squeezed my eyes shut and screamed, "Get the hell out of my house!"

Everything stopped.

Silent.

Still.

I opened my eyes and blinked at the spaghetti sauce boiling on the stove. The shattered pieces of plate lay scattered across the tile. The glass crunched under my shoes, and the fear in my chest started to drain. She was…gone. My fingers shook around the half-charred leaves in my fist.

"It worked," I laughed, though it sounded more like a sob, and forced my fingers open. The leaves dropped onto the tile.

And then everything exploded.

Kitchen cabinets and drawers burst open. Silverware turned into shrapnel. Wine glasses burst like grenades around me. The pot of spaghetti sauce erupted like a volcano, and the loaf of bread I'd been baking shot out of the oven and slammed into the wall.

I dropped to the ground, slapping my hands over my ears, and scrambled into a corner. Across the room, cans started to fly out of the pantry. Above me, forks whistled through the air and jammed into the wall. I curled into a ball and wrapped my arms around my legs, pressing myself as close to the wall as I could get. I could feel her. She felt like ice, a prickling cold against my skin. I couldn't think. Couldn't breathe. All of those incantations I'd read about…I could only remember one.

"This is a house of the living. Not a place for the dead," I whispered into my knees. "You are not welcome here." I could smell spaghetti sauce burning along with the sage, but I couldn't make myself move. All I could do was say it over and over until my lips felt numb. "This is a house of the living. Not a place for the dead. You are not welcome here."

I didn't stop until everything got quiet and the cold bled out of the room. Was she gone? I wasn't waiting around to find out. My knees almost buckled as I pushed myself up and brushed the glass off my jeans. I couldn't deal with this. Not now. Trying to suppress a sob, I ran down the hallway and into my room, then collapsed onto my bed. With the darkness of my pillow blocking the rest of it out, I could think.

The sage may not have worked, but the chant must have. Maeve wouldn't have gone on her own. Not unless she'd gotten what she'd wanted. I rolled over, mind reeling, and exhaled a shaky breath. "Thank you," I whispered. I wasn't sure who I was talking to. God maybe.

"Emma." Finn started across the room and I sat up.

"Maeve…she was here," I said, my voice hoarse from screaming.

"Are you okay?" He placed his open palms on either side of me and leaned in so close I could feel his warmth reaching out to my skin. "Emma, answer me."

"I…I'm okay." I stared at him and the fear in my chest eased. "She is gone, right? I can't feel her anymore."

He nodded.

"Why is she doing this?" My voice cracked.

"She's angry at me," he said softly. "It's not your fault. None of this is."

He looked sad and tortured and I couldn't stand it. I couldn't stand any of this. I pushed myself up off the bed and made my way back into the kitchen. It looked like a disaster area. Like a freaking tornado had roared through our house and turned my baking refuge upside down. Trembling, I touched a steak knife sticking out of a cabinet. How the hell was I supposed to explain this to Mom? An entirely different kind of terror washed through me. If she saw this, she'd think I did it and send me back to Brookhaven. She couldn't see this. I pulled out the trash can and a broom and started to sweep.

"Emma," Finn said from behind me.

I focused on the broom in my hands. Solid. Steady. I dumped a pan full of broken glass into the trash can.

Finn pulled the broom out of my hands. "Look at me."

I wouldn't look at him. I couldn't. I was about to shatter. "Do you have any idea what Mom will do to me if she comes home and finds this? I can't…she can't see it."

He didn't say anything else, but he didn't leave either. Out of the corner of my eye, I saw him throwing broken things into the trash can. He dismantled the chairs and placed them back around the table. Jerked the forks and knives out of the wall and tossed them in the trash, too. When we'd gotten the kitchen into somewhat-decent shape, I stared at the holes the forks and knives had left behind, trying to come up with a good lie for why they were there. Mom would freak out if she saw them. I'd have to drive to a hardware store first thing in the morning and buy something to cover them up before she noticed.

Finn followed me down the hall, and when I crawled back into bed, he lay down beside me. His cheek pressed against the pillow next to me, but it didn't crease or dent under the weight of him.

"The kitchen still looks awful. Do you think she'd believe me if I told her I threw a party?" I laughed. Sort of. I pressed my fists into the mattress. Why couldn't I stop shaking? "Maybe she'll be too distracted with her new boyfriend to notice all the holes in the wall."

"Do you like him?" he asked, softly, trying to change the subject. I could have picked a better one.

"I don't want to like him," I said. "I want my Dad back."

Finn reached up like he was going to brush the hair from my forehead, but stopped. He let it rest in the space behind my pillow instead. "You can't have him back," he whispered. "Don't punish her for that."

"I'm not trying to punish her." I shut my eyes and let myself feel Finn's heat against my face. I wanted him to touch me. To make me forget what had just happened. To finish what he'd almost started in the living room what felt like a lifetime ago now, but he didn't. "It just hurts."

"I know it does."

"I want to know how to stop her, Finn," I said. "More than just incantations and sage. Tell me what to do to stop Maeve. I'll do it."

He watched me silently, like he didn't know what to say. "I don't know how to stop her. But I'm going to figure it out."

Taking a deep breath, I opened my hand and reached out to touch him. He watched my fingers silently until I was just a breath away from his chest.

"Don't," he whispered.

I looked at him surprised. "Why?"

Finn's green eyes held mine, and something in me clicked into place at that moment. He'd looked at me like this before. I remembered. Or I at least remembered the feeling inside me.

Electric. Achy. Overwhelming and right.

"Because if I touch you, I won't be able to stop touching you."

I pulled my hand away, but never broke eye contact. I didn't want to lose this feeling that was making me dizzy all over. Not trusting my hands, I folded them between my face and the pillow.

"Then just stay with me," I said.

Finn nodded against the pillow. "Okay."

Chapter 20

Finn

At times like this I thanked God I couldn't feel. November wind rushed through me, knocking the last of the leaves from the trees around me as I waited outside Emma's school for the bell to ring.

There'd been no sign of Maeve for almost a week. As much as I didn't want to be away from Emma, I couldn't stand the monotony of going through her classes with her anymore. Maeve's silence was the perfect opportunity to get away from the useless information being pumped into my head. I'd never been great in school. While the other kids had their noses diligently shoved into books, I was somewhere else all together, staring out the window, my head in the clouds that I would eventually die in. I guess that's why I jumped at the chance to actually fly in them. I could still hear Mama as she slammed the dishes around in the metal sink so hard I thought they might shatter.

"Finn, you can't go. They can't make you. You're still a child. You haven't even finished school." She was crying, tears flowing down the crevices that years of worry and hard work had already carved into her cheeks.

"For the last time, they aren't makin' me, Mama. I want to go. It's what's right." I'd never sounded so uncertain. I was like a dog with its tail between its legs, afraid of being scolded. But then again Mama could drive the fear of God into the toughest of men, so I shouldn't have expected to be any different. *"And I'm not a kid anymore. I'm eighteen."*

"What about the farm? You know your daddy's getting too sick to do it alone. He needs you."

I looked away. *"Henry can help. He's sixteen now. He's old enough."*

"You can't wait to get out of this place, can you; away from us. Just be a man and admit it. You don't want to end up a poor hick farmer like your daddy." Her words trickled through me, burning holes as they went, until every emotion was draining from me like water through one of Mama's metal strainers she used for noodles.

"I am being a man. When I come home a war hero, you'll be proud of me. You'll see." I was trying to swallow back the useless tears, but they refused to be quieted. Instead of finishing the speech I had prepared, I walked over to her and placed my hands on her shoulders, smoothing out the wrinkles in her sunflower-print dress. *"I love you, Mama. I'm sorry."* I placed a kiss into the brown curls that were fastened behind her ears and walked away, only stopping long enough to grab my duffel bag, which carried everything I owned in the world.

It was the last time I saw her. It was the last thing we'd said to each other.

I shook off the last of the memory that was eating me from the inside out when the bell rang. It always took Emma a few minutes to grab her books and pry herself away from the crush of students, so when I heard my name I knew it wasn't her. I tensed when I felt it. The cold crawling up my spine. The breath of death prickling my senses. I didn't even have to turn around to know it was her. Maeve.

"Whatcha doing out here, Finny?" Maeve danced around me, pirouetting like she was part of the wind. She was a shimmery pixie with silver and red hair blazing like fire around her pale face, a complete contradiction to the cold that surrounded her. "Shouldn't you be inside?"

I crossed my arms over my chest, feeling the anger blaze through me like a flame. After last night…after I'd had to fight her off, and bait her to get her away from Emma. She was getting ruthless. I didn't know what to do anymore.

"Oh, come on. I'm here to play nice." She stopped dancing to stand in front of me, her red hair blocking out the sun behind her.

"What do you want this time?"

"Besides the obvious?" She glanced back and grinned when she saw Emma walking out of the school. The wind immediately picked up her blond hair and tossed it into her face. "You know, that wasn't very nice of you last week. Spoiling my fun like that."

"You think it was fun for her?" I snapped.

"Though I have to say it *was* entertaining. Did she actually think her little chant and some burned leaves would be enough to get rid of me?"

"Get to the point, Maeve."

"Relax, it's not like she can see me. Or you for that matter." When I tensed she stopped looking back and forth from Emma to me. "She can't see you, right Finn?"

I clenched my jaw, wanting to take back my reaction. This would definitely piss her off. The fact that I'd found some kind of happiness. It was going to send Maeve's madness into overdrive, and I'd just thrown fuel on the fire. Panic started a slow burn in my chest.

To my surprise, she visibly calmed herself. "Well, isn't that nice. Regardless, we can call a truce for now. I'm too busy working on something to bother with your screwed-up love affair."

"On what? What kind of game are you playing this time?" Emma was almost here, swinging her bag as she hurried across the crowded parking lot. The fear of having them this close to each other twisted me into knots.

"Who said it was a game?"

"It's always a game with you, Maeve."

"Have you spoken with Scout lately?" she asked a little too innocently.

I shot Maeve a look that could have cut through steel. "Why? Have you?"

Emma stopped by my side and gave me a wide smile. "You're here."

Maeve's form vibrated with the blackness of her rage. "You really want to be with her? In the flesh?" she asked, her voice shaking. "Go see Scout. He's got a really interesting operation going on. You might even find it useful yourself." A cruel grin on her face, she blinked out of existence.

"Hey, pretty girl." I tried to smile at Emma, tried to feel the warmth of her presence. But no amount of Emma's warmth could cast off the cloud of worry that had settled over me. What had Scout gotten himself into? If Maeve had anything to do with it, it couldn't be good.

Chapter 21

Emma

"What's wrong?" I looked around to make sure there wasn't anyone close enough to hear me talking to myself, worry curling around my spine like a vine. Finn was staring at nothing beside me, his brow creased, a frown ruining the happy look that usually accompanied his face.

He snapped back to reality and smiled at me, shaking off whatever had been bothering him. "Nothing. Are you ready to go?"

I shivered as a bitter gust of wind blew over me, biting at my nose and cheeks. Winter was close. "Yeah, we better before I get frostbite." I bounced on the balls of my feet to keep warm, tugging my gray stocking cap over my tousled hair to cover my ears. Finn gave me a distracted smile, and followed me toward my worn-out blue Jeep Wrangler. It was spotted with rust and the air conditioner didn't always work, but it was mine.

"So, what are we doing today?" I tossed my bag into the back of the Jeep and cranked the ignition, praying that the heater wouldn't take a century to heat up. I had wanted to try out a new hiking trail and load up my camera with landscape shots, but today was way too cold for that. Any minute now, snow would start dumping from the sky in buckets.

Finn stared out the windshield at an approaching SUV. "I don't know about us, but it looks like *you* have company."

I slipped off my gloves and shoved my numb fingers against the vents to thaw them out. Cash's black Bronco ground to halt in front of us, blocking in my Jeep. He jumped out of his truck, shivering as a rush of wind blasted his face, turning his cheeks pink.

I gave Finn a meaningful look and he groaned. "So, what? Am I supposed to go stand out in the cold now?"

"You can't even get cold," I said.

"Point taken."

"Seriously," I said. "Just give me a minute with him."

Finn gave me a small smile and nodded, barely giving me time to blink before he was gone. I watched him until all I could see was the flicker of his gray shirt near the tree line, but then it was gone, too.

Cash climbed in the passenger side and slammed the door shut behind him. "It's cold enough to freeze Hell over out there." He rubbed his hands together and blew hot breath into them.

"Here." I cranked the heat up another notch and turned a vent in his direction. "Better?"

He nodded and settled back in his seat.

"So what's up?"

He looked at me and raked his fingers through his thick

black hair. "Funny. That's exactly what I was going to ask you."

I averted my gaze, watching a whirlwind of tawny-colored leaves dance over the hood of my Jeep and get stuck in my windshield wipers. I'd been avoiding Cash for more than a week—pretty much since Finn had popped into my life. Honestly, I was surprised it took him this long to corner me and demand an explanation. Mom would've demanded an explanation for my behavior days ago had I not patched up the holes in our kitchen walls while she was at Spin class. I took a deep breath and said, "I'm sorry."

"Sorry?" Cash asked, his stare burning a hole through me. "Don't say sorry, just tell me what I did that's making you dodge me in the halls and not answer my calls. And what the hell is up with the new lock on the window?"

"I didn't do the window," I said to my lap. "Mom did after she caught you in my room the other night."

"So, what, then?" he asked. "Is it because I didn't believe you about the pictures? The ghost crap? Did I fuck up?" Cash leaned across and grabbed my arm. "Talk to me, Em. What?"

I stared down at his hand. "You didn't do anything, I swear. I've just been dealing with some stuff lately." It wasn't a lie, but I wasn't willing to give him the details. Not even Cash would accept what was going on in my life as reality.

Cash stared blankly out the windshield. "You used to let me help you deal with stuff. Now it just feels like you're shutting me out." He wiped his palms over his jeans and laughed bitterly. "You're my family, Em. You're the only one who gives a damn about me, so I'm asking you to let me in. Don't try to do this on your own again. We both know it doesn't work. If you're going through something, then I go through it, too. Got it?"

"Okay." I nodded, wanting so badly to tell him about the boy who had saved my life. In more ways than one. I wanted to tell him how wonderful Finn was. I wanted him to be alive so Cash could see for himself.

"So…we're good?"

I shoved the things I wanted to say back into the place in my mind just for me and nodded. "Yeah, of course."

"Do you want to hang out tonight? We could go to the old drive-in. It's cold as hell, but I got the heater fixed in my truck." Cash pulled out his phone and started Googling show times. "We can hash out these problems of yours over a hot box of popcorn. Unless it's gross girl stuff. If that's the case, I take back what I said about us going through everything together."

I peered out my window, looking for Finn. I spotted him lingering at the tree line, hands shoved in his pockets as he kicked a few rocks waiting for me. "It's not gross stuff. Why aren't you going out with Tinley tonight?"

"She's grounded," he said. "Hey, *Zombie Apocalypse Two* is playing at seven thirty."

I sighed. More dead people. Just what I needed. "Perfect."

Cash finally slid his phone back into his pocket. "I'll pick you up at seven." He lightly punched me in the arm and climbed out of the Jeep.

Once the black Bronco was out of sight, Finn slid into the front seat. "How bad was it?"

"He's fine," I said, pulling out of the parking lot and starting the fifteen-minute drive home. "Just worried about me. He wants me to go out tonight. He probably thinks I'm on the verge of a mental breakdown."

"You should go."

I stopped at a stop sign and glanced over at Finn, who

looked completely at home in my Jeep. He looked like he belonged there. With me. "What about you?"

"I have somewhere I need to be. I'd rather you be with him so he can keep an eye on you."

I lifted my chin. "I don't need a babysitter 24-7." It may not have been the most effective way, but I'd gotten rid of Maeve at the house. I could do it again if I had to. And chances were, I would. I couldn't expect Finn to be with me every waking minute.

"I know that," he said, but didn't sound like he really believed it. "But it'll make me feel better if you're with him."

I pulled my Jeep over to the side of the road under a canopy of pine trees and turned so he couldn't see my face, my bleary gaze spilling out onto the empty highway. I wasn't in control of my own life and after two years, I was finally tired of it. I was tired of being afraid. I was tired of people looking at me like I might snap at any moment. I was tired of Finn treating me like he was my bodyguard when I wanted him to be something else.

"Emma… What's wrong? What are you thinking?"

"I think you've spent the last two years trying to protect me because, for some reason, you feel guilty. Like it's your job, or something. You constantly say this isn't my fault, but it's not yours either. You didn't *do* anything to her. Nothing that would justify this, or obligate you to keep me safe all this time. I just…I wish things were different."

I wished everything were different. I wished I could have a normal life, that there wasn't some crazed soul out there hell-bent on me dying. I wished Finn could be here because he *wanted* to be, and not because he felt that he had to protect me. It hurt to admit even to myself, but I wished Finn was alive. I wanted him to be able to hold my hand. Kiss me. Do everything I could do and not worry about the consequences. I wanted so many things from him that he couldn't give. And it wasn't fair.

"I don't need you safe because of some obligation," he said, his voice tight. "I need you safe because if something ever happened to you it would rip me apart! Don't you see that? I need…" He laid his hand in the seat between us and stared at it. "I need *you*, Emma. I need you more than I've ever needed anything."

"Finn…"

"I'm not trying to be an ass. I just need you to trust me when I say that something is dangerous. I have to go somewhere and I need to know you're safe while I'm gone. The only way I'm going to be comfortable leaving you is if you stay with Cash."

"Cash isn't going to be able to protect me from Maeve."

Finn's fingers carefully brushed against mine. The warm spark ignited by his fingers sent a rush of heat racing across my skin. "He won't have to."

I took a deep breath, heart pounding with want, and watched his hand pull away. He was right. I would protect myself. Maybe it would work. Maybe it wouldn't. But I wouldn't go down without a fight. No matter how screwed up and unfair it was, I wanted more of whatever it was that Finn and I had too much to give up now.

"I'll be okay," I finally said. "I promise."

"You're sure?"

"Yeah. Just…" I glanced out the window at the cars buzzing by, trying to force some confidence in my voice. "Just come back, okay?"

Finn scooted across the seat. I felt the warmth of his lips shimmer against my cheek. "I'll always come back to you, Emma."

I shut my eyes again, trying not to think about how badly I wished that kiss could have been real, and when I opened them he was gone.

Chapter 22

Finn

The club I tracked Scout to was up on the mountain. It would have been about an hour's drive past the reaping border, but it only took me a few minutes. One perk to being a dead guy—no traffic. Peak was the closest thing to a club you got in this part of the state, and it seemed like every drunken single person within a fifty-mile radius had made it out despite the crappy weather. I dreaded going in. The music was loud and the obnoxious drunks were even louder. It wasn't anywhere close to where I wanted to be, but I had to do this. I had to at least see what Scout was up to. Not to mention find out what in God's name he could possibly be doing with Maeve. I was almost afraid to find out.

I dissolved through the cold steel doors and into a smoke-filled room packed with bodies. The music was so loud, I could barely hear myself think. Where the hell was Scout? A better question—what was he doing here?

"Finn?" I stopped when I heard Scout's voice next to the bar. Spinning around, I accidentally dissolved through a girl and came out the other side reeking of cigarette smoke and apple martinis.

I made my way over to him. He looked like the same old Scout, but something was different. His eyes...he looked... *alive*.

"Holy Hell, Dr. Death. I didn't think I'd be seeing you again after that meeting. Seriously, what did you do? Balthazar looked *pissed*."

"You know me. I've never been very good with rules." I looked around, getting dizzy as my eyes flickered from face to face. "Can we go outside and talk?"

Scout smiled and I followed him, cutting through the crowd to an emergency exit, and slid silently through the door. The sleet had picked up, but it was so black outside, the only place you could see it was under the orange glow of the streetlights, tiny flickers of ice in a frenzy to coat the earth.

Scout leaned against the brick wall and crossed his arms over his chest. "What's up?"

"You tell me. Why is Maeve saying I should come see you?"

"Probably because I told her to tell you to come see me," he said.

Yeah, this was going nowhere fast. "Okay, better question. Why the hell are you talking to Maeve in the first place?"

Scout raised his hands defensively. "She came to me. I told you before—you and her, your girlfriend, the drama... Count me out, man."

So much for loyalty. I blew out a long breath and leaned

against the wall next to him. "What's the big secret?"

"I did it." The look on Scout's face was nothing short of triumphant. "I found a way back in."

"Back in where?"

"Back in there." He pointed at a couple around the corner, laughing and kissing. I froze, paralyzed by a thousand different emotions: fear, disgust, but the most unsettling...*hope*.

"I can get into a body, Finn. I found a way."

I shook my head. Back when he was just a newbie and I was dumb enough to hang around him, we'd tried a lot of stupid crap, this particular stunt being the most moronic by far. "You can't. We tried, remember? It doesn't work."

"It does," he argued, his blue eyes intense. "They just have to be inebriated. Alcohol, pills, sleep aids. Anything to lower their defenses, make them cloudy, and I'm in. It only lasts for a few hours, though, but that's long enough to have some fun." Scout bounced on the balls of his feet, smiling. "You have no idea how good the cold feels. You'd think it would suck as much as these yahoos complain about the weather, but it doesn't. It's amazing."

"I don't believe you," I finally said. I didn't want to believe him. If it was true, it meant way more bad than good.

"Seeing is believing, friend." Scout winked and backed up, watching the couple he'd pointed to stumble around the corner, laughing. Idiots. They were going to freeze in this weather, but they were probably too drunk to notice.

"What are you doing?" Stepping away from the wall, I watched Scout approach the redheaded guy's back. Something inside me twisted. This wasn't about to happen. It couldn't.

Scout took a deep breath and dissolved through the thick denim jacket of the redhead, who now had his tongue shoved halfway down his girlfriend's throat. But that wasn't the disturbing part. Scout didn't come out the other side. He was... gone.

"No," I whispered stumbling back against the wall, balancing myself on my heels before I went spilling through the brick wall. I clenched my jaw and focused. The shock of what was happening was making it hard to stay in one piece. "What did you do?"

The redhead backed away from the girl and cleared his throat before casting me a quick glance. "Baby, why don't you wait inside? I'll be there in a minute, just want a quick smoke before we go." She smiled and nodded before heading inside, swaying her hips when the stream of music poured through the open door into the night air.

The redhead pulled a pack of cigarettes from his pocket and shivered as he lit one up. The red glow from the end of the stick lit up the dark shadow he stood in. After he'd taken a long drag, he threw his head back and groaned, blowing smoke out the side of a grin.

"I forgot how much I liked smoking," he said. "The last kid didn't smoke. I lucked out this time." He tapped his pocket where he'd shoved the pack, then strode over to me, smiling. "What do you think, Finn?"

I didn't know what to say. This meant a lot of things, but the most important to me at the moment was that Maeve knew there was a way in, too. And if Maeve knew...son of a bitch! I gripped the back of my neck, trying to think.

"I pray to God that you weren't stupid enough to tell Maeve about this."

He frowned and took another puff of the cigarette. "I don't get you, man. I'm standing here telling you I found a way in. A way to actually freeze from the cold, savor the sensation of a drink sliding down your gullet, feel the wind in your hair!" He ran his fingers through his short red spikes and frowned. "Well, not this kid. This kid doesn't have the greatest hair for that. But that girl in there." Scout lifted his chin and laughed, smoke sliding past his lips with the sound. "I'm going to feel that, too."

I wanted to puke. In that moment I wished more than ever that I still had that human function so that I could expel whatever it was that I was feeling. The whole thing was disgusting. "And the girl? Or should I say 'girls,' since it looks like you've been doing this a while. What do they think about it?"

"Trust me. They have a good time. It's not like most of them know the guy they're with any better than they'd know me. And the guys waking up next to a hot chick—you think they're complaining? Nope." He made a popping sound to exaggerate his "nope," then flicked his cigarette to the ground and rubbed his arms.

"I'm telling you man, the cold hurts, but I can't get enough. It makes me feel alive." He laughed and the sound felt stale, leaving a bad taste in my mouth, just like the cigarette smoke. "You want to try it? I'm sure we could find you someone, too."

This was sick. And I was screwed. I couldn't help but wonder where the hell the real Scout had gone, because this wasn't him. "Balthazar is going to let you burn for this."

"Whatever, man," he said. "Don't tell me you haven't been dreaming about this very thing for years. Don't tell me you wouldn't do it to be with Emma."

"Not like this. This is wrong, Scout. These people don't know you any more than they know what's happening to them. It's screwed up and you know it."

"Bullshit. You are so full of—"

I cut him off, watching his breaths come out in foggy puffs of white that looked like clouds wandering into unfamiliar darkness. "Tell me you didn't show Maeve. Please, Scout, just give me that."

His eyes, which strangely enough were Scout's eyes, stared back at me as if I should've already known the answer. "She's known for a week."

Stupid, stupid, stupid! He knew what would happen. How could he… Something inside me broke in half, a dam breaking, flooding me with rage. "What the hell did you do? You knew what she'd try to use this for. You *knew*!" I pulled out my scythe and backed him into the bricks, not really sure what I was planning to do with it.

"I'm sorry! What do you want me to say? I thought if she could figure out how to use this maybe she'd give up on Emma."

The sleet pelting the asphalt was the only sound to break the bitter silence that hung between us. It didn't matter that he was sorry. It didn't matter what he thought. It didn't even matter that a lost soul like Maeve might not even be able to pull this off. I couldn't take chances with Emma.

I backed away, losing my steam. "Good-bye, Scout."

Chapter 23

Emma

Cash fiddled with the radio until he found the station that would provide the sound for the movie while I leaned out the window and snapped a picture of three girls sitting in the back of a pickup, blankets wrapped around them like cocoons. As crazy as it sounded, I almost liked taking pictures for the yearbook now. I could control the orb problem now that I knew what was causing them, and when people weren't posing and acting stupid, I realized it wasn't all that different from landscape photography. My shots were getting better, that's for sure.

I took a few more pictures of random things that I thought might make a neat collage, and after I'd gotten what I needed, pulled off my coat and tossed it in the backseat. "Can we turn this down?" I asked Cash, messing with the heater.

Cash batted my hand away. "Are you kidding? It's effing

cold in here."

I rolled down my window a crack and sat back in my seat. "Maybe for you."

"So, are you going to spill, or am I going to have to force it out of you?"

I didn't know what to say. I knew what he wanted to hear, but I wasn't a very good liar, so it didn't leave me a lot of options.

A couple of seniors I knew walked by on their way to the concession stand and I grabbed my camera to snap a picture of them. On the big screen, a hot dog in a top hat danced, while popcorn boxes sang in the background. I couldn't help but wonder where Finn was.

"I just feel lost," I finally said, letting the camera hang from my chest. It wasn't the whole truth, but it wasn't a lie. I felt lost in the impossible, in the way I was starting to feel about Finn. There was a silent tug-of-war ripping me apart inside. One side telling me to do what was sane, the other pulling me over the edge of reason where nothing made sense. "I feel like I'm coasting on fumes and I don't know where I'm going to land and it terrifies me."

"I think everybody feels that way sometimes." Cash stared out his window. He drew the outline of a woman's profile on the fogged-up glass with his fingertip.

"What happens when you *always* feel like that?" I asked. "What happens when you finally run out of gas?"

He sighed and leaned his head back on his seat to look at me. "Then you realize that I'm right behind you with a can of fuel and you stop worrying so damn much."

I smiled and we both laughed a little. Cash turned down the heater and slid on his jacket as the movie started. It opened with a desolate street and a lone man walking through a city empty of living things. It didn't take long for the dead to rise, though. Rotting and starving, they filled the alleys, consumed every hollow space, like cattle called to feed. Cash yelled at the screen, calling the man an "effing idiot" when he got himself cornered in an alleyway. I sighed. Whoever came up with this grotesque concept of living dead had obviously never met a soul.

"I'm back," Finn said behind me. "Get rid of him. We need to talk. Now."

Something in the tone of his voice made my chest constrict. I knew it wasn't fair that I was sending him out into the cold so I could have a conversation with a nonexistent person, but hopefully whatever Finn had to say wouldn't take long. "Cash, could you get me a Coke from the concession stand?"

"You have two feet last time I checked."

"Yes, and I'll kick your ass with one of them if you don't get over yourself and be a gentleman."

Cash frowned. "What's a gentleman?"

I forced a laugh, needing him to leave. "Please."

"Fine." He nodded and grabbed my purse out of the floor to dig for my wallet. "But you're buying."

"Deal." When he was gone, I spun around in my seat. Finn looked upset and, for the first time since we'd met, disheveled. Was that even possible for a soul? "What's wrong?"

"Something's happened. And I'm not sure…I don't know how to handle it. But I don't want you freaking out on me. I'm going to figure it out." He braced his palms on the seat and stared at the floorboards like he was trying to calm himself. "I'm going to figure it out," he whispered to himself again.

"Just say it," I said, forcing the tremble out of my voice. "I can handle it." It's nothing I hadn't been through before. Two years of this…was there really anything he could say that could surprise me?

"Emma, look at me." He leaned close enough that I was enveloped in the warm scent of Finn, trapped in my own personal summer while the rest of the world battled the cold outside. I stared into his green eyes, churning with emotion. "It doesn't matter. I'm going to keep you safe. There's no sense in you worrying about something that you can't do anything about."

"But that's just it. I *can* do something. I stopped her, Finn." I grabbed the back of the seat. "At the house. I used a chant, and she left."

Finn shook his head and looked away. "Emma…"

"No, I'm serious. I'm more than capable of—"

"She left because of me," he said, softly. "The sage, the chant… They're just as useless as the Ouija board. None of it works."

My vision blurred as my gaze drifted to the window. Cash was making his way through the row of cars, a Coke in each hand. The colored lights from the movie screen reflected off the shiny black leather on his jacket, making him shimmer like Finn.

It hadn't worked. Oh my God…it hadn't worked.

"Just calm down. Breathe," Finn whispered into my ear.

I closed my eyes, took a breath, and nodded.

Finn stiffened, peering out the back window into the night. "Emma…" he started, never taking his eyes off of whatever he saw out the window. "Stay in the car."

A gust of wind ruffled my hair and before I could say anything, Finn was gone. He was gone, and Maeve could be anywhere. I braced myself on the dashboard. My breaths were coming in too fast, making me dizzy. I fumbled with the glove compartment and popped it open. Cash used to keep a utility knife in here.

Cash swung open the door, and I crammed the napkins and papers back into the compartment and slammed it shut. I felt stupid for even looking. A knife wasn't going to stop Maeve. And the sage, the chants…none of that had worked. I didn't have anything to defend myself. I felt like I was bobbing in open water, waiting for a shark to finish me off.

Cash shoved a cup into my hand and nodded at the glove compartment. "What were you doing?"

I grabbed both drinks as he shivered and shook like a wet dog once he was in the safety of the truck. "N-nothing. Just looking for a napkin."

He grabbed his drink and looked me over. "You're being weird tonight. What's going on?"

"Nothing. I'm fine." I took a sip of the Coke, letting the caffeine race through my system and chase away the violent, unraveling feeling inside me. Peering into the night and not finding a trace of Finn, I couldn't stop shaking. She was here. She was here and Finn was out there trying to stop her.

Cash set his popcorn on the seat between us and stared at me.

I couldn't look at him. All I could think about was Finn. What had he seen out there? Where had he gone? What if he couldn't stop her?

"Em…"

I shook my head, knowing that if I didn't get out of that truck within the next ten seconds, I was going to lose it in front of him. "I'm going to go to the bathroom. Be right back."

Chapter 24

Finn

Maeve. I may not have been able to see her, but I could feel the wintry chill trickling down my spine. The whisper of nearness that another soul left across my skin. I made my way through the menagerie of cars, letting the soft pull in my veins guide me. To my right, I heard a shrill peal of laughter echo across the lot. I catapulted over a car, heading in the direction of the sound, then stopped. The chill faded and the pull tugged me in the opposite direction. I spun around, shaking my head, trying to clear it. To get some focus.

"Maeve!" I rounded another car and started across the lot. "I know you're out there." But the pull faded again, and then pulsed with life, tugging me in the opposite direction. What the hell? I rolled my shoulders and gritted my teeth. *Get it together, Finn.* I stopped, looking for anything—the hint of a red shimmer, a spark of silver—anything to tell me which way to turn. There were too many people here. Too many ways for her to bait me. Realization hit me.

She's trying to bait me.

I spun around, slid over the hood of a yellow Volkswagen. I had to get back to Emma—

"Looking for someone?"

I froze at the sound of Maeve's voice. She stood on the roof of an old pickup that once upon a time had probably been red. Now it was mottled with rust and made creaking sounds every time the kids inside moved.

"There are so many options here. So many ways to die, don't you think?" She tapped her finger on her chin, calling attention to the black veins standing out on her throat. A dull silver color was strangling the lively red from her hair one strand at a time.

"Don't do something stupid just to prove a point," I said.

Maeve glared at me. Her black pupils ate up the green that had once been around them. "And what point is that? That I have wasted the past seventeen years of my existence for something that should have been mine in the first place? Well, no more waiting, Finn. I'm taking what's mine tonight."

What? Her words tumbled around inside my head before clicking into place. She didn't want just anyone's body, she wanted…Emma's?

She twitched as the right side of her face morphed into a screaming shadow before returning to pale-colored skin again. She grabbed the sides of her face and an agonized scream exploded from her throat. She was about to turn. I slipped my scythe out of its holster and climbed onto the hood. "You're not taking anything."

Maeve straightened her back and laughed, the shadow

flickering over her features. Before I could blink, she leapt over me, what was left of her red shimmer blurring across the dead black sky. I spun around, looking up, down, left, right, until the stars in the sky blurred together. Where could she have gone? What was she—

An ice-cold hand wrapped around my ankle and jerked me off the hood of the pickup. I landed on my back. Swirled into nothing resembling a man. I focused on pulling myself back together, and when I did, Maeve was standing over me, red hair blowing around her pale freckled face. Rage had consumed her to the point she was shaking. I glanced at her hand. It was wrapped around a blade. *My* blade. My scythe. It looked so awkward in her white fist. Mine felt so incredibly empty without it.

"Maeve…" I held my hand up and tried to ease up. "Don't do—"

She swung out. The blade sliced through my thigh, and all that existed was pain. I clutched at my thigh and groaned. Black oozed from between my fingers, glittering like stars in the night.

"Oh, does that hurt? Poor little reaper. Maybe you should have picked someone else's life to ruin. I could be happy right now! I could be alive. I could be in love. I didn't get the chance to have *any* of that my first life. And you made sure I'd never have it again. You call me a bad person, Finn? What about you? You walk around like there's a halo on your goddamned head, but you're just as bad as me and we both know it."

"Her time was up!" I shouted, panic and anger fighting for a place in my chest. I clutched my head to stop everything from spinning. "You could have had another chance!"

"Once my name was called, it was over for me, too. There

was no second chance for me. There never is, but you didn't stop to find that out before you ruined my life, did you? But now…now, I'm taking my chance. If I can get into her body, there is no way in hell I'll let you take it from me again."

I opened my mouth, but stopped, processing her words. *Take* it from her? Scout said a possession would only last a few hours. This didn't make sense…unless she'd found a way to make it permanent. No. She couldn't have. I had to believe that. "That's not even possible. Just…think about this. Think about—"

"I'm done thinking about it!" A shadow slithered over her face and she sobbed. The black veins in her neck pulsed with darkness. "Look what you did to me!"

She swung my scythe again and I grabbed her wrist. Twisted her until she landed on top of me. The blade clattered to the ground. She screamed and turned to a vapor in my grasp.

"Maeve!" I shouted, grabbing my scythe and shoving it into my holster. I vaulted to my feet, and my vision blurred out of focus. The anger was burning me up. Turning my insides to ash. "You want the truth?" I spun around and stumbled. "I don't regret it. I'm not sorry. You didn't deserve that body. And there is no way in Hell I'd let you have it now!"

An engine started behind me and roared to life. I turned on my heel and squinted into the headlights that engulfed me. There wasn't anyone inside. *How…*

The car leaped into action, accelerating, and I stumbled back. I barely had time to think. I focused on making myself solid, lunging for the young blond girl carrying a box of popcorn in the car's path, but spilled right through her. I flexed my fingers and they scattered like stars. I couldn't keep it together. Couldn't touch her…

I took a deep breath and shouted, "Move!" She spun around in time to see the car and horror registered across her face. She stumbled back out of the way, falling into the gravel.

Across the lot another engine roared to life. I staggered through the cars. The groaning sounds of the undead on the screen filled my ears. The thought of Emma being in this parking lot while Maeve was going on a rampage made my head spin and my legs pump a little faster. The car revved, churning a cloud of dust into the air, and rolled forward. I ground to a halt in front of the car, expected it to fly through me like everything else, but it stopped, the bumper an inch from touching my chest.

I bent over and grabbed my knees, dizzy. The hole in my thigh oozed and ran down my leg. I couldn't stay like this. I felt... I closed my eyes and focused, but no matter how hard I tried I could feel myself losing it. Energy was leaking out of me, leaving me wispy and weak. I'd never been this drained. I limped over to Cash's Bronco, slid through the metal and into the seat. "Get Cash to take—"

My lips froze around the words. Emma was gone.

I grabbed the door handle, hoping to catch Cash's attention, but my fingers slid right through it. Trembling, I reached out and tried to knock the bag out of his hands. Nothing. She'd drained me. Something hot swept through my chest. Panic. Terror. She'd planned this. Set me up to fail so she could get to Emma. I slid back through the door of the Bronco and looked across the crowded lot. Maeve was out there. So was Emma. And there was nothing I could do about it.

Chapter 25

Emma

"Finn?" I whispered as soon as I pushed through the swinging door to the bathroom. The silence that answered me stung like lemon juice in an open wound. I braced my hands on chipped tile counter. Where could he possibly have gone?

Something dark like a shadow flashed behind me in the mirror, then disappeared.

"Finn?" I whispered. He didn't answer. Nobody did. I walked over and grabbed the door handle, but the big metal door wouldn't budge. A thread of fear seeped into my abdomen, tying into knots. The lights flickered and buzzed. Cold slithered over my skin and I shuddered.

I wasn't alone.

I spun around and pressed my back against the cold metal, lifted my camera, and snapped a picture of the open air in front of me. A dark-colored orb, nothing like Finn's, filled the far corner of the room.

Something hit the door behind me and I screamed. It sounded like a battering ram and had enough force to make my bones rattle. Shaking, I located the one window in the room, the only way out. My only chance.

I ran for the window, my body bracing for the pain that was going to come with barreling through a glass window. Something hard slammed into me and I flew back across the room. My back slammed into the wall and I choked the breath back into my lungs. I scrambled to my feet, ignoring the ache in my back, and snapped another picture to see how close she was. Before I could get the display to show, the strap around my neck snapped and the camera flew out of my hands, smashing into the wall beside me.

Behind me the grimy bathroom stalls shuddered with what sounded like thunder. One of the stall doors flew open, slamming into the wall, knocking over a trash can. Toilet paper unraveled into a pile on the floor, then slowly rose and began to swirl around me. A cyclone of filth.

"Stop!" I screamed, running for the door again. I beat on it until my fists turned red and throbbed. "Let me out! Somebody let me out!" Fear ripped the words out of me like razor blades.

One by one, the stall doors flew off their hinges and into the big wall-length mirror above the sinks. Glass shattered and flew through the room like shrapnel. Finn was right—she wasn't going to stop until she got what she wanted. But he was wrong about her wanting to hurt me.

She wanted me *dead*.

The tissue fell into limp heaps and the lights flickered again. I squeezed my hands into fists. This couldn't be happening. Not now. Not in a filthy theater bathroom.

The lights dimmed, then flared back to life. When the last stall door flew off its hinges, I didn't see it coming. Pain burst like darkness behind my eyelids and I crumpled to the floor. My hand reached for something, anything, to grab onto. Blood trickled into my eye and I managed to swipe it away with the back of my wrist. "Please don't do this…"

The lights stopped flickering and the room went silent and still. Could she be listening to me? Trembling, I pushed myself up. "I'm not going to pretend to know anything about what happens after you die, but I do believe there is something better out there. I have to believe it. Just like I have to believe there's something like that out there for you. Maybe Finn can help you find it?"

Nothing happened. I let out a shaky breath and tried not to cry. She'd heard me. Listened, even. Finn was wrong. I could still do something—

A long shard of glass dragged itself across the tile floor, the scraping sound enough to make me feel sick to my stomach. One by one, the larger pieces of broken mirror rose into the air. Something dark flashed in the surfaces. The glass sliced through the air and I screamed, pressing myself against the floor to avoid being hit. Pain pulsed, burning hot from my neck to my shoulder. A piece had gotten to me. I could feel it lodged in my neck.

Silence spread through the room, thick like darkness, and then…the lights flickered again. I started to climb to my knees, but something knocked me back. My head hit the floor and the room spun in circles above me. This was it. She was going to win. I couldn't do anything about it.

And then I felt it—the icy sensation I'd associated with Maeve, slithering over my skin like it was looking for a way in.

Something heavy and cold pressed me into the floor, pushing the breath out of my lungs. Frantic, my soul pushed back, clinging to my skin as it forced her away. This wouldn't be my end. I was not losing my life to some crazed poltergeist bitch.

"Help! Somebody help!" I screamed until my throat felt raw. "Cash! Finn?" *Someone, please find me,* I pleaded silently as I crawled to the door, one hand clutching the wound on my neck. Sticky liquid seeped between my fingers, churning my stomach. I didn't have to look to know it was blood. The way the room was spinning and turning dark around the edges was enough to tell me that.

The window blew out like it had been hit with a wrecking ball. I tried to crawl away but white-hot pain bit into my calf, the fiery sensation of metal grating against bone. I closed my eyes, praying for anything that would make the pain stop. *Make it go away,* I prayed through the pounding in my head. Steady as a drum, it pounded louder, louder, louder, until a final burst drowned the sound out with shouts and screams.

"Emma. Oh my God, Emma, what happened?" Cash's breath was warm on my face, his hands replacing mine around the wound on my neck.

I screamed. The sound choked off into a strange gurgle as he slid the piece of broken mirror out of my skin. Everything was blurry even behind my closed lids, a gray catacomb of never-ending fuzziness pulling me deeper into an ocean of forgetting. I fought it, concentrating on the feel of Cash's fingers on my face. I needed to talk. I needed air. I needed…

"Finn," I whispered, and then everything went black.

Chapter 26

Emma

"Don't you dare die, Em." Cash's voice sounded like he'd been wrapped in cotton. "I mean it. I'll follow you to the grave and kick your ghostly ass if you don't stay with me."

My eyes rolled around behind my eyelids. I couldn't open them. Couldn't make my lips move to tell him not to worry.

"Sir, we're going to need you to back up," a woman's voice said. I felt pressure against my neck. So much pressure. A prick in my wrist. A plastic mask around my mouth. Then warm, familiar fingers laced through mine. Cash.

"He really cares about you," a girl said.

I blinked, confused by the fact that I was suddenly sitting on a bench next to the drive-in concession stands with a girl I didn't know. In front of us, the back of the ambulance was a flurry of action. I had never seen a pair of hands move so fast as the paramedic worked at bandaging my neck. Cash rocked back and forth, staring at our linked fingers. My body looked pale and empty on the gurney.

"I'm dead," I breathed. I looked up and had to blink away the golden spot that bloomed across my vision before the girl came into focus.

She smoothed her white dress over her legs. "You're not dead."

"Then what is this?"

She cocked her head to the side, inspecting me with golden eyes. I watched her thumb rub the pearl handle at her side. "You're close," she said. "But I think you're going to be fine."

"Th-then why are you here? What do you want?" The back of the ambulance started to spin. I gripped the sides of my head and stared at my lifeless body.

"We're losing her!" Monitors started to wail. A choked sound seeped from Cash's throat.

"Okay, I don't have much time," the girl said. "Come here."

I jerked away from her touch. "Why?"

She sighed. "Because I've been given permission to show you something that I think you need to see. The only reason I can show you now is because you're straddling the line. After they finish with you"—she nodded to the paramedic—"I lose my chance."

Hesitantly, I nodded.

"Trust me. You'll thank me later." She smiled and raised her palm to my forehead, pausing just before making contact. "Oh, and Emma?"

"Yeah?"

"Tell Finn he owes me."

She pressed her palm to my forehead, and I was engulfed in light.

• • •

The shock of cold was too much. It burned through me until it was something else altogether. Cold like this wasn't just a temperature. It was pain. Throbbing. Cutting. Consuming. I tried to gasp for air, but nothing came in. Nothing got out. Ice laced with the blood in my veins. My legs felt like slabs of concrete.

A hand touched my cheek. Peace flooded through those fingertips like warm honey. Numbing me. Calling my name.

"What the hell do you think you're doing?" a rough voice said. The hand was jerked away. I felt lost without it. Cold. "You don't touch them. Ever."

"I wasn't—"

"I don't know what's going on with you today. Just do your job. Got it?"

The voices stopped and the snow crunched beside my face. The warmth moved away. And then…pain. Darkness. Everywhere. I screamed inside my head but I couldn't feel the sound on my lips. Couldn't find the light with my eyes. Something sharp sliced through me. Splintered me in two. And then I was weightless. Blissfully numb.

I opened my eyes and blinked at the shadow of a boy who stood in front of me. His green eyes swept over me thoughtfully, like he was waiting for me to break. Or at least realize what was happening. I glanced behind me at the body lying in the snow. Her lips were blue. A red halo of blood stained the snow around her blond head of hair.

She was me.

"I-I'm dead." I stumbled back, feeling afraid and hopeless, but two hands caught my shoulders.

"It's going to be okay," he whispered. "I'm going to take you

somewhere now. Somewhere safe. Away from this."

I turned around in his arms and nodded against his chest. This was what was supposed to happen when you died. Just like Mama said. I shouldn't be afraid anymore. The nothingness was something to be afraid of. Not this. I looked around, waiting for my tunnel of bright white light. The one they talked about in church. "W-where's the light?"

The boy cleared his throat and put a little distance between us. "Actually, you're going somewhere else."

"Where am I going?"

"The Inbetween."

I gaped. "The what?"

The boy grimaced and stared up at the dull, dimming sky. "The Inbetween. It's a sorting ground for souls. This is where you go until they see you're fit for another chance."

"Another chance? Like reincarnation?"

"Among other options, yes. When and if they think it's right, you'll get the chance to go somewhere else."

I looked out at the blue Chevy half-submerged in the icy river, then down to the lifeless body of Zach Murray. I was supposed to ride home with my sister, but I made her cover for me so I could ride with Zach. I didn't know he'd been drinking till we were on the road.

"You don't have to be afraid," the boy said. "Not of me. Not of this place."

I nodded again and placed my hand in his. His touch felt cool now. Comforting. He pulled us forward until the world blurred around me, turning everything gray and dull. I blinked when I saw the gates. They loomed before us like pewter-colored shadows, surrounded by mist. I squeezed the boy's hand, needing that contact more than anything in that moment. To my surprise, he squeezed back.

"Don't you want to know my name?" I asked.

He stopped when we reached the gates and gave a two-finger wave to a man in a gray robe. He slid me a sideways glance that looked perplexed. "Do you want me to know your name?"

"I wouldn't have asked you if I didn't."

He grinned and looked down at his shoes. "Well, now I think you better tell me, or I'll have to nickname you Smart Ass."

I smiled. "It's Allison."

He nodded and greeted the man unlocking the gates. The big silver bars eased open and we slipped inside.

"Aren't you going to tell me yours?" I asked.

"Why do you want to know?"

"I don't know anyone else here."

The boy looked at me, sadness creasing the corners of his eyes. "Trust me, Allison. After today, you won't want to know me."

I folded my arms across my chest. "Are you going to tell me your name or not?"

He waited for the guard to back away and finally said, "Finn. My name's Finn."

I slipped my hand into Finn's and forced him to shake on it. Daddy always said it was polite to shake someone's hand when they gave you their name. Finn stared at our entwined fingers, brows drawn together like he didn't know what to think. Our flesh glimmered and glowed. It took my breath away.

"You're an angel, aren't you?" I marveled.

Finn pulled his hand out of mine and shook his head. "Not even close."

He nodded to the guard who was watching us warily and

backed out of the gates. I wrapped my fingers around the bars after they closed. "Are you coming back?"

He rubbed his hand over the back of his neck and looked around like someone might be listening. "I'm here every day. It's my job."

My chest fluttered where my heart used to be. "So, if I wait here tomorrow, I'll see you again?"

Finn wrapped his fingers around the bars above mine. "Why would you want to see me again after I brought you here?"

"I could use a friend up here," I whispered, though really, I didn't know why I needed to see him again. Something inside me just…knew. And the emptiness in those haunting green eyes said that he needed it, too.

Finn rested his forehead against the bars. "I'm not supposed to. It's against the rules for me to even be talking to you like this."

I opened my mouth, not entirely sure what was about to come out, when a voice parted the shadows. Finn stepped away from the gate. From me. He raked his fingers through his hair and nodded at a pretty girl in a white dress who looked like she was waiting for him. Of course there was someone else. I don't know why I hadn't thought of it. The fluttering feeling sank, and I slipped back from the gate and into the mist. Into death. "Good-bye, Finn."

"Hey, wait." He clutched the blade at his hip and glanced around, then let his eyes fall on me. "I…I'll see you tomorrow. If you still want to after today. All right?"

I nodded, feeling something I thought I'd left behind with my flesh. Hope.

• • •

My eyes opened and I gasped, choking for air, clawing at my

mask. The bed I was on rolled through a doorway. There were so many doctors talking that their voices blurred into one. Anaya leaned over me, perched on the side of my bed. The fluorescent hospital lights seemed dim compared with her. She clasped her glowing palm over my forehead.

"Just a little more, Emma." She smiled and ran her thumb over my cheek. "Just remember a little more."

I didn't have a choice. My eyes followed her orders and closed against the light.

...

Finn's breath was warm on my neck. His chest firm against my back. His lips brushed the once-tender spot just behind my jaw.

"Finn," I breathed. My insides buzzed with fear and desire. "Someone will see."

His arms looped around my waist and his lips touched my hair. "It doesn't matter. Not now."

It did matter. This might be the end for me, but it wasn't for Finn. He couldn't risk that. I couldn't let him.

"They'll banish you." Warily, I watched the souls fill the meeting square. This was it. This was my last chance. No amount of Finn's kisses was going to make that any different.

"I'm not trying to get banished," he said. "I'm trying to get a kiss."

"You know we can't do that out here in the open. If Balthazar sees—"

I yelped when Finn yanked me into the shadow of a hemlock and pressed me into an invisible wall. I gasped when he kissed me.

"Now they can't see," he said softly, and kissed me again.

"You're just trying to distract me."

"*Is it working?*"

I realized that this might be the last time I kissed him. If I was chosen to go back, Finn couldn't follow. If I was tossed to the Shadow Land, I wouldn't want him to. No matter what the outcome was today, it meant saying good-bye to Finn. A desperate feeling gripped my chest and I clutched him closer, but I couldn't get close enough. Finn must have felt the same way because he crushed his mouth against mine.

I lost myself in the moment. Lips tangling, our breaths mixing and melting on my tongue. His kisses felt so good, his lips so gloriously solid against mine, it took my breath away.

The trumpets sounded, and he pulled away slowly. His green eyes were vibrant against the shadow of his face, reminding me of the day we'd met. The day he'd collected me. "Come on, they're starting."

Finn took my hand and pulled me into the hazy gray twilight that always hung over this place. He stopped just shy of the crowd, leaving us cloaked by souls. Reapers created a wall on each side of the lectern, standing firm against the group of desperate souls pressing forward. They looked fierce and ready for the danger the souls not chosen for reincarnation or Heaven might pose. A ring of guardians formed a protective circle around the porthole glowing behind them.

Finn should have been up there with the reapers, fighting for order. Instead, he was with me. "Shouldn't you be up there?"

Finn shook his head, watching a guardian knock a soul back from the porthole. "No. I'm exactly where I need to be."

I stood on my tiptoes and found Maeve. She smiled and gave me a little wave. I didn't know how to be that confident. This was my last year. For souls like me—souls that had done something irreparably wrong, whether they knew what it was or not—there were only ten years before the decay set in. For the madness to take over. For the transition to a shadow to begin. I turned my hands over to expose the black spiderweb of veins crawling up my arm. I didn't have to look to know my neck looked the same, or that the darkness had eaten away nearly all of the blue in my eyes.

Finn pulled my hand away and turned it back over to make me stop looking.

"I need all remaining reapers and guardians to the front please!" Balthazar shouted.

Finn looked torn, not wanting to let go of my hand.

"Just go," I whispered. When I looked up, fear swallowed me. Balthazar's careful eyes were watching us. He met Balthazar's gaze. After a long moment, Balthazar nodded. Finn held my hand tighter and pulled me forward.

I yanked against his grip. "Stop. You'll get in trouble."

"That doesn't really matter now, does it?"

"Attention!" Balthazar's voice thundered across the crowd, leaving a wave of silence in its wake. "The decision has been made!"

There were thousands of souls here, their energy pulsing, pulling, pressing in on me like a rip current. I knew the odds weren't good, but I forced myself to imagine my name rolling off his tongue. Finn gripped my hand. I could feel him shaking.

"Anderson Mills," Balthazar announced, "Faye Dunn, Tommy Gilford, Samantha Monroe. Can you all approach the porthole?"

I closed my eyes. He'd only say a few more names.

"Ryan Butler and…" He crinkled the thin paper in his hand and squinted at it. "Jonah Bates."

Finn wrapped his arm around my waist, pulling me close. I

buried my face into his shoulder. I couldn't look. He pressed his lips into my hair.

"Shh," he whispered. "They'll say your name. They will. You're going back today, I promise."

"All right, just one more," Balthazar said. "As for the rest of you, better luck next year."

There was no next year for me. Next year I'd be in the Shadow Land, a hungry, empty thing with no memory of who or what I once was. No memory of Finn and his kisses. I held my breath and tried to count to ten. I only made it to three.

"Maeve McCredie. Today, the seven of you will be born again."

My heart sank, but the silence of Balthazar's announcement erupted into chaos as the crowd pushed Maeve to the front. I tried to smile, but I could feel it mangle into something that felt more like a kick in the gut than a congratulations for Maeve. Maeve had only been here two years and had been nothing but rude to the few souls who'd attempted to befriend her. Worse, she still had time. I didn't.

Maeve breezed past me and winked. "Hey, Emma. You're looking a little…dark. It's amazing your reaper boy can stand being that close to you with how deathly you smell."

I blinked away the hurt and the shock as I watched her weave through the crowd. Some were bright-eyed as they pressed forward, anxious to get a glimpse of what might be their future. Others looked dark and hopeless, trying to get a glimpse of what they'd never have. Finn squeezed my hand and a dark sound rumbled in the back of his throat.

"Finn!" Balthazar moved through the crowd, but Finn wouldn't let go of my hand. "I need you closer."

Finn looked back at me, jaw clenched in frustration. "Can I stay with her? She's close to transition."

Balthazar looked me over and pursed his lips. "Bring her with you."

"Come on." He grabbed my hand and pushed through the souls until we were huddled against the portal, watching the chosen souls fall into the light to be reborn. The portal was beyond beautiful, with blinding streaks of color permeating its golden glow. We were so close, I could feel its warmth. If I reached out, I'd be able to touch it.

"One step through that light and you're reborn," Balthazar said to the sixth soul in line, a younger boy who'd been in the Inbetween for barely over a year. "Don't be shy, son."

For a fleeting second, I imagined myself grabbing Finn and leaping into the light together, but quickly pushed the thought aside when a guardian pinned me with a dark look, as if he could read my thoughts. I ignored him and turned my attention to the only soul left in line. Maeve. Her red hair spilled around her shoulders, and her hazel eyes glittered with excitement.

Finn dragged me even closer, and Balthazar's brows pulled together when he noticed. I thought for sure he'd pull Finn away from me in that moment, but he turned his attention to the guardian watching me.

"Joseph," he called over the crowd, motioning for the guardian to follow him with two fingers. He slid one last careful glance my way, then turned back to the crowd.

Finn held me close. "Ally," he started, then shook his head. "I love you. And I'm sorry it took me so long to tell you that. I'm so sorry I waited until now." He held my face between his palms, stealing the words from my mouth. "Remember that. No matter what happens, hold onto it, because I will see you again. Promise me you'll remember."

"You're scaring me."

"Promise me!" he demanded.

"I promise."

His lips brushed my ear. His voice lingered there, making my chest ache with want and what could have been. "Please forgive me for this, pretty girl."

Without warning, he grabbed my shoulders and shoved me forward. I gasped and stumbled into the light. Behind me, Maeve screamed.

"Finn!" I cried against the wind. "Finn, wait!"

But no one answered. I soared through cerulean blue skies, puffs of billowing clouds whispering through my hair. I was free at last, my reaching arms turning to wings as I spiraled through the shimmering facets of color.

And within seconds of dissolving into the precious warmth around me, I couldn't remember who I was reaching for.

Chapter 27

Finn

She's alive. That's all that matters.

I kept thinking it over and over, but I wasn't fooling myself. Emma had almost died again. Because of me. I closed my eyes, forcing myself to remember what she'd looked like that last day. When the darkness was ready to swallow her. I needed to see it so I could justify what I was doing to her now. What I'd done to her seventeen years ago when I'd pushed her into a life she didn't choose.

I stepped into the quiet hospital room and found Anaya lighting up the corner of the room, her eyes focused on Cash asleep in a chair on the other side of the bed.

"Hey," I said, softly. "Everything okay?"

She watched Cash a few seconds longer, then gave me her attention. "He hasn't left. Not even to go to the bathroom. Do you find that odd?"

I leaned against the wall next to her. "No. He cares about her like family. Don't you remember what it's like to care about someone like that?"

Her gold eyes dimmed. "Sometimes, it's so easy to forget."

"Why do you think I always loved her?" I watched Emma's chest rise and fall beneath the blanket, feeling my chest swell with warmth. "She doesn't let me forget."

When Anaya didn't say anything I nudged her shoulder. "Thank you for not leaving her."

She smoothed her hands over her dress. "It's the least I could do. She didn't deserve to go through something like that."

Guilt burned in my chest. No. No, she absolutely did not deserve any of this.

"Besides," she continued, nodding to the soundless television flickering in the corner of the room. "I got to catch up on modern television."

"You don't even have the sound on."

She laughed. "That's the only thing that made it bearable."

I noticed Anaya's scythe pulsing with light at her side. "I've got it from here if you need to go."

She looked at Emma and a soft smile tugged at her lips. "I know you do. Regardless of what you think, Finn, she's lucky to have you."

Her hand settled on my shoulder and a second later she was gone, leaving me alone with the sound of beeping machines and Emma's ragged breathing.

I sank into a chair next to the bed and rested my elbows on my knees, choosing to look at the heart monitor instead of Emma. She was too black and blue. Too broken to keep my eyes on her for more than a second. It was hard to face something so horrific when I knew I'd been the one to cause it—the one to cause everything. Leaning over the bed, I kissed her on the top of her head. It wasn't the real kind of kiss, the kind I wanted to give her, but it would have to do.

I pushed myself up and walked over to the window to keep myself from doing something stupid. The moon glowed between the skeletal treetops, casting a spiderweb of shadows across the sparkling white parking lot. Stars winked. Burned. Taunted me with memories of the Inbetween.

If I couldn't protect her from this, I was useless to her.

Behind me, the door opened and a nurse crept into the room. She pushed Emma's hair out of her face then checked her vitals, doing her job quickly and efficiently, the way I had been expected to do mine for the last seven decades. The difference between us? She was in the business of preserving life. I was in the business of ending it. After she was gone, my gaze drifted over to Emma. She moaned in her sleep and turned her head so that the puffy line of stitches that ran the length of her slender neck were visible. So many things burned through me. Rage. Guilt. Pain. I clenched my fist and listened to the reassuring beep of the heart monitor, letting the rhythm of the life flowing through her veins soothe me.

It didn't take long for the pull to interrupt my thoughts. The cold crept though my insides, crackled in my skull. My fingers wrapped around my scythe and it pulsed under my palm. Trying to fight it, I braced myself on the wall, not wanting to leave her. Not now. Not after what had just happened.

"Finn?" Emma mumbled, her eyelids cracking open.

Thank God. I started forward, but my scythe stopped me in my tracks before I could get to her.

"I'm here," I whispered, hoping she could hear. "I'm right here."

Emma moaned and settled back into sleep. I took one last lingering look at her, at what I had done, and I let go.

Chapter 28

Emma

I bolted upright in the bed. My stomach felt empty, sick. I couldn't escape the feeling of falling. The screaming until I couldn't breathe. Finn's lips, his voice in my hair. I gripped the sides of the bed. *Finn*. I remembered Finn. I remembered where I'd been, who I was...what he'd done. Oh God, what had he *done*? I had to write this down. I had to get it out of me before I forgot.

I scrambled for the table next to my bed and jerked open the drawer. Gauze, sanitation wipes...where was it? My journal...my journal. Frantically, I looked around. I was in the hospital, not my bedroom. My journal wasn't here. My fingers searched for a notepad, aching with the need to preserve this memory before the truth was taken away from me again.

"I need some paper!" I shouted, yanking the drawer off its tracks in my desperation.

"Emma!" Mom rushed into the room and pulled the half-emptied drawer from my hands. "What's going on?"

I tumbled off the bed and one of the stitches in my leg popped open. I cried out, one hand flying to my leg, the other grabbing onto the nightstand.

"Oh my God!" Mom grabbed me and helped me back onto the bed. "What are you doing?"

I fell limp into the pillows. It was already fading. I couldn't hold onto it. "I need something to write with. Anything," I sobbed. "Please, Mom."

She looked me over, bit her lip, and nodded. I waited while she hurried across the room to her purse and came back with a little notebook and a pen. I plucked the remainders of the dream from my mind, cursed the empty spaces where the memory had already disappeared. There had been something wrong with me, but I couldn't remember what. I skipped over that part and focused on what I knew. Finn was a reaper, and Maeve wanted me dead because he'd stolen her chance at life and gave it to me. And he *lied* to me about it. About all of it. My heart felt like it was being disassembled and stitched back together. I'd trusted him. I was falling in love with him. And he just kept it from me like that? My life was a lie. It didn't even really belong to me. I scribbled so hard the pen ripped through the paper as Mom patiently waited, patting my good leg. I stopped when I felt her tugging at the bandages around my calf.

"These need to be changed," she said, quietly. The bright red spot of blood had grown while I wrote, soaking through the gauze. "I hope whatever you had to write down was worth it."

I looked down at the words. Half-broken memories. The truth. "It was."

She made a face and pushed the call button beside my bed. A nurse in pale pink scrubs rushed in and shook her head as she cleaned my wound, then wrapped it in a fresh bandage. Mom leaned up and touched the one on my neck. "How's this one?"

I flinched away. "Fine." It wasn't, but I didn't want her poking at it. It hurt bad enough as it was. *Everything* hurt at this point.

Mom nodded and picked at a loose thread on the stiff blanket covering my other leg. "Were you dreaming about your Dad?"

"Yes," I lied, hugging the notebook to my chest.

"That's good," she said. "It's good that you remember."

Mom was the queen of avoiding the past, I realized. She filled up her days with nonsense meetings and nonsense people until there wasn't room for anyone or anything real. After everything I'd been through, I didn't blame her. It had to be easier than facing the pain. In that moment I would have given anything to not have to face the pain that Finn and his lies had caused. "That story you told me about Dad…your kiss. That was nice. You should tell me stuff like that more often."

"You're right. We should remember more."

I thought about how hard most of the memories in my head were to relive. The old ones. The new ones. "Easier said than done, right?"

She cleared her throat, and tucked her wavy blond bob behind her ear as she stood. "You hungry? I could have them bring you some soup. Or Jell-O? They must have something good around here."

"Sure." I wasn't really hungry, but I did want her gone. I needed a minute to myself to soak in the words that were living on the paper against my chest. They were whispering to my heart, screaming against my ribs, begging to be read.

Mom paused in the doorway, watching me. "Honey, I want you to know that Parker is doing everything he can to catch this guy. He won't give up until they have him."

So he was a cop. I nodded, thinking he'd be looking forever then. "Tell him…thank you."

After she was gone, I read the memory over and over again. I didn't remember it all, but I remembered how he touched me. Remembered that he loved me. I remembered that he lied to me. I closed my eyes.

"Are you awake?" Finn's voice ran through me like syrup, coating everything with a sweet sensation that I couldn't wash away if I tried. But there was something bitter inside me now, too. A painful regret, the kind that came with knowing the truth. He'd kept everything from me. Betrayal throbbed in my chest, painful and sharp. I opened my eyes, temporarily blinded by the buttery sunshine spilling through my window and the shimmering outline of Finn. When I lifted up my hand to shield my eyes, he jumped up to pull the drapes closed.

"You're awake," he said.

"I'm awake."

"I never should have left you. God, I'm so sorry, Emma." He looked like he was out of breath, though I knew that wasn't possible. I gazed at him, mapping out his face line by line, comparing it to the perfect memory in my head.

"You lied to me," I finally said, considering my words very carefully. Forcing myself to stay calm when all I wanted to do was scream. I swallowed past the burning lump in my throat and focused on the throbbing pain that radiated from the gash on my neck instead. Concrete pain like that was easier to deal with than the emotional kind.

"What are you talking about?"

"You lied to me about everything." I twisted the blankets in my hands until my knuckles turned white. "Maeve. What we were to each other. God, Finn, what did you *do*? You…you took her life away from her and you forced me to be involved. I didn't want that. I didn't want this. It's no wonder she wants me dead. She has a right to!"

"Emma…" He looked panicked, placing his hand on the mattress next to my arm. I jerked it away from him and he flinched. "Wait—"

"What are you, really?" I said. "You're not just a soul."

Finn looked away and rubbed his palms over his knees. "Why do you need me to say it if you already know?"

"Because I want you to tell me the truth. After all of this, I deserve it."

"Fine. You want a technical term? I'm a reaper. You want the truth? I'm death." A holster materialized on his hip. He grabbed the curved blade it held and flipped it open. "I rip souls from their flesh, and I don't take them to a happy place."

On the other side of the hospital room door, a nurse laughed. A cart rolled past. A sob welled in my chest, refusing to let me breathe.

"I took you," he whispered, his eyes burning a hole in my floor. "I was supposed to take you again two years ago."

"I know. A girl in a white dress showed me. She said to tell you that you owe her one."

"That's Anaya. She's one of Heaven's reapers." Finn scooted closer to me, staring at the book. "What else did she show you? Exactly how much do you remember?"

I swallowed, stretching my stitches. "You said you loved

me," I said. "Did you?"

Before he could answer, I turned away to hide the tears rolling down my face. Even through the anger I was feeling, the need to touch him was so intense that my chest ached until I couldn't breathe. As if he could read my thoughts, Finn moved. He touched my open palm, and his hand turned to iridescent particles that sifted between my fingers.

"Yes," he whispered.

I didn't know what to say to that, so I just nodded. There was still too much hurt inside. Far too much for three little words to erase it all away.

"You were out of time," he continued. "I don't know if you remember what was happening to you, but I was losing you. And I couldn't let you go like that. Not when it was my fault you were damned in the first place. I knew relationships between souls and reapers were forbidden, but I thought *I'd* be punished, not you. I wasn't thinking. I should have known…" Finn stopped and his voice sounded strained. "Despite all of that, despite knowing I'd been unforgivably selfish, I couldn't let you go. I still can't."

I absorbed the missing pieces to the puzzle, bits of what the girl in the white dress had given me coming back. The black veins. The Shadow Land. My mind wandered through the newly familiar memories that still didn't quite feel at home in my mind, trying to remember feelings that belonged to another girl. My heart fluttered just thinking about the way Finn had looked at me. The way he'd touched me. "I don't want you to let me go."

I may have been angry and hurt and confused, but I at least knew that much. I wasn't ready to let him go, either. Even after all of this.

Finn kissed my wrist, his lips dissolving into a fine mist as they moved slowly down to my palm. My breath caught in my throat and my fingers curled around the shimmery particles. He pulled away, his skin weaving back together as he sat up. Once he was whole again, he grunted and grabbed the blade at his hip.

"Don't go." I sat up, reaching out for him, but he pulled away.

He stood up, regret and want swirling in the green depths of his eyes. "I don't have a choice. Please don't hate me."

"Wait!" By the time the word had passed through my lips he was gone. My gaze drifted down to the places he'd touched that still felt warm and tingly. I could still feel him on my fingers. In my veins. And none of it was enough.

Chapter 29

Finn

I couldn't tell where the hell I'd landed. Shadows slithered over my vision. Hundreds of them. They screamed, writhed, twisted until I dropped to my knees and slapped my hands over my ears. My knees sank into dirt and ash and God only knows what. This was not the time for me to get dragged away. Not when I didn't know where Emma and I stood. I had to make her understand. I couldn't just leave things this way.

Easton slapped me on the back. "Smells like home."

I looked around. Flashes of shimmering light punched holes into the dark. Reapers. At least twenty of them. "Why are they here?"

"Too many," Easton said. "Body count's going to be over a hundred."

He pointed over my shoulder. Flames stretched so high into the darkness, they could have touched the stars. A massive hunk of metal burned, bordered by fir trees and flames. Jet fuel fumes ate away at the fresh air. A charred wing jutted up from the wreckage, branded by a blue and red airline logo. A plane. A plane full of burning people. My body heaved. God, I wished I still had the ability to throw up. I took a step back and stumbled right into the heat of a memory.

Heat licked at my neck. Something stung near my elbow. I punched at the controls of the airplane. Just a little farther…

"Finn?"

Smoke choked me. Something hot scorched the back of my neck, my shoulder. "Son of a bitch!" I slapped at the flames crawling down my sleeve. The plane shuddered just before—

"Hey." Easton knelt beside me, his brows drawn together, as he snapped his fingers in front of my face. "Snap out of it."

He stood and held a hand out to me. I looked at it like it was a snake ready to strike. Groaning, he grabbed my wrist and pulled me up.

"Look, I know this is hard," he said. One of Heaven's reapers, a boy with blinding white hair and alabaster skin, walked past us with his arm around the trembling soul of a woman in a flower print dress. "You can do this. You've had to do it before, and as long as these stupid humans keep trying to fly, you're going to have to do it again. So I need you to take this."

Easton slowly pulled the scythe from my holster and folded my fingers around it. I felt numb. I couldn't even feel the blade in my fist. I didn't want to feel it. I wanted to run away from this.

"Hey." Easton snapped his fingers again, bringing me back. "Stay with me."

I nodded and swallowed. "Okay."

Easton smiled. "Okay?"

"Yeah." Not even close to okay, but the lie didn't taste too bad in my mouth. It was better than admitting I was terrified to someone who faced Hell on a daily basis. Easton nodded, looked me over once, and turned away. "Hey, Easton?"

He stopped and looked over his shoulder.

"Are you still pissed at me?" I asked, wanting him to say no.

He rolled his eyes and twirled his scythe between his fingers like a baton. "Nah." He paused, considering. "But for the record, I do still think you're a dumbass."

"Fair enough." I didn't think he heard. He was already gone, tearing the soul from some poor bastard's chest.

I closed my eyes and put one foot in front of the other until the heat consumed me. I opened my eyes. Flames licked out, teased my chest, the toes of my shoes. Someone stepped up beside me.

"I've already had to take three kids," Anaya said. She chewed on her bottom lip. "I don't know how you do it."

"I try not to think about it."

"Then that's what you need to do here."

I glanced back to the plane. "I know."

"You're welcome, by the way," she said. "Things will be so much easier now with all of the secrets out of the way."

"You're welcome?" I glared at her. "Do you understand how pissed off she is at me right now?"

"She'll get over it. Trust me." Anaya held out her hand to me. It was so small and slender compared to mine, her skin just a shade darker. "Come on," she said. "We'll do this together."

I stared at the silver shimmer that swirled like smoke where our palms connected, and took a deep breath. I didn't need it, but I wanted it. If after seventy years I couldn't forget the feel of my flesh melting from my bones, I didn't think I'd ever escape those memories. I squeezed Anaya's hand and stepped into the flames.

Chapter 30

Emma

Cash walked into my room holding a mug of hot chocolate. I could smell it from here, sweet and rich, mixing with the cool scent of peppermint.

"How you holding up?" he asked.

"I'm fine," I said, setting down the book I'd been reading. "You don't have to keep checking on me, you know. I'm a big girl."

"Hey, you're lucky I don't set up a cot and move in after what happened the last time I left you alone." He was trying to joke, but he wasn't pulling it off. I knew he was serious. That he felt responsible. And I hated myself for making him feel that way.

I cured my fingers around his arm. "It's not your fault."

He shook his head. "You were upset. I shouldn't have just let you run off like that. If I'd come after you sooner, that guy wouldn't have had the chance…"

My throat closed up. More lies. I'd had to tell him the same thing I'd told the cops. That some guy on drugs had attacked me in that bathroom and gotten out through the window. If I'd told them the truth, that it had been Maeve, I'd be in Brookhaven right now. I was getting so tired of the lies. Tired of Finn's. Tired of my own.

Cash sighed and set the steaming cup down on my nightstand. "I thought it might feel good on your throat."

"Thank you. That was really sweet." I smiled. "You get bonus points for that one."

He stretched out across my bed while I took a drink. "Bonus points?" He raised a brow. "Can I use them now?"

I slapped his leg with my book. "Gross. The hot chocolate's not worth that."

He flashed me a lopsided grin and winked. "Hey, don't knock it till you try it." His words didn't quite match the worry written all over his face. The dark circles under his eyes. The way his hair stuck up in every direction like he'd run his hands through it a hundred times.

"Enough. What's up? What do you want?"

Cash propped himself up on his elbow and squinted at me, like he was trying to unravel all of my secrets. I hated it when he did that, because he usually could. "Who's Finn?"

Heart thudding, I asked, "Who?"

"Don't give me that crap. You said his name right before…" A guilty look flashed across his face as he messed with one of my pillows. He cleared his throat. "Right before you passed out at the theater."

"He's…no one," I said, my hot chocolate suddenly leaving a bad taste in my mouth.

Cash sat up, brows pulled together. "Seriously? I tell you everything. I tell you shit you probably don't even want to know about, and you're going to hold out on me now? Come on, Em. Are you dating the guy? If you are, I want to meet him. Does he go to our school?"

"You can't. He's…" I paused searching for the right thing to say. "He's out of reach. He's always out of reach."

"So does that translate into it's a long-distance thing?"

"Yeah, I guess you could say that. An extremely long-distance thing." He was dead. I was alive. Long distance was an understatement.

"How did you meet him?"

I couldn't say anything. I didn't want to lie to him anymore. And I didn't want to talk about Finn. Not yet. There was still too much anger and hurt there. Yes, he'd given me this life. Kept me safe. But at what cost? I didn't know whether to be grateful or angry. Love him or hate him. I couldn't balance all of the feelings inside of me and it was making me nuts.

When I didn't answer, Cash went on, "Please don't tell me you met him on the Internet. Have you even met the guy in person? They never look like their pictures. He could have a mullet. He could have a third nipple or something—"

"Oh my God! I did not meet him on the Internet."

Cash laughed and I was grateful for it. "Calm down. I'm just messing with you." He snagged my hot chocolate cup out of my hand and took a sip. "But if you're going to continue to be a dirty little secret-keeper, I'm taking this back."

"If it will get you to leave me alone, take it." I picked my book back up and peeked at him over the top.

Cash reached across the bed and pulled the book out of my hands. "Hey, why don't you come over?"

"Seriously? I look like a zombie." I spread my arms, feeling like something out of a Tim Burton movie. Black and blue and stitched all over. There was no way I was hiking across the yard to his house. "I'm not even supposed to get out of bed. Besides, I really don't feel like watching you and your skeevy friends get wasted and pretend you know how to play guitar."

Cash threw my book across the bed and frowned. "I can play." I raised a brow and he laughed. "Okay, I can play a *little*. Come on. It won't be as fun if you're not there to laugh at me. I could carry you? You wouldn't have to walk at all."

My battered reflection in the vanity mirror caught my eye and I looked away. "Even if I could, I'm not going anywhere looking like this."

I also wasn't going anywhere until Finn came back. There were still too many things left unsaid. He still owed me answers. Cash sat up on my bed and nudged my foot.

"You don't look that bad, Em," he said. "Believe me. The guys I'm having over will still totally hit on you. I don't think a few bruises and stitches will deter their inappropriate behavior."

"Is that supposed to make me feel better?"

"I just…" The humor drained from his voice. "I don't want to leave you alone, okay?"

The guilt in his voice made my heart hurt. I couldn't stand him thinking any of this was his fault. "I'm fine. I swear. Besides, Mom's home. I won't be alone." I grabbed my book from where he'd tossed it onto the pillows. "I just need a quiet night. No drama unless it's the fictional kind."

"Fine." Cash ran his fingers through his messy hair. "Have your nerdfest. But I'll call you later to check on you."

"One of your famous 2:00 a.m. drunk calls?" I smiled.

"Can't wait."

Cash disappeared out the window, shimmying it closed behind him. I listened to the cold November wind pulse against the walls of the house. Just the sound of it made me shiver. I tugged my red cardigan around my chest to hold in the warmth and burrowed into my covers, flipping the pages of the book I was reading.

I'd made it through three more chapters by the time Finn came back, stumbling through the wall like he'd been shoved into the room. He braced himself on the sill, pulling back the parts of himself that had seemed to melt right through the Sheetrock and cursed under his breath.

"You're not very good at that, are you?" I asked, feeling relieved and upset all at the same time.

He glanced at me over his shoulder, then cast a haunted look back out the window. His eyes flickered with the movement of whatever he was seeing. Snowflakes, probably. Even from my bed I could see the eerie ballet of white dust against the black velvet sky outside.

"Were you…" I hesitated, searching for the right word. "Were you collecting a soul?"

"Where's Cash? I thought he'd be with you," Finn said, carefully deflecting my question. He didn't have to answer, though. I could see it written all over his face. The pain and regret. The mask of horror that death brands into a person's eyes.

I turned my attention back to my novel, pretending to read so I wouldn't have to look at him. "He's drinking with some of his buddies. They're forming a garage band," I said. "Not my thing. Besides, you and I never got a chance to finish talking."

Finn didn't say anything right away. He didn't even look at

me. But after a few moments of silence, he sat down beside me on the bed. The mattress didn't give. The blankets didn't shift. So close and still so far away.

"If you're waiting for me to tell you I regret it, that's not going to happen," he said, his voice sounding tight and uneven. "I don't. I wouldn't take it back even if I could. You deserve to be here, and you sure as hell didn't deserve to be cast off as the scum of the underworld for the rest of eternity because I made a mistake. If that makes me a bad person, if it makes you hate me…then I guess it is what it is."

I opened my mouth, then closed it again. I was afraid of what would happen if I let the words out. I didn't hate him. I… loved him. He'd risked everything for me. He was *still* risking everything for me. How could I hate him? I was just angry, and no matter how hard I tried, it wouldn't go away.

"I am sorry I lied to you," he whispered. "I'm sorry I got in the way of who you were supposed to be. If I had just left you alone that first day…"

"Don't say that." I moved closer. "I *want* to be here, Finn. I want to be alive."

"You could be in Heaven if it wasn't for me. Do you realize that? You could still have that if I could just let go."

"I don't want Heaven. Not yet anyway," I said. "I want… this." I reached out, but Finn jerked away like I'd burned him.

"I can't…I don't trust myself with you right now."

"What's wrong?"

Finn scrubbed his hands over his face. "Nothing. Okay, not nothing. But I'll get over it soon."

I bit my lip and watched him. "If it helps, I don't hate you."

"You should."

The lights flickered above us, the wind outside waging a

war with the power lines. Without thinking, I leaned across Finn to grab a candle and a lighter from my nightstand drawer. My arm sank through his shimmer and dissolved through his arm. He inhaled sharply and I froze. My hand glittered like silver dust beneath his.

"I'm sorry," I said without moving. I could feel his warmth against my cheek as I hovered over him.

"Emma…please," he said breathlessly. He shut his eyes, like he was trying to get some control over himself. "No. I should go."

"Please don't." The lights flickered again, so I pulled away to light the candle, then set it on the opposite nightstand beside me. "Talk to me."

He watched me for a moment, his gaze jittery. His hand moved across the mattress between us, but he yanked it back before it got to me. "I don't…I don't deal very well with, um…" He swallowed. "Fire."

"Is that where you were? A fire?"

He nodded. "A lot of people died. You'd think I'd be used to it by now."

"That's how you died, isn't it? A fire made your plane crash?"

He looked away, a pained expression on his face. "How do you know I was in a plane crash?"

"I researched your name on the Internet."

"Why?" He still wouldn't look at me. I wanted to make him. It felt necessary to life that he look at me at that moment.

"Because I care," I said. "And because I feel like I should know these things, considering what you are to me."

"And what am I to you?" Finn asked just as the lights gave a final flicker and went out. The candle glow made him look ethereal in the dark, his skin like caramel, his eyes the deepest shade of jungle green.

"I…I feel something when I'm with you that I've never felt before," I whispered as if anyone else were there to hear. "Like we're two halves of a whole."

"You feel that way even after everything I did?"

"Yes. Don't you feel it?"

He finally rested the back of his head against the headboard and stared at the ceiling like he was looking into a nightmare. "I was a fighter pilot in World War II. My plane was shot down at the Battle of Midway. I was only eighteen. I didn't even finish high school," he said in a flat voice. I had a feeling it was the first time he'd ever said it aloud since his death. "My mom begged me not to go, but I went anyway. At the time, it seemed right. I remember thinking I'd come home and show them all when I was a war hero." He laughed, but it sounded bitter. "I did come home a war hero. Or at least the letter and medal that represented me did, all wrapped up in a pine box. I really showed them, huh?"

"I'm sorry." It sounded so inadequate but it's all I could think of to say.

"It's okay. Ancient history, right?"

"And they made you a reaper right away?"

"Yes."

"Did you hate it?"

"Not always," he said. "Not until I had to take you."

I shifted so that I was close enough to feel the warm energy coming off of him. "Tell me what happened."

"You were with a boy. His truck went over a guardrail into a river." Finn dropped his head and stared at his clenched fists in his lap. "I'd never doubted what I had to do. Never gave it a second thought. But after seeing you lying there in the snow, knowing you'd dragged yourself out of that river and died alone…for the first time in over forty years, I hated what I had to do. I hated myself."

He stopped to rub his hands over his face again. I didn't say anything. I didn't know what to say to this boy who had seen me die. This boy who was doing everything in his power to make sure it didn't happen again.

"When I came back the next day, you were at the gates, waiting," he went on. "I thought for sure you'd hate me. Most of them did. Not at first, but after they realized how trapped they really were, what kind of fate waited for them, they always hated me."

"But I didn't." Hesitantly, I met Finn's intense gaze. "I didn't hate you, did I?"

"No." He shook his head. "No…you loved me, I think."

I nodded and forced myself to look away. I already knew that part. I knew because it was still inside me, filling up my heart, making it feel like it was ready to explode being this close to him.

"Anything else?" His voice sounded gruff.

"Why me?" I finally decided to ask. "What made me different?"

"Before you, there was only dark." He stopped, but his voice was still unsteady when he started again. "You lit up my whole world, like the sun bursting through the clouds on a stormy day. You made me remember what it was like to feel alive. You made me believe I was something more than death. You made me believe in something that I didn't think existed anymore."

My heart pounded in my chest, a steady beat that thudded

harder with each passing second that he wasn't touching me. I'd never wanted anyone to touch me as badly as I wanted Finn to in that moment. "Could you touch me right now if you wanted to?" I asked in a shaky voice.

He raked his hands through his hair and tugged. "Don't ask me to do that. Not now. I'm too messed up to think straight and there are rules…"

He sounded torn, but for once, I didn't want to think about what was right—I wanted *him*. Whatever that meant. There were too many memories in my mind. I didn't want memories. I wanted the real thing. Here. Now. Finn jumped off the bed and started to pace, his jaw clenched in restraint, the muscles in his forearms flexing. I hauled myself up behind him, heart in my throat, but pain throbbed through the stitches in my neck and leg. I gave up and leaned against the bed.

"Don't leave. I won't ask again. I pro—"

I stopped when I heard it. Static electricity seemed to crackle in the air between us, then the floorboards under Finn's shoes groaned with his weight. He took a deep, shaky breath, and his gaze… His gaze looked *reckless*. And then—

He kissed me.

I froze as his warm, solid lips pressed against mine. This… this couldn't be happening. Finn was kissing me, *really* kissing me. My lips parted in surprise, my neck stinging, but the pain was worth it. He moaned against my mouth, and the sound ran through my body like fire in gasoline. One of his hands slid down my jaw, cradling my face to deepen the kiss. The other hand brushed down my ribs to touch the bare strip of skin where my shirt rode up. My arms wound around his back to close any space left between us.

His weight made me stumble against the bed and I winced,

pain shooting up my leg as though I'd been stabbed all over again. Finn jerked away, but his hands held me in place. "Oh God…did I hurt—"

I pulled him back to me and sealed our lips, trapping the rest of his words inside. It *did* hurt. Everything did, but I didn't care. Finn's lips worked against mine and he shuddered, his hands careful of all the places that hurt.

"God," he groaned resting his forehead against mine, shaking. "I want to feel this, Emma. I want to feel *you*, and I can't."

I frowned, but he kissed me again as if he could will himself to be alive and held my head in place, giving my neck the support it needed. I wanted him to be able to feel me, too. Wanted him to feel the fire in his veins like I did, and didn't understand why he couldn't.

All at once, there wasn't room for any of the anger or the hurt over the lies. There was only room for Finn. The memories of this might have been good, but they were nothing compared to the real thing. His hands settled on my hips, gripping my flesh like he wanted more of me than he could get.

"Finn," I whispered against his kiss, needing so much. Too much. I never wanted this to end. My hands slid around to his back, and his body slowly softened. Melted into a cool vapor against my skin. A burst of energy ripped us apart and he scattered into a thousand particles before he managed to pull himself back together. Once he was solid again he reached for me, but his hand turned to vapor against my skin.

"Damn it," he said, dropping his hand. "I can't…I can't keep it together."

Pain seared my neck and my need for Finn took my breath away. I reached for his shimmering form, needing to feel him again, but all that was left was a translucent version of the boy I loved. I clutched my chest where it hurt, and a choked sob ripped its way out of my throat.

"Emma, stop…don't cry," he pleaded. His gentle fingers, their breathy warmth touching my face, only made it worse.

"It's not enough," I cried, unable to stop myself. "This will never be enough."

It hurt, loving him like this. It hurt knowing everything about our past, but knowing we didn't have a future. I wanted to go to sleep and wake up to find it all a dream, because this kind of pain was going to kill me long before Maeve ever could. I wanted so many things I couldn't have. I wanted him to be alive.

His eyes raked over me, a desperation in them that I'd never seen before. "Did you say Cash was drinking tonight?"

I nodded. Finn hopped up and went to the window. "If Cash comes to your window, let him in."

I could barely see the fading shimmer of his outline in the moonlight. "What are you going to do?"

He squeezed his eyes shut and shook his head. "Just let him in." With that he dissolved through the wall and into the darkness, leaving me aching and alone.

Chapter 31

Finn

I didn't think. I just moved. Kept moving until I was sinking into a bleary-minded Cash, who was sitting on his sofa strumming a soft tune on his guitar. If I thought about it, I'd remember what I said to Scout that night on the mountain, and what a disgusting excuse for a person I'd become the second I decided to do this. I told myself I didn't have time to think about it, but as the dizziness swept through me from the feel of new blood rushing through my veins, not thinking was impossible.

Seeing Emma crumble, hearing her cry that what we had wasn't enough, shattered what was left of my already shattered soul. I thought about the look in her eyes, the eagerness of her kisses, the way her hands seemed desperate to touch every part of me... I hadn't been able to feel any of it. Not the heat of her skin against mine or the taste of her kiss. Going corporeal, risking everything to be with her—it was nowhere near enough to fill the gaping hole in my chest that cracked open when I stumbled into her room tonight. I hoped I had enough time to at least get Cash over there before Balthazar sent Easton to drag me to Hell. Even if the idea of me in her best friend's body freaked her out, I didn't want to leave her alone.

And I was going to Hell, all right. At least Easton and Anaya would watch over Emma after this. Anaya would for sure. Easton would probably be too pissed off at first, but Anaya would never let an innocent like Emma die. Especially not knowing what she meant to me.

I set the guitar on the floor and stood up, stumbling into the table in front of me as I worked out how to use my new legs. I felt like I was made of rubber, bending and wobbly in all the places that should have been supporting my weight. Disoriented, I shook my head. Things began to focus but when I spotted the empty beer cans on the coffee table I figured out the root cause of most of my problem.

"Where are you going? It's freaking cold out there," a blond kid slurred from a recliner in the corner of the room. I paused at the door and looked back at him, surprised for some reason that he could actually see me.

"I'm going to Emma's." My mouth snapped shut involuntarily when I realized it was the sound of Cash's voice instead of mine. Damn it, this was weird. And if I thought about it much more, I wouldn't be able to go through with it.

"Dude! What's up with your eyes?" The kid sat up and squinted at me. "They're green. Like, crazy green, man."

Not wanting to open that can of worms, I stumbled outside. It was eerily quiet this time of night. No crickets, no hiss of tires gliding along the icy streets. Just the sound of Cash's boots crunching through the freshly packed snow that spanned from his house to Emma's. When I rounded the corner, I could see her. Her window was open and her face was there, scanning the darkness for me.

I stopped just short of the light spilling out onto the snow and watched her. Her face was flushed, her cheeks and nose pink from the cold. Her pale blond hair looked almost white in the moonlight, and her blue eyes were luminescent enough to cut through the night and right through to my core. I filled my lungs with icy air and took a step forward into the light. "Can I come in?" I asked in an unfamiliar voice.

She nodded and moved aside, watching me warily as I climbed clumsily though the window, then shoved it closed.

"Cash?" she asked, her voice a whisper.

I shook my head. I didn't want to talk. I couldn't stand hearing my words come out cloaked in his voice.

Emma looked into my eyes and eased back onto her bed, her eyes wide with shock. "Finn?"

I nodded and took a step forward.

"Oh my God…Finn, what did you do? Is Cash…is he…?"

I knelt down in front of her. "He'll be fine." I, on the other hand, wouldn't be very soon. Balthazar had to know by now. I had maybe a minute or two before they dragged me through Hell's gates.

"Why?" Her voice broke and a tear rolled down her pale cheek before landing on her collarbone.

"I want to be able to feel you like you feel me. To be with you without any limits, even if it's only once," I whispered. My fingers twitched, aching to touch her.

I couldn't make myself finish. Instead, I leaned up until I was close enough to feel her breath fanning across my lips.

Connection sparked between us, reeling me closer.

"But you're not you," she whispered.

"Look into my eyes, Emma." I placed my palms on either side of her face, and the shock of her skin on mine, the heat…I shut my eyes and a breath shuddered out of me. I forced my eyes open, needing her to understand before they came for me. "It's me. It's Finn."

She nodded. Her blue eyes fixed on mine. "You're Finn."

"Please say this is okay," I said, the urgency drowning me.

She nodded and I couldn't hold back any longer. I didn't have time to. I kissed her, and the paper-thin space between our lips was crushed out of existence. Her mouth immediately opened, letting me in, and I slid my hands up her thighs to the edge of her cotton shorts. She tasted like chocolate and peppermint and life. Her smooth skin felt like silk. I needed more of her. All of her. I could barely breathe through the amount of want building up inside me. I didn't want to waste time breathing.

My heart pounded so loudly I thought for sure she could hear it. It was a strange sensation after not having a heartbeat for seventy years. I leaned into her and my hip bumped her injured leg. Emma gasped against my lips.

"Damn it. Sorry." Gently, I shifted her back farther on the bed. I wanted this, but I knew how much pain she had to be in. My palms pressed into the mattress on either side of her head as I leaned over her and touched my bottom lip to hers. I wanted to kiss her again, but didn't know how to do it without losing control.

"Don't stop," she whispered, and her words left the thin wall of self-control I had built up crumbling.

"I don't want to hurt you." Not more than I already would

be. I kissed her throat, tasting the spot just behind her jaw. Emma made a frustrated sound, pulling my face up, and our lips collided with so much force I groaned.

Emma whimpered and I swallowed the sound as her fingers found their way into my hair, tugging at the long spikes. Unfamiliar tingles danced across my scalp. I felt dizzy. I felt drunk. Completely intoxicated from all things Emma— her smell, the feel of her skin, her taste. It was driving me mindlessly over the edge.

She scooted back onto her bed, grabbing a fistful of my T-shirt to take me with her. I followed. I would have followed her into the fiery depths of Hell if she'd asked me to in that moment. Twenty-seven years of wanting her spilled into me, refusing to be satisfied. A desperate hunger twisted my stomach into anxious knots.

Her fingers tugged at the hem of my T-shirt and I broke away to help her pull it over my head before diving back in. Little whimpers and moans escaped her until I couldn't tell the difference between pleasure and pain. But she wouldn't let me stop. I didn't want to stop. An involuntary moan rumbled somewhere deep in my chest. She felt so warm beneath me, so alive. God, I wanted her more than I'd ever wanted anything in my life.

"You taste so good," I whispered against her moving lips. "You taste like peppermint. I almost forgot what that tasted like." More importantly, she tasted like home. My hands inched up her tank top and touched her bare stomach, something I'd dreamed about doing for months. Last summer when she'd laid out, trying to tan her pale skin, all I'd wanted to do was touch her stomach. And now that I could, it was so damn worth it. I'd go to Hell a thousand times over to have my hands were they were now.

"What in the *hell* are you doing?"

Every muscle in my body tensed at the sound of Easton's voice. I rolled away from Emma. He stood at the end of the bed, his eyes dark, angry. The blade in his hand flashed.

"Finn…what's wrong?" Emma touched my hand.

I laced my fingers through hers and squeezed. *Not yet. God…I'm not ready yet.* "I love y—"

I didn't get the words out. Not before Easton's scythe pierced Cash's chest and jerked me out in one swift tug. Pain sliced through me as I separated from blood and skin and bone, and a choking sound escaped my throat. He grabbed my arm, singeing my skin. A familiar black cavern of screams opened at our feet. I couldn't look at him. My gaze was riveted on the porthole to Hell.

"I hope it was worth it," Easton said.

I glanced over my shoulder at Emma, shaking Cash's shoulders, trying to rouse his unconscious body. I'd never hold her again. Would never taste her, talk to her, or hear her laugh. There wasn't going to be any "get out of jail free" card for me. Not this time. It was over.

I didn't know what I could say to change anything, so I just said, "It was."

Chapter 32

Finn

Everyone's version of Hell is different. Or so Easton tells me. Some burn in fire. Some die in ice. Most drown in their nightmares, or choke on twisted fears and mangled memories. Only one thing is certain here—whatever your poison, it's sure to last an eternity.

Easton tugged me down the ash path, through the blazing gates, and to the smaller iron gate where we'd deposited the two souls. He rapped his scythe on the bars and I knew I should have been afraid, but instead, I thought of Emma. I wanted to remember her warmth. I wanted to remember her breath in my mouth and my hands in her hair. I wanted to remember her like the dream she was before they turned her into a nightmare.

The gates opened. "Let's go."

It was dark here, and the heat strangled me. In the distance, screams morphed together into one long, continuous moan that felt infectious. Like the sound was reaching down into my belly trying to pull my scream up to join them. I flinched when the buzzing sound of a chainsaw echoed down the corridor. Something wet splashed under my shoes, but it felt too thick to be water. Smelled too metallic to be anything other than blood.

Someone cleared their throat and Easton stopped. A soft glow lit up the dark cave, splashing light onto the stone walls like melted gold. A rush of cold turned the sweat dripping off of my nose to ice.

Balthazar.

He folded his hands behind his back and sighed. Behind him, yellow glowing eyes blinked from the corners.

"You just couldn't listen, could you?" he said, stepping toward me. He looked over my shoulder at Easton and jerked his chin. "You can go. I'm sure you have plenty of other work to do."

Easton squeezed my arm once before releasing me. "What are you going to do to him?"

"That's none of your concern." Balthazar's eyes glowed as he narrowed them on Easton. "But if you're intent on staying, maybe we could arrange something for you, too."

Easton hesitated in the doorway, his violet eyes burning with regret. Then he stepped into the darkness. I stood still, listening to the splash of his footsteps until he was gone. Lifting my chin and tamping down the fear inside of me, I looked at Balthazar. He had his own brand of regret settling across his face, but it wasn't enough to change anything. He was probably more upset he was soiling his bright white robe, which was soaked in blood from the ankle down.

"Possessing a human?" Balthazar hissed. "Are you trying

to make a fool of me? Did you honestly think it could go unpunished?"

I shook my head and considered ratting out Scout, who clearly wasn't on Balthazar's radar, but I didn't. I'd known the consequences of my actions. They were mine and mine alone. "What's next?" I asked, bracing myself. Balthazar didn't answer right away. Instead he strode forward and nodded for me to follow. He ducked under the low, dripping rocks and when we came up on the other side, we were met by a crystal clear pool of water. Not understanding the compelling need to see it, I stepped forward. A rippling reflection of myself stared back at me, stone-faced, afraid. Something dark swam under the surface and my reflection smiled and waved, then burst into flames. Black skeleton fingers broke the surface and pulled the reflected Finn into the depths.

I wiped the sweat out of my face and swallowed a fresh batch of fear down my throat. "What is this?"

"Your worst fears. Your nightmares." Balthazar looked into the water and smirked. "A place where they all come to life. Everyone's Hell is different. This one is about to be yours."

I closed my eyes and inhaled the rotten smoldering stench of this place into my lungs. I'd known this was going to happen. I'd been leading up to this moment for the past two years. But knowing didn't make it any easier now that it was here.

"Please take care of her," I said. "I might deserve this, but she doesn't. Assign her a guardian. Send someone after Maeve. Anything. Just don't leave her alone with my mistakes."

"Emma is not my concern," he said, grudgingly, as he turned to leave. "And she's not yours anymore, either."

"Balthazar, wait!" I reached out, but he was gone. A cool white fog lingered where he'd been standing, but the heat was quick to snuff it out.

Before I could pull in another acrid breath, the air was suctioned out of the room. My lungs burned and my eyes watered. The walls began to weave together, black vines crawling, braiding, and locking me in. I spun around and the glistening reflecting pool was gone. All that was left was a gaping crater. Vines crept up from the center, piling on top of one another until they spilled up over the edge. They smelled like they'd been soaked in jet fuel. I couldn't breathe. I didn't want to breathe. But God...I *needed* to breathe. I hadn't needed to breathe like this in seventy years. One of the vines at my feet sparked and a slim flame swirled around the stem. The black leaves burst into ash as it danced closer and set another vine ablaze.

"Not this. Please," I whispered to myself, and only to myself. Anyone here would only roll on the floor laughing at my plea for help.

Another vine went up and scorched the toe of my shoe, and I stumbled back, tripping over my own legs. One by one, the vines caught fire. Closing me in. Tighter. Tighter. I pressed my back against the heated stone wall behind me and curled into myself in a nest of vines. The black billowing smoke blinded me and fear took over.

The ground shuddered under me and I grabbed at the vines on either side of me. But I didn't find vines. I found the sides of a sweaty vinyl seat. I looked up and the cockpit was filled with a choking black smoke. A flame stretched up from the back and licked my shoulder. I slapped at my jacket, trying to put it out.

"Not real. Not real. Not real." I repeated it like a prayer, knowing it wouldn't matter. My fist battered the dashboard as

I watched the gauges spin out of control. I jerked at my seat belt, but it wouldn't budge. The buckle to my harness had melted under the heat. A high-pitched whine filled my ears. I looked up a second before the ocean crashed in through the big cockpit window. Broken glass slapped me in the face. Salt water stung my charred back. I sucked in a lungful of…water.

Shit!

I sputtered in the black water and sucked in another gulp of wet brine that set my lungs on fire. I couldn't tell up from down. My fingers grasped for something solid but found even more water. And when the world started to go black…it felt way too good not to let go.

My eyes flew open and a gut-wrenching scream ripped through the cave. It took a second to realize it came out of my mouth. That I wasn't in the plane anymore. Flames crawled up my pants. My shirt. I shut my eyes and choked when the flames leaped onto my face. Through the inferno, Emma held Henry's hand. They were burning, too. Burning and melting and reaching for me and I couldn't move. I couldn't breathe.

"Stop!" I screamed through my ruined lips. They felt numb now. At least there was that. Slowly, the red world in front of me turned to ash. Gray. Cold. I closed my eyes and shivered, curled onto my side. The flames were gone, and for a moment I thought they might have mercy. I thought they might just let me stay numb. But when I opened my eyes again, a new nightmare unfolded like an origami bird, slowly stretching out before me.

Pop's farm.

I sat up and ran my hands over the frost-covered ground. The peach trees, brittle and dead, swayed under the cold pewter sky. An empty whistle of wind swept past me, stirring their branches. This wasn't right. This wasn't home. Ash, soft as petals, fell from the sky as I blinked at my surroundings.

"Pop!" I stopped to listen. Someone whimpered behind me and my muscles locked in place. It sounded far away and faint, but it was a whimper. I skirted through the peach trees. Trees I'd climbed in and broken bones in as a kid. Trees that had given us purpose. A life. I laid my palm against the crumbling bark of a tree and it turned to ash beneath my fingertips. The whimper crept up my spine, this time from behind me. I spun around and found Pop leaning against a tree. Black and charred. Clinging to life.

A sob welled in my chest, and I fell to my knees in front of him. His calloused hands reached out for me and I grasped one of them in mine, ignoring the way they scorched my skin.

"Pop...no."

"You left," he gasped. "You left us." He said it over and over until my ears wanted to bleed. Behind me, trees erupted in flames until the field consisted of nothing but heat and ash and disfigured memories. I backed away from Pop and winced when a flame sprang to life on my back. It crawled down my arms, setting my fingertips ablaze.

He was right. I'd left. I'd burned. And now I was dead.

Chapter 33

Emma

"Cash?" I shook Cash by the shoulder, feeling so raw and afraid inside that I could barely breathe. He didn't move. I pressed my ear to his chest, listening to his heart pound out a steady rhythm. "You have to wake up. *Please* wake up."

He'd been out an hour. That couldn't be normal. What was I saying? None of this was normal. I'd just made out with my dead boyfriend while he was in possession of my best friend's body. Any shot I had at normal was long gone by this point. All I could think was that we'd broken him. If this had hurt him, if he didn't wake up…

No. He'd wake up. He had to. And where was Finn? I needed him right now. He'd just disappeared. No warning. I realized he had an unconventional job, but after what had happened between us, a little warning would have been nice. I slid off the bed and began to pace. My head was spinning with memories. Finn's hands and lips. Cash's hands and lips. Oh my God. What did we do? How could I have let that happen?

Cash groaned and relief exploded to life in my chest. I sank down onto the bed and pulled my fingers through his hair.

"Cash," I said, softly. "Are you okay?"

He squinted up at me. "What happened?"

I smoothed my hand over the comforter. "You…um…you passed out."

Cash sat up and rubbed his head. "Shit. I feel like I got hit by a truck. How much did I drink?" He looked around and his brows pulled together. "And how did I get over here?"

I opened my mouth but the words refused to come out. I'd already used him—I didn't want to lie to him, too.

"Hey." Cash leaned in to touch my arm, but I jerked away before he could make contact. I couldn't have him touching me right now. Not after Finn had just been touching me with those same hands. "What's wrong?"

"Nothing."

Cash ran his hand over his bare chest, then froze. His gaze wandered over his body, as if he was taking inventory of every detail. With a gasp, he scrambled back and fell off the bed, then jumped up, breathing hard. "What…what did I do?" He motioned between us. "What did *we* do?"

I stood up too, knowing I needed to look at him, but I couldn't. Not yet. I stared at the wall beside him. "You didn't do anything."

"Don't give me that bullshit, Em." Cash shoved his fingers through his dark hair and leaned on my vanity, then shot back up like he couldn't keep still. He rubbed his lips and groaned. "I can taste that peppermint lip crap you use, for God's sake!"

"Cash…" I couldn't finish. I didn't know how to. I wanted

to say I was sorry. I wanted to hug him and beg him to forgive me. None of that would come. The pain and guilt in my throat wouldn't let it.

"Look at you. You can't even look at me." Cash strode forward and reached out as though he was going to touch me, but he stopped as if he didn't know if that was okay anymore. "Please tell me what I did. Please? I'm sorry, Em. I am so—"

"We kissed, okay?" I sucked in a deep breath, feeling dizzy with the force of my words. This half of the truth was the only answer I could give him, and the only thing that would make him stop feeling guilty. And I was terrified it was going to change everything. "You were drunk. And we kissed. And now...now we're going to forget it ever happened. Okay?"

"Did I hurt you?" He looked horrified, his eyes wide. He looked ready to break.

"God, no!" I grabbed his hand and forced him to sit on the bed with me. "It...it was just stupid, okay? It didn't mean anything. Right?"

He looked me over, uncertainty coloring his features. "Do...do you want it to mean something?"

I sat back, brows pulled together. "N-no. Do you?"

He stared at me for one terrifying second, then shook his head. "No. I don't want to ruin this. I don't...I can't risk losing you, Em. If I ever went there with you..." He swallowed and dropped his gaze. "I'd ruin it. I would."

"Hey." I nudged his leg, feeling relieved and guilty all at the same time. "You didn't ruin anything. I'm still me. You're still you. And we're still us. Nothing's changed."

Besides the fact that I am officially the worst friend in existence.

Cash rubbed his jaw and shook his head. "I have *got* to

stop drinking. I really am the king of asshats when I'm drunk."

I listened to another gust of wind beat the side of the house and shivered. Cash wrapped his arms around my shoulders and rested his chin on top of my head. I sat there quietly, trying to dissociate the feeling of his touch from Finn's.

"I really am sorry," he whispered.

I shook my head, the guilt eating me alive. "I don't deserve you, Cash." He needed to know. I could never tell him the whole truth, but I'd at least give him this. "You are a better friend than I'll ever be to you. You should know that."

Cash pulled away and smiled, his lips tilted in that crooked little-boy grin that he never seemed to outgrow. "I think that's the craziest thing I've ever heard you say."

I stared out the window, at the snow piled up outside and the foggy film forming across the glass. I couldn't look at Cash. Not when all I could see was Finn.

Chapter 34

Finn

"Get up," a familiar voice said above me.

Easton? I tried to pry my eyelids open, but they felt like they'd been melted together. They probably had. My palms found the warm wet stone beneath me. It felt sticky under my cheek. I wanted to get up. I wanted to get the hell out of this place but my limbs wouldn't work. Pain burned under every inch of my skin. My skull. The dull echo of horrific memories pulsed behind my eyelids.

"Don't be a pansy, Finn. It's only been forty-eight hours. Get. Up."

I swallowed and pushed, but the movement only ground my cheek further into the muck underneath me, which smelled like blood and ash. "Can't." My voice sounded like sandpaper. It felt like it, too, as it crawled its way up and out of my throat.

"Son of a—" Boots scraped along the stone in front of me

and stopped. "Can somebody take care of this? This wasn't the deal. I can't do anything with him like this."

After a few more seconds of agony, something started to happen. A tingling sensation started in my toes then blazed through my legs, my fingers. Something swelled in my chest, then raced up my neck until it burst like gold behind my eyelids. And then…nothing. A familiar numbness swept over me. No pain. No nothing.

I cracked an eye open and blinked at the black combat boots a few inches from my face.

"Time to get up," Easton said. "Humpty Dumpty's together again."

He offered his hand to help me up, but I slapped it away and climbed to my knees. "What's going on?" I swayed. "Is this…is this real?"

"You're free," Easton said. "Balthazar made his point."

"Made his point?" I glared at him. "Are you fucking kidding me?"

I stood up and the room tilted off-balance, so I closed my eyes again. It was over? God….it was finally over. I patted down my body, making sure everything was as it should be. When I was sure I was still me, I turned and stomped out of the cave. No vines or flames blocked my escape. I shook my head, feeling sick inside.

Easton followed behind me. "Finn…wait."

"Don't." I held up my hand and blindly hiked through the screams. "Just…don't."

"I was following orders. Besides, if you'd have stopped being such a dumbass, this wouldn't have happened. But you'll go right back up there and do it again, won't you? And Balthazar will give you another waste of a chance."

I stopped when we reached the iron gates and clenched my fists, feeling like I was about to snap in half. I couldn't take anymore right now. I was too raw. "I can still feel the flesh melting off of my goddamned bones, and you're going to give me crap about Emma right now? After *you* dragged me here?"

"I didn't have a choice!" he shouted. "If you want to blame someone for this, look in a goddamned mirror."

"Screw you."

I didn't wait for his reply. Instead I barreled out into the whirlwind of ash outside the gates. I closed my eyes, immersing myself in the fiery wind around me. When I opened them again I was standing in Scout's uncle's garage, vibrating with rage. And pain. And things I didn't want to think about ever again. I knew it was my fault, damn it. I'd known going into it. But I was starting to think too much had built up between Easton and me. I wasn't sure if we'd ever get back to the way we were before. And that bothered me more than I wanted it to.

I took a deep breath and shuddered. If Scout wasn't here, I didn't know what I was going to do because it would be a cold day in Hell before I went back to that bar, and I needed his help before I could deal with the Emma situation. Clenching and unclenching my fists, I scanned the dusty garage. I still didn't trust him after finding out what he was doing with the humans at that bar. I was still pissed. But I wouldn't be a hypocrite after what I'd done. And I'd have to get over it if I wanted his help.

"Why don't you just punch the damn wall and get it over with?"

I spun around too quickly and silvery tendrils of vapor went in every direction.

"Hope you didn't come for a fight. I've never been any

good at fighting." Scout fell back onto the dusty sofa, twirling a piece of a truck engine in his hand. "And if I'm being honest there's no way I'd try to hit you. Not when you're carrying around that crazy-ass scythe. You've had more experience with yours than I've had with mine. It wouldn't be a fair fight and you know it."

"I didn't come for a fight." I glanced from the red F-150 parked on the other side of the room, then nodded to the piece of metal in his hand. "What's that?"

"I don't know." He shrugged and a familiar grin caught both sides of his mouth. "But the old man won't be able to start his truck without it."

"Why do you still torture him? He is your family, you know." Remembering all of the stupid stunts Scout had played on his uncle over the years, it was a wonder the old guy hadn't had a heart attack by now.

"I'll stop messing with him when he stops messing with me. One trick all those years ago and he still messes with the Ouija boards and crap. Like I'm some ghost of Christmas past that's going to come back and tell him how to fix his screwed-up excuse for a life. Do you know how much the man spent on phone psychics last year? Enough to buy a freaking new car, that's how much. The man's a moron. And until he stops being a moron I'll continue to screw with him."

He laughed and it suddenly felt like old times with Scout. When we'd sit in his garage and try to figure out a way to live like humans even though we were anything but. "Besides, it helps to pass the time in between my reaps. We don't get as much action down here as you guys do up north." When I didn't respond, Scout set the engine part on the couch, and rested his elbows on his knees, staring at the floor like it held all of life's answers. "I thought you hated me now," he said more to the floor than to me.

"I don't hate you. You just…" I stopped searching for the right thing to say. "You just screwed up, okay? You screwed up, and with Emma, I can't afford those kinds of screwups."

"I know."

"I'm not going to say I get it. I'm not even going to say it's okay, because it's not. But I'll get over it."

"She got hurt, didn't she?"

"Yeah, she got hurt."

We both froze when his uncle stumbled into the garage and climbed into his truck, cursing as his foot slipped out from under him twice before he could make it in.

"He still drinking?" I asked.

Scout nodded. "Stupid old drunk. I'm doing the community a favor keeping him off the streets." The old man cranked the ignition and when all that resulted was a clicking sound, he erupted. A stream of obscenities bounced off his tongue so fast you could barely keep track. Scout looked tired as he watched his uncle dig under the hood and come out looking white.

"You're in here, aren't you?" the old man called, his eyes searching the garage, but only finding a floating brigade of dust particles illuminated by the sunshine spilling in through the one window that wasn't covered with plastic.

"Oh, I'm here all right," Scout grumbled and kicked an empty can across the room.

The old man jumped back two feet with a gasp. The can hit the toe of his shoe. "Damn it, Scout! Stop with these games! I'm getting too old for this crap. I can't believe your mama hasn't come to drag your ass back to the afterlife yet." He continued to mutter to himself as he let himself back into the house then slammed the door, knocking an old can of nails off his workbench and onto the floor.

Scout picked up the engine part and tossed it into a pile of junk in the corner of the room. "Wouldn't he just shit a brick if he knew I was the one to drag her ass to the afterlife?"

"You took your own mother?" I said. "Isn't that a conflict of interest?"

"It's not like I planned it. I was just covering for one of Heaven's reapers that day and her hourglass ran out of sand." He shrugged. "At least we got to say a proper good-bye that way. It wasn't a big deal."

I pressed my lips together into a hard line, trying not to torture myself with not knowing who had taken Mom and Pop. And Henry. It was too much to think about.

"Why did you stay?" I finally asked. It was the question I'd always wanted to ask him. The one I wasn't sure I wanted to hear the answer to.

"What do you mean?"

"After Balthazar hired you on. You requested this territory. Why in God's name would you want to be in this place? Watching the people you knew die again and again."

He smiled and looked out at a memory that I couldn't see. A stream of sunlight spilled across the dusty space illuminating the pain beneath his smile. Pain that looked way too familiar for my liking. "A girl, of course. Why the hell else would I stay here?"

"A girl? You put yourself through this kind of hell for a girl?" I asked, a little disbelief seeping out with my voice. Scout had never seemed like the romantic type.

He raised a brow. "Like you're one to talk."

"So what happened? Where is she now?"

He crossed the room and fiddled with something on his uncle's workbench. If I knew Scout, he was just trying to hide his emotions from me. I let him.

"I don't know," he finally said. "Last time I checked in she was married, had two kids." He glanced back at me and shrugged. "It *has* been twenty years, Finn."

"Did she ever see you?"

"No. I didn't want her to." His voice turned gruff. "I stuck around for a few months after the funeral. To be honest I didn't really know where else to go when I wasn't rubbing elbows with the dead." He chuckled, but it sounded bitter. "After I watched her cry herself to sleep every night for three months, listened to her talk to me in the dark while everyone else in the world was sleeping…I couldn't take any more, so I left her alone."

"She talked to you?"

He turned to face me. His eyes grim, years of pain finally being set free. "Of course she did. She could feel me. Even if they can't see you, Finn…they know. They always know. Just like on some level, Emma knew way before you ever made a physical appearance."

Scout took a step closer and knelt down in front of me.

"They can't move on while we're still around. You know that, right? Emma won't ever move on as long as you're there. Just like Sophie wouldn't have if I hadn't left when I did." He finally plopped down onto the dusty concrete beneath us, looking whitewashed, exhausted. "Just because we're stuck like this doesn't mean they should be. They deserve more than that."

"How did you let her go? How were you okay with her

having a life with someone else?" I asked.

Scout rolled his eyes as he wrote a message to his uncle in the dust with his fingertip. *I'm watching you.* "You think I'm okay with it? No, man. I'm not okay with it. Watching her chase after kids that are half him, half her. Seeing her curl up next to him in bed at night, watching him touch her in all of the places that only I used to know." He ground his teeth together and closed his eyes. "No…I'm not okay with it."

He opened them again and sat back on his elbows, nodding to the message in the sand. "But I keep busy. And she loves him. Knowing that she was able to love somebody again, that she found some kind of happiness. Knowing I was strong enough to give that to her. It makes it easier."

I stared at my empty hands. Hands that had held Emma a little more than forty-eight hours ago without feeling her. Hands that would never hold her again once this was finished. This had to work. Because I was done torturing her. I was done torturing us both. Scout was right. She deserved more than me. More than I could give her.

The inside of my chest fractured, tore, and ached. Now that I'd come to terms with the decision, I felt hollow. For twenty-seven years, she had consumed every thought. My heart. My soul. She was my purpose. And now…who the hell was I supposed to be if I wasn't this? Was there even anything left inside me if I wasn't loving her? In that moment, it didn't feel like it.

Scout cocked his head to the side, watching me. "You don't have to do this, you know."

"But you said—"

He didn't let me finish, making an irritated sound in the back of his throat. "Screw what I said. I am the most miserable creature in existence. Emma's different and we both know it."

She was. And staring into Scout's empty eyes, I saw my future. He was strong, cut from steel…and facing an eternity of loneliness. Scout was giving me an out that I would've taken forty-eight hours ago, but I refused to do this to her anymore. I was going to take care of Maeve once and for all, and then I'd do what Easton and Anaya had always wanted me to do.

Walk away.

"I think," I said slowly. "If you can find time to stop screwing around with the living, you can help me."

He sat up, smiling, and rubbed his hands together. "You need my incredibly talented and genius-like mind, of course. Where do we start?"

I blinked. "That easy?"

"Well, I do sort of owe you. What are we doing?"

"We need to find a way to get rid of Maeve. And I mean for good."

Emotions unfolded across his face. Shock dissolved into contemplation. "You mean—"

"Gone. Whatever that means. I couldn't care less. But preferably Hell if we can get Easton on board. I don't know, though. We're not on the best terms right now."

Scout stood up and started pacing, the wheels in his head that had already achieved the impossible beginning to spin. "Don't worry about Easton."

I nodded, glad I didn't have to ask.

"It's possible. I've thought about it before, but it would mean going to extremes, and unless you could get her right where you wanted her, it would never work," he explained, setting me up for disappointment, if I had to guess. There was no way Maeve would ever trust either of us enough to get her to play along.

"How?"

Scout leaned against the door and looked me over, then shrugged as if it were obvious. "We have to kill her."

I rolled my eyes. "She's already dead, boy genius."

"Not when she's in a host body, she's not."

Disbelief rippled through me as each of his words sunk in. He was right. But that also meant—

"But you'd have to kill the host for that to work, and even then, there's no way to guarantee she wouldn't get away."

"Not if there were a soul there to guide the original one back into its body and another to take her to Hell," he countered with a smile. "And I'm guessing with all of the nasty tricks Maeve's been up to, Easton would be the one sent to collect. We'd just be speeding the process up a bit."

He had no idea just how willing Easton would be to take Maeve out of this picture. Because if Maeve was no longer a threat, there would be no reason for me to be with Emma anymore. And as much as it hurt, I was finally ready to make that compromise.

Hope surged through me. God, this could happen. This could actually work. And he was right. With everything Maeve had done, she'd sealed her fate. There would be no white light waiting for her when she exited the body. No Inbetween, no Heaven. The only thing waiting for her was a one-way ticket to Hell and Easton's smiling face to take her there. And when he came for someone, he never left empty-handed.

Scout interrupted my thoughts. "It would take two of us for sure."

"Us?"

"I'm bored as hell. You don't think I'd let you go it alone, do you? Besides, you need me." He went to dig in the junk pile, retrieving the unknown car part, then put it back where it belonged under the hood.

"Finn."

We both looked up at the sound of Easton's voice. I gritted my teeth. "I haven't been out long enough to screw up."

Scout punched me in the arm. "Way to piss off the missing piece to our puzzle."

Easton ignored Scout. "That's not what this is about."

I studied the panicked look in his violet eyes and shot up. "What's happened?"

"It's…it's Emma."

I narrowed my eyes. "You followed her?"

He groaned and shoved his scythe in its holster. "Fine. Yes. I watched her and Cash sit in her room like awkward little kids while you were in Hell. I'm not as big of an asshole as you think."

I raised a brow.

"Something bad's going to happen," he said. "I just came from there. It's Maeve. She's there, and there's no talking her down this time."

I didn't need to hear anymore. Fear pierced my chest. Throbbed in my ribs. I looked at Easton and he nodded. In a flash I was gone.

Chapter 35

Emma

Two days.

It had been two whole days since Finn had kissed the breath out of me and started to tell me he loved me. That kiss...that moment...it had been earth-shattering. Reckless. Perfect. How could he stay away that long after what happened between us?

I pulled the milk out of the fridge and set it on the counter next to the flour, sugar, and bag of chocolate chips. After crossing that line, feeling him touch me, he was all I could think about. All I could dream about. Without him...I felt like I was in the dark. Like I couldn't see what was coming, and I hated it. What if something happened to him? He'd touched me and he wasn't supposed to. What did they do to souls who broke the rules?

I stared at the ingredients in front of me, not really seeing them. Seeing Finn's face instead. Why did I let him touch me? Why did I touch him back? If he was okay, he would have come back by now. My mind wouldn't stop. It was out of control, thinking about what could have happened to Finn, not to mention the fact that a soul could even possess a body like that. Could Maeve do it, too?

I grabbed the phone off of the wall and called Cash, needing to hear someone's voice. Needing to not be alone right now. If I was alone, my thoughts were going to eat me alive.

It rang and rang. When it went to voice mail I hung up. Crap. He was probably still freaked out about our "kiss." I slid down the kitchen wall, careful not to mess with my stitches, and buried my face in my hands, trying to make sense of the screwed-up mess that my life had become. It felt like a tangled, silver web I couldn't escape, and the fact that Maeve was still out there was the spider coming to finish me off.

"Emma, I'm home!"

I jerked, startled, when Mom stumbled into the kitchen laughing, Parker on her heels. A gust of cold air swirled into the house, stirring the edge of Mom's red dress, as he closed the front door shut behind him.

"Hey. You're home early." It was only eight, far earlier than they typically came home, but I wasn't complaining. At least I wouldn't be alone. I hopped up, wincing when I tweaked the stitches in my neck and leg a bit too far, and headed for the refrigerator. "Did you guys get a chance to eat? I can make something if you want."

"We had dinner," Mom practically purred. She grabbed Parker's shirt and hauled him closer, kissing him like she wanted to taste his tonsils, then broke away and ran her fingers through his hair. "I think we're more interested in dessert."

My mouth fell open. "Mom, gross!"

Parker held her at arm's length, his eyes wide. "Okay, sweetheart. I think you had a little too much wine." He smoothed a hand down her arm and gave me an apologetic smile. "Looks like I should have cut her off earlier."

You think? I wanted to ask, but I forced myself to focus on the ingredients on the counter. Milk, flour, sugar, chocolate chips. For the first time, I wasn't sure baking would occupy my mind enough to calm down.

"How are you doing, by the way?" Parker continued. "I want you to know we're not going to stop until we catch that guy. Everyone in the department is putting in their time on this one. We'll catch him soon, Emma. I promise."

Mom snorted and muttered something under her breath, and both Parker and I frowned. I'd seen Mom tipsy before, but never rude like this. Parker helped Mom slide onto a barstool and kept his hand on her shoulder to keep her from tumbling off the side. She leaned into his chest and nuzzled into his neck, breathing deeply.

"Um," I began, not quite sure what to say. "I was going to bed anyway, so you two have fun." Abandoning my cookie ingredients, I fled to my room. Watching Mom date was one thing. Seeing her shove her tongue down some guy's throat was another. I'd never even seen her act like that with Dad. Not in front of me anyway, thank God.

I heard the static and hiss of radio followed by a dispatcher's voice out in the living room. A few seconds later, Parker said something about having to leave for work. I sagged against the door in relief. At least I wouldn't have to hear their *fun* through the wall.

Safe in the confines of my room, I crawled into bed and

buried my nose in the bedspread. I breathed in the last of Finn's scent as if I could hold it in me forever. "Please come back," I whispered into the blankets.

Mom opened my door, a lazy smile spread across her face. I peeled myself away from my memories of Finn and sat up, knowing I was probably going to be forced to listen to her gush over Parker. Her arm slid up the doorframe and she sagged against the doorway, sighing. "I almost forgot what that was like."

I rolled my eyes. "I really don't want to hear this."

She stepped in and shut the door behind her, then pressed her back against it. "You know, I almost bailed on my plans for you so I could take that man to bed. He was *delicious*."

"Mom…" I carefully slid off the bed, my stomach twisting into uncomfortable knots. I wished she'd just pass out already and stop acting like a lovesick college girl. "Maybe you should go to bed. Come on. I'll help you."

She threw back her head and laughed, dancing past me. "Oh, Emma. This is going to be more fun than I thought."

She twirled some kind of tool in her hand. Just the sight of her holding a simple screwdriver was cause for concern. Mom plus tools equaled broken things; lots and lots of broken things.

"What are you doing?"

One by one, she jammed the screwdriver into the screws beside the lock on my window and twisted until they were half way up, then wacked the screws to bend them over. "There. I don't think you'll be unlocking that window any time soon."

I gaped at her. "Have you lost your mind? Mom, seriously, I think you've had too much to drink."

Mom sauntered back to the door and tossed the screwdriver across the room. "What a sad, sorry excuse for a girl you are," she said. "You should be thanking me for putting you out of your misery. Pining away for a boy you can't have, not willing to trust anyone but your best friend and mother. Really, I couldn't have planned this better if I'd tried." She gave me a wicked grin. "Time to hand over that body, Emma."

The fear that been building in my chest exploded and I stumbled back, catching myself on the edge of my bed. My stitched leg slammed into my mattress. Her eyes. Tonight, they were hazel green with flecks of gold. Nothing like the jewel-tone blue eyes that had watched me grow up for the past seventeen years. She'd done what Finn had done to Cash. Maeve was in there, and Mom… Oh my God. "What did you do to her?"

"What dumb luck that your mom chose tonight of all nights to get sloshed!" Maeve laughed. "It was easy. Too easy really. Just a bump on the head in the restaurant bathroom. And the fact that your mom likes her wine definitely helped things along."

She inspected Mom's nails. "I apologize for dragging this out. I really do. I'd planned to get this out of the way at the theater, but there were…technical difficulties." She grinned and dropped her hand to her side. "See, you weren't *dead* enough. But I'll fix that tonight."

My breath hitched in my throat and I started for the door, but Maeve stepped in front of it again and shook her head. "Do you actually believe I'd let you out of here?"

I balled my hands into fists at my side, trying to think. I didn't know what to do. Where to go. Yeah, she was in a body… but it was my *mom's* body. I couldn't hurt my mom. And she knew it.

Something thick and heated tainted the air and I scrunched

my nose. The dark smoke billowing under the crack of my door drew my attention to the floor.

"Y-you started a fire?"

She sighed. "Well, yeah. But I'm not going to *burn* you to death. I'm aiming for the smoke to do the trick."

I shook my head furiously. It was all I could do, because the words wouldn't come. I didn't want to die. Not yet. I hadn't even gotten a chance to tell Finn I loved him, or to make up for what I'd done to Cash.

"Just think of how close you are to going to Heaven!" Maeve leaned against the door. "You'll get to be with your dad. Oh wait… That's right. He's not up there."

My breathing hitched, then stopped altogether. My dad *was* in Heaven. Finn told me he was. He'd watched him go.

"Oh, Finn didn't tell you?" She touched her mouth in mock surprise. "Finn always was good at keeping secrets. And *lying*. But you already knew that."

"No…" I gripped the bedpost to support myself. Blood rushed to my head, making me dizzy. She was lying. She had to be.

"Poor Daddy," Maeve said. "How many times do you think he's burned over the last two years? It's got to be thousands. Maybe that's why Finn lied. He wanted to spare you the pain."

"You're lying." I slid along my mattress until my hip hit my nightstand. The smoke was so thick my eyes watered. My lungs burned.

"Am I?" She raised a brow. "Or is Finn? He's lied to you before."

I coughed and sucked in another lungful of smoke, feeling dizzy and off-balance. My hand curled around the lamp. I had to get Mom out of here. Even if that meant hurting her.

"What's the matter, Emma? You look a little pale." Maeve giggled, and it sounded so wrong coming out Mom's mouth that it made my stomach turn.

"I don't blame you for being mad," I said to her. I stood up and dragged the lamp off the nightstand with me. Maeve's eyes darted to the lamp and back to my face. "I'd be pissed, too. But I didn't choose this. I wouldn't have taken this from you. I never would have chosen myself over you."

I took a shaky step closer, the lamp cord dragging behind me, and Maeve tensed. "And now?"

"Now…" I stopped to cough again. The room was starting to fade around the edges. "Now you've involved my mother, and I won't let her die for this. Not for you. Not for me."

I didn't wait for her to answer. I lunged forward with as much force as my stitched leg would let me, the lamp raised above my head.

Mom's body collapsed.

The lamp clattered to the floor, forgotten. Coughing and sputtering from the smoke, I knelt down and pressed my fingers to Mom's throat. She was alive. Thank God.

Something fell to the floor and shattered behind me, and my hand froze against Mom's neck. Her pulse beat against my fingertips. Fear as thick as the smoke choking me swirled inside my chest.

Maeve. She was still here.

We weren't safe yet.

Slowly, I stood and something brushed the stitches on my neck, feather soft. Cold crept along my skin even after the touch was gone. And then…pain.

The stitches along my neck ripped open in one swift tug. My knees buckled and the side of my face hit the hardwood floor with a sickening thud. Pain spread across the right side of my face, and tiny incandescent lights floated at the edges of my vision. I ran my tongue along the sides of my teeth to make sure they were still there and tasted blood.

The room was a nightmare around me. Glass shattered. It sounded like the walls were splintering, tearing in two. Or maybe that was just in my head. I reached out and dug my fingers into the floor, crawling forward until I reached Mom's leg. Her limp body was blocking our only escape. I had to get her out.

"Mom…" I croaked, grabbing onto the edge of her dress to pull myself forward. "Please wake up. Please."

She didn't move, so I forced myself up onto my knees, vaguely realizing the pain was starting to fade, and reached for the doorknob. My fingers were wet with blood and slipped on the knob, but it opened an inch. Smoke and heat spilled into the room. My lungs burned and my chest tightened. My head felt fuzzy and my insides tingled. I gasped for oxygen that wasn't there and collapsed next to Mom.

I blinked against a darkness that had nothing to do with the smoke-filled room and everything to do with the fact that the life was bleeding out of me. I could feel it. Cold. Final. My eyes fluttered closed and hopelessness swept through me. I was going to die.

Chapter 36

Finn

I appeared outside Emma's with a flash. The world around me was white, covered in untouched crystalline snow that was packed around the quiet house. But something didn't fit. The smell of smoke lingered in the air, growing stronger with every step I took toward the house, igniting a panic that blazed through me to the point of pain. I started forward, but stopped when a glimmer of gold caught my eye. Anaya.

She stood, hand on her scythe, face solemn, waiting. "I'm so sorry, Finn."

"No." I stumbled back and Scout gripped my shoulders. I couldn't...I *wouldn't* let her do this. I'd been to Hell and back for this girl. Literally. I grabbed the scythe at my hip. It didn't burn with cold. It wasn't being called to be used. But I'd wield if I had to. "I won't let you take her. I'll stop you if I have to."

Anaya narrowed her eyes. "Don't be a fool, Finn. Don't get

in the way. Think of what he'll do to you."

"I don't care."

Easton melted up from the ground beside me, his gaze fixed on Anaya. "Go," he said to me. "Do what you need to do. I'll stall her."

"Thank you." I backed away from Anaya, arm extended behind me, feeling for brick. In my mind, flames licked the insides of my skull, demanding to be seen. I closed my eyes and blocked them out. I didn't have time for them. Not now. *Emma. Emma. Emma.* Her name was the only thought running through my mind. I had to keep her safe.

I slipped through the brick wall and stumbled into the room, disoriented by the smoke that billowed around and through me, leaving me saturated in its dangerous scent. *The high-pitched whine of the plane rang in my ears and smoke made it hard to breathe—*

"Where is she?" Scout asked as he seeped through the wall behind me, interrupting the memory.

"I don't know. Just…start looking." I pushed my way through the smoke. "Emma? Damn it, Emma, answer me!"

The sound of a window popping somewhere on the other side of the house broke my shouts. I felt my way through the room, running my corporeal hands over what I guessed was the vanity. Glass bottles toppled over its edge in the wake of my clumsy fingers. Cursing, I found the wall, her closet door, the bed… I ventured out into the center of her room until, finally, my foot hit something solid and a muffled moan rose up from the floor.

"Emma!" I sank down, my hands finding her before my eyes with all the smoke. I barely recognized her. Her hair was matted with the blood coming from the busted stitches on her neck. Her face looked pale, and her lips were turning a terrifying shade of blue. She groaned again and her eyes fluttered open for a fraction of a second before falling closed again.

Scout stumbled into the center of the room. "Finn, I can't—" Seeing Emma, he breathed a curse, and knelt beside me. "What do we do?"

I swallowed through the rage building in my throat and closed my eyes to steady my breathing. "We get her out of here."

More glass popped, this time a little closer. Maybe the guest room across the hall? I tried to lift her up, shoving my shoulder under her arm, but fear and exhaustion that ran soul-deep swept through me and I dissolved. I couldn't keep it together.

Scout shook his head. "There's no way you're going to make it all the way out of here with her. Hell drained you, man."

"Then help me!"

"Finn…" Scout hesitated, looking torn. "He'll know if I touch her. I can't risk that."

I knew that. I knew I shouldn't have even asked. But… *damn it*! I motioned to the window, trying to gain some kind of control. "Go get help. There's a kid next door. Do whatever you have to do to get his attention. Get him to look out his window, anything. Just get him over here."

Scout nodded and took off. A few seconds later, I heard one of Cash's windows explode.

I turned back to Emma and smoothed the bloody hair from her cheek. "You have to help me, pretty girl," I pleaded. "I can't get you out of here by myself, okay?"

Tears leaked from her eyes. "Finn…"

"I'm right here." I grabbed her hand, feeling like my chest was being torn in two.

"S'okay. Doesn't hurt anymore." She blinked, her eyes unfocused. "I love you." She squeezed my hand and her eyes slid closed.

My lips froze around the words in my mouth. I'd waited a lifetime to hear her say those words, but the way she'd said them… They were a good-bye.

"No." A breath shuddered on its way out of my lungs. I focused on each part of my body, trying to will my skin into existence, but…nothing. Not even a spark.

Rage like I'd never felt before burned through me. I would not let Maeve take this girl's life before it was her time. I'd burn for an eternity before I let it happen.

Shaking, I stood up. A violent flash of black curled around me before disappearing into the smoke. Maeve. And she was on the verge of changing. "Get out here, you coward! I know you're here, and you have lost whatever is left of your twisted, sadistic mind if you think I'm letting you take her!"

Laughter echoed off the walls, as thick and deadly as the smoke that hid her from me. "What are you going to do, Finn? There's no way out now. Just face it. I won. You lost. Game over."

"This isn't a game. This is somebody's life you're playing with."

"You're right. It's *my* life," she whispered behind my ear.

I spun around to face her but all I got was a face full of smoke. How could Emma breathe in this? God knows I hadn't been able to all those years ago. There were a lot of things that could have killed me in that crash, but the smoke had been the worst. Burning my lungs, my throat, my eyes. Eating up the oxygen until the world went dark.

Hatred coiled in my gut. "I'll kill you! I'll freaking kill you the second you're alive. Do you hear me?" I staggered through the room, head spinning as I searched for Maeve's shadow, and dissolved through several pieces of unidentified furniture before making my way back to Emma. I reached out and realized there was a body next to her. Her mother.

I stopped, a realization stirring the fear in my gut. It wasn't the fire I needed to worry about—it was the smoke. Maeve wouldn't let anything permanently damage the body before she could take it. She couldn't care less about what happened to the soul inside. But I did. I blinked against the smoke and the heat, refusing to let my fear get in the way. There wasn't room for that. Not anymore.

"Wake up, pretty girl," I said to Emma. I managed to push the damp hair away from her face before my fingers fizzled out. Outside, Cash pounded on the locked window. "Help is coming. I swear I won't let you die like this. I swear it." My voice faltered as it made promises I wasn't sure I could keep. What if this didn't work? What if she died on the floor of this smoke-filled room? Or, worse, the flames got to her before Cash did?

The silvery outline of Maeve's shape shimmered in the far corner of the room. "You're just going to get the boy killed. You do realize that?"

I couldn't think about that right now. "I meant what I said. The minute her eyes open…" I swallowed. "If those eyes aren't blue…if it's you there instead of her, I swear to God I'll kill you myself. I'll find the first drunk on the street and use him to rip your freaking throat out. Do you hear me? Are you listening?"

"You wouldn't dare." Her voice quivered like water rippling out across a puddle. "They'd send you straight to Hell and you know it."

"Oh, I would." The words rumbled, sounding more like a feral growl than my real voice. "See, I just got out of Hell, and I'd go back in a heartbeat if it meant saving her life, but don't think for a second that I won't take you with me."

"Emma!" Cash's muffled voice shouted from the other side of the door, followed by a round of ragged coughs. He tried to open the door, but Rachel's unconscious body was in the way.

How was he in the house? I could feel the heat of the flames pouring through the door. He got it open enough to slip through the gap and felt around for what was blocking his way in.

"Shit…Rachel?" He knelt down and touched Emma's mother's face, then shoved his arms underneath her and carried her out.

"No! Come back, you idiot!" I shouted, ready to smash my fist into something.

A few minutes later he stumbled back into the room.

"Emma?" he managed to wheeze between the coughs that made him double over every few steps. *Crap*. Maeve was right. All I was going to do was get them both killed.

When he found her, he collapsed to the floor and pulled her into his arms. He struggled to stand, gathering her close, and backed out of the room in stumbling steps. I stayed behind them, whispering to Emma as he walked, but the second he made it to the doorway, a black blur darted in front of me and slammed Cash into the wall. He grunted and collapsed, his head slapping the floor with a final-sounding thud. Emma rolled out of his grip.

"*No.* Get up. You have to get up." I knelt over Cash, whose face had already faded to an ashy gray color. The red spot under his head grew quickly, sticky and wet. *Blood.*

Down the hall, flames licked the living room ceiling. At least she'd started the fire on the opposite end of the house. If it had been closer, there would be no way out of this. As it stood, there was only one way out of this. I had to get it together. Find the strength. If I didn't… *If you don't, she'll die in this fire. She. Will. Die.*

I closed my eyes and took a deep breath, feeling gravity take hold of my body, and pulled Emma up into my arms. Her skin was pale and slick with sweat, little wisps of crimson-stained honey-blond hair stuck to the side of her face. All I could think about was our last moment together. Kissing her until I couldn't breathe. Telling her I loved her and then disappearing.

My fingers gripped her tighter as the pain overwhelmed me, drowning me in desperate waves of regret. I looked over at Cash, limp and alone. Would he die because of me? Emma would never forgive me for that. Never. From the color on his face and the growing puddle of blood beneath his head, he didn't have much time. I couldn't see his chest moving anymore, couldn't hear the reassuring wheeze of his labored breathing. Death lingered like a stale stench in the air. It was so close, I could taste it.

Emma gasped, shuddered, and fell limp beneath my fingertips. The world ground to a sickening halt. I crawled over her body and pressed my ear to her lips. Her heart. It was still beating but only barely. She was so still. So empty. I focused on staying solid as I pressed my fingers to her neck to try to stop the bleeding. "Stay with me, Emma. You can't leave now. I won't let you. You want to be alive, remember?"

"Finn, stop," Easton said from behind me.

I pressed harder and the blood slowed. "You stay the hell away from her," I choked. "Forget Maeve. I can do this. I can save her."

Easton gripped my shoulder, his touch burning, and jerked me off of Emma's limp frame. Pain blinded me. Rage consumed me. I reached for my scythe, but Scout grabbed my other arm. The flames crawled closer. It was too hot. Too much... "She's going to die if I let her go!"

"She won't, I swear it. We can save her *and* take out Maeve, but you need to calm down and let me do my thing," Easton growled against my ear. "Remember the plan you and Scout came up with? I'm here to do my part." He stepped back and pulled his scythe out from his belt and looked at Scout. "You're going to have to hold him."

Scout sank down behind me, gripped my arms, and locked me in place. "Do it."

Easton raised his scythe and swung, ripping through Emma's soft flesh. I choked. Scout held me tighter as Easton peeled Emma's soul away from her flesh.

The world stopped. She blinked at me, shimmering, beautiful, and confused, looking totally out of place next to Easton.

"You guys need to move," Anaya gritted out. "I can't hold out much longer. I'll take her. I won't be able to stop."

"Finn?" Emma's mouth moved around a whisper and I scrambled to get to her, but before I could, a screaming flash of black ripped between us. The shadow hovered over Emma's empty body, twisting and writhing with need. Maeve's face broke through the shadow's oily surface, and with a screech, she dove into the lifeless flesh.

"She's in!" Easton shouted. "Get Emma out of here, Scout. She doesn't need to see this part."

Scout hurried over and wrapped his arm around Emma's willowy shoulders. They stirred and turned to vapor at his touch. She opened her mouth, flailing for words as Scout pulled her away. Away from me.

I clenched my teeth and jumped up to go after them but Easton's voice stopped me. "The sooner I get Maeve out of there, the sooner I can take her and the sooner you can put Emma back in."

He nodded to Emma's body. I gritted my teeth and I waited for her chest to start to rise and fall. And then it happened. Emma's chest rose with an unsteady breath, then fell.

But it wasn't Emma inside. No…this was Maeve.

Her eyelids twitched and another breath filled her lungs.

Easton lunged forward. "Now!"

I scrambled back, watching him rip Maeve out of the girl I loved. Watched the fire eat the walls. Turn them to ash. My mind was a jumble of memories. My flesh melting. Charring. Eating me alive. I gripped the sides of my head and groaned.

A scream ripped through the air. Emma's back bowed, then collapsed to the floor as Easton tore Maeve from the flesh, her shadowy form twisted around Easton's scythe. A puddle of shadows gathered around his ankles.

"Scout!" Easton shouted. Screams erupted from the oily surface beneath Easton's feet. With a grunt, he grabbed Maeve's wrist.

She screamed. "*No*. No, no, no way. I'm not going with you!" Easton spared me one glance that told me to finish it, and then he was dissolving into the sulfur-scented shadow beneath him, a screaming Maeve in tow. I turned my head away and squeezed my eyes shut, my stomach churning, as the screams funneled away like bathwater down a drain.

"Finn," Scout said, pulling Emma into the room behind him. "She's ready."

It was time to get the girl I loved back where she needed to be. I jumped up and grabbed onto Emma's hand. She looked horrified, staring down at her body.

"Hey." I touched her chin. "Wake up, okay? Wake up because…I need you. No good-byes. Not yet."

She nodded. I kissed her once, then knelt with her beside her body, guiding her back into her flesh. Slowly, her soul melded with skin as each part of her gave in. She blinked two shimmering eyes at me and then they were gone too, replaced by warm, closed eyelids. I hovered over her body, holding her shimmering shoulders to keep her inside. After taking life for so long, giving it back was…beautiful. Once I was sure she was in, I pulled my hands away.

And then there was just Scout and I staring at her chest. Waiting. Praying.

"What if she doesn't—"

"She will," I snapped.

Her chest rose with a wheezy breath, then she coughed and I was drowning in relief. Scout laughed and slapped me on the back.

"She made it." I rubbed my hands across my face and smiled.

A fireman sprinted up the hall and crashed through the bedroom door. Shouts echoed, muffled by smoke and sirens. Then Emma was in his arms, being carried away.

I was only dimly aware of Anaya. She knelt over Cash, a prayer on her lips, as his soul rose from his body. Anaya placed her palm over his chest and pressed him back into his flesh.

"Anaya!" Scout bellowed. "What in God's name are you doing? Take him already."

Anaya ignored him, tucking one of her braids behind her ear and tilting her head to study the unconscious boy. She smoothed the hair back from his head, something I'd never seen her do, and whispered another one of her prayers.

"Aren't you going to take him?" I asked.

She shook her head and smiled. Touched the tip of his nose. "No. Not this time."

To my amazement, Cash began to cough. His lungs began to fight for air. I glanced up at Anaya. She had the strangest look on her face. "What did you—"

"We have another one over here!" a fireman shouted, distracting me. By the time he scooped Cash into his arms, Anaya was gone.

I sighed, feeling sweet relief wash through me as I floated out onto the lawn. Emma was there, a bloody, frail body melting a hole into the melting snow. She didn't stay there long, though. Within seconds, she was loaded onto a stretcher and shoved into the back of an ambulance.

Police cars and fire engines littered the street, casting a blue and red glow across the white snow. Rachel was lying on her own stretcher. Before I could see anything else, the world began to spin. I felt like a toy top, spinning so fast the world melted into a quiet blur, my existence fading right before my very eyes. Memories poured down like rain. Mom standing at the kitchen sink crying, Pop running the tractor through a swaying mass of golden wheat the color of Emma's hair, the Inbetween sitting gray and empty, and Emma—always Emma—bright and full of life. The memories unraveled so quickly, I couldn't hang onto them. They spun away like a ribbon into the distance until there was nothing else left. Only darkness.

Chapter 37

Finn

White. Everything was a beautiful, blinding white, no end and no beginning. I sat up, rubbing my eyes to clear my bleary vision.

"He's up," Anaya said from the corner of the room where she and Easton stood waiting.

"Anaya? What's going on?"

"Good, you're awake." The timbre of the low voice behind me sent fear-induced shivers racing down my spine. I spun around on my heel, squinting as the blinding shimmer around Balthazar came into view. He smiled and my muscles coiled.

"You're wondering what you're doing here," Balthazar said casually.

"No, I think it's obvious."

"Can I ask you a question?" he asked, walking the perimeter of the room we were in. A cloud of white mist gathered around his ankles, following him like fog over the lake on a cool spring morning.

I swallowed the fear lodged in my throat and cast a wary glance over at Anaya. "You're the boss."

"Do you regret it?" he asked, never turning to face me. His gaze had settled somewhere on the horizon.

"Which part?"

Balthazar laughed. The sound echoed from walls that I couldn't see or feel.

"All of it." He slid me a careful glance. "Do you regret taking away Maeve's chance at humanity? Do you regret giving that chance to Emma?"

Those were questions I didn't have to think about. Images of Emma limp and lifeless flashed across my mind. If Maeve was capable of such things, she didn't deserve a chance at humanity because there was nothing human left inside her. Then again, if I'd never given Maeve a reason to hate me, it wouldn't have happened in the first place. I shook my head. "I…I don't know."

His white robe rustled with a breeze I couldn't feel. Balthazar sighed. "I don't regret any of it."

Shock fizzled through me. Had I heard him right? I couldn't have.

"The things she's done are unforgivable. And God knows where Emma would be if you hadn't dedicated yourself to her safety the past few years. She's a good soul. That can't be denied. She was not to blame for the transition that condemned her to the Shadow Land, as you well know."

I did know. Unable to speak, I watched him pace, his eyes fixed on the horizon. The fact that he was seeing light in the darkest thing I'd ever done was enough to leave my head spinning. This didn't happen. In a place this close to the Almighty, exceptions were never made.

I swallowed and gathered up the courage to stand beside him. A valley stretched out below us, gray with mist, every inch shimmering with a silver dust. The Inbetween. "What are you going to do to me?"

"We'll get to that in a moment, but first, I have a confession to make."

I raised a brow. "You do?"

He nodded. "I never should have made you a reaper. It was never your calling. And that day, when Allison's name wasn't drawn, I knew you'd push her through if I allowed you to get close enough. I let it happen."

"What? W-why would you do that? Why let it happen just to punish me for it over and over?"

He sighed. "I needed her gone. I needed to rid you of the distraction so you could become what you were always meant to be."

I narrowed my eyes. "And what, exactly, am I meant to be?"

He faced me, a look of pride pulling up the corners of his lips. "A guardian, of course. If your silly obsession with that girl has proven nothing else, it's proven that you have the heart of a guardian. You were meant to protect. Not destroy."

This had all been his plan. I didn't know how to feel about any of this. "I…don't know what you want me to say."

"I have orders to offer you a position as a guardian, Finn."

I couldn't seem to form the appropriate reaction. I knew I should've dropped to my hands and knees to thank God for giving me an opportunity like this, but all I could see when I thought about that life was a world that didn't include Emma.

"Do you dare deny me, when I'm offering you what your brother and sister over there only dream of?"

Easton spoke up from the edge of the room. "Take it, Finn. Don't be stupid."

"It's not in your heart, is it?" Balthazar's bright gaze swept over me thoughtfully. "No… there's no room left in your heart for anything else, is there?"

"I'm sorry," I whispered, wondering what kind of consequences awaited me after turning this down. As far as I knew, no one had ever turned down an offer like this.

"You realize I can't let you keep going on like this," he said, sounding tired. "I can't trust you to stay away from her. I can't continue to allow you to break our laws for a mortal who means nothing in the grand scheme of things. So, what do we do?"

I watched a shadow twist on the horizon, feeling hopeless. "I don't know."

"What do you want, Finn?"

Without thinking, my lips desperately formed Emma's name. "Emma. I want Emma. I want to be…alive."

He took a deep breath, his eyes calculating as he circled me. "What would you give? An eternity of service perhaps?"

"What?"

"Would you take us up on our offer to make you a guardian?"

An eternity without Emma for a lifetime by her side? Thoughts overwhelmed me before I could fight them off, each one leaving me weaker than the last. Her laugh, rich and radiant like music in my ears, the feel of her skin moving beneath mine, the taste of her lips on my tongue.

"Yes." I whispered before I lost control completely. I

dropped to my knees, the pain of almost losing her still fresh in my chest. "I'd do anything."

"Very well." Something in his voice sounded so final it rattled me with a strange mixture of fear and hope. "There's only one thing to be done, then." He turned to face me, the light around him shimmering so brightly I had to shield my eyes with my hand. Fear rippled down my spine as a porthole appeared behind him.

"W-what's happening?" I stuttered, unable to move. The light was swirling, pulling me in like a whirlpool. And Balthazar's intense gaze drove me further against my will. The porthole flickered and moved until a thousand rainbow colors melded into a light so bright it burned.

"Balthazar?" I dug my heels into the ground, only to find there was no ground to save me. I was so close I could feel its heat on my face. Easton's hand rested on my shoulder to guide me forward. He wouldn't meet my gaze.

"Don't forget what you've agreed to, Finn," Balthazar said as I stepped into the portal. "I'll see you at the end of your mortal life to collect."

Chapter 38

Emma

I should be dead. It was I could think. It was all I could feel. I didn't remember everything from the fire, but I remembered enough. The re-stitched side of my neck pulsed with pain and I reached up to brush my fingers over it. I'd almost lost everything because of Maeve. My mother. My best friend. My life. There were too many things in this world I wanted to do now, and I wasn't going to give any of it up without a fight.

I tried to recall the fire, two days and what felt like a hundred oxygen treatments ago, but smoke clouded my memories, making them fuzzy and weak. I did remember Finn. I would always remember Finn. Something ached in my chest at the thought that I might never see him again.

The steady beep of a monitor pulsed behind Cash's head, and the smell of antiseptic and sickness hung in the air like a fine mist. When he made a groaning sound in the back of his throat, I raked my fingers through his hair and adjusted his blanket. His pierced eyebrow twitched.

"Stop messing with me. I'm fine," he grumbled. His words had the sort of slip and swirl that only really good pain meds could provide. I leaned back and smiled when he opened his eyes. Muddy brown. The soft spaces underneath dark and bruised. Those telltale signs were all the proof I needed to know he hadn't been sleeping. He turned over onto his side and stared past me. His gaze tracked something behind me I couldn't see. "Are they letting me out yet?"

"Not yet," I rasped, and covered my mouth to cough. "I think your dad's trying to work something out, though. They said something about wanting to keep you one more night for observation."

Cash's eyes drifted over me like he was taking inventory. "You sound awful." He sounded almost as bad as I did, but he sounded guilty, too. And he shouldn't have. Not after what Finn and I did to him. After what he'd done for me. For Mom.

"I'm getting better." I held up a duffel bag. "I brought you some clothes and a magazine."

"Thanks." He nodded. "I'm getting tired of these nurses staring at my ass."

"Since when are you tired of anyone staring at your ass?"

Cash rewarded me with half of a grin. "Touché."

The light from a pair of headlights in the parking lot collided with the blinds and sent shadows swimming across the wall. Cash flinched and closed his eyes. I could practically feel the fear radiating from him. I touched his leg and he flinched again.

"Hey…what's wrong?" The words felt so inadequate I wanted to be sick. I squeezed his leg through the blanket.

"Cash?"

"They're everywhere," he whispered.

"What?"

"*Them*."

I followed his gaze to the walls around us. I didn't see anything but pasty white walls and medical equipment, but whatever Cash could see was making him terrified enough for the both of us.

"What are they?" I asked, softly.

Cash grabbed my hand and stared at our intertwined fingers. "I believe you."

"What?"

"Everything." His fingers fell out of my hand and he turned away. "I believe everything."

I swallowed the lump in my throat and closed my eyes. Focused on the blood rushing through my veins and the air in my lungs. I needed Finn. He'd know what to say. He'd know what was happening with Cash. He'd be able to make everything all right with just a look, a touch, a whisper in my ear. But I hadn't seen him since the fire. I didn't know if I'd ever see him again after what he did for us. Alone, I just felt useless and terrified of the world lurking around me that I couldn't see.

"Emma," my mom said from the doorway. "The police want to ask you a few more questions."

"In a minute," I said over my shoulder.

She nodded. "I'll wait in the hall."

"Cash, it's going to be okay. Everything is going to go back to the way it was. I promise."

"That's crap and you know it." He wouldn't look at me and I wanted to make him. I wanted him to make me believe my own lie.

"It's not—"

Cash looked at me and the words stuck to the insides of my mouth.

"We shouldn't be here," he said. "In a world that makes sense, we shouldn't have made it out of that fire, Em."

I bit my lip, not knowing what to say. I didn't want to lie to him anymore. "You don't know that."

"We shouldn't be alive." Cash's eyes darted across the ceiling. He clutched the covers and hunkered down into the sheets. "We should be dead…and *they* know it."

I touched his leg. Anybody else would have thought he was crazy. But I knew better. My best friend had risked his life to save mine and now something was wrong. Something had gone inconceivably wrong in that house and I didn't know how to help him. How to take it all away.

"I have to go talk to the cops, but I'll be back later. Promise."

Cash didn't look at me. Just nodded into the pillow and closed his eyes.

When I stepped into the fluorescent-lit hall, my chest twisted. Two detectives wearing suits were speaking to my mom in hushed voices and writing in their annoying little notepads. They both looked up when I walked in. The one with salt-and-pepper hair smiled and stuck out his hand.

"Hi, Emma. I'm Detective Monroe. You mind if we ask you a few questions about the fire?"

I tugged on a strand of hair coming loose from my ponytail. "I already told the cops everything when I woke up yesterday."

He nodded and looked at his partner. "Right, but you were still in pretty bad shape then. Thought you might remember some more now."

I took a deep breath and nodded. This was such a waste of time. I followed Detective Monroe into the waiting room and sat down in a faded dove-blue chair.

"So, the intruder," he started. "What exactly do you remember about them?"

"Red hair. Sort of hazel-colored eyes." I wrapped my arms around myself and looked away. Just thinking about Maeve made me sick.

"Okay. You said she was a woman, right?"

I nodded.

"How old?"

"A little younger than me, I think." At one time, anyway.

He scribbled in his pad then tapped on his knee with his pencil. "So, not the same person who attacked you at the theater? Correct?"

I finally met his gaze. "What?"

He flipped through his notepad. "You said that was a *man* who attacked you there. But this was a woman?"

"Umm…" I tucked my hair behind me ear. "Yeah. That's correct."

"That's pretty odd, don't you think?"

He had no idea just how *odd* this all was. "I guess. Why?"

"I need to ask you something, Emma." He waited for me to look at him. "Does your mom have a drinking problem? Does she treat you badly?"

"What? No!" I sat up in my chair. "Of course not. What the hell does that have to do with some cracked-out guy attacking me in a theater bathroom?"

Detective Monroe slipped his notepad back into his pocket. "Okay. Just calm down. With the extent of your injuries and the fact that your mother had been drinking, not to mention that we don't have one witness who saw this woman or the man, I have to ask. I'm just trying to help you."

Help me? I wanted to laugh. His badge wasn't going to do me a bit of good. Not against something he probably didn't even believe in.

"You can help me by leaving us alone."

I got up, expecting him to stop me, but he didn't. Instead he sighed and said, "You know where to find me if you change your mind."

. . .

Parker drove us back to his house from the hospital in silence. After my conversation with the cops, I didn't really feel like talking to him about any of it. The more people I had to lie to, the more complicated this was going to get. So I went with silence, which was broken up by the occasion cough from me or my mom. We finally pulled into a gravel driveway that led to a sleepy white house set back in the trees. Through the big picture window in front, I could see a few lights on in the house.

"Do you have kids?" I asked.

Parker shook his head and ducked out of the car to open my door. "Nope. It'll just be us."

An hour later, after we'd eaten pizza that Parker had ordered, he showed me to the guest room. I almost fainted when I spotted the black and white print of me at Lone Pine Lake hanging from the wall. I traced the shimmer next to me and my heart fluttered painfully at the thought of Finn. I wondered if he'd ever come back.

"I can't believe you saved this," I whispered. Parker leaned on the wall next to me and looked at the picture.

"Sorry I wasn't able to get your books." He slid a box over to me with the toe of his boot that was full of secondhand paperbacks. "I picked these up today. I think there are even a couple of your dad's in there. Your mom said you liked to read. Maybe we can rebuild your collection."

I stared down at the books, images of Dad flashing through my mind, and my vision blurred with tears. "Thank you."

"Okay, well, I'll let you get settled. Good night." Parker turned and left me in the room full of unfamiliar furniture. It smelled like fresh paint. Mom lingered in the doorway, watching me after Parker had gone.

"So how long are we staying here?" I picked up a paperback and pretended to read the blurb on the back. When she didn't answer I tossed the book back in the box and looked at her. "Earth to Mom!"

She blinked like she'd been somewhere else and smiled.

"Are you still upset about the cops questioning you?" I asked. "I told you everything was fine. I gave them a description of the girl who did this." A description of a girl they'd never find, considering she was dead.

She shook her head. "I'm upset that there is obviously some person out there intent on hurting you and I couldn't do anything to stop it. If I hadn't been drinking, none of this would have happened. You could've *died*."

"But I didn't." I eased down onto the unfamiliar bed and patted the spot beside me.

Mom flashed me a tight smile and took a deep breath, settling down next to me. "Are you okay with this? Staying here? I know I should have asked you." Mom twisted to face me, waiting for my approval. "We can stay in a hotel if you want."

I thought about Dad. About his smile and the way he always smelled like pine needles and coffee. The sound of his laptop soothing me to sleep at night. Parker wasn't Dad. He wasn't ever going to be Dad. But maybe if he made her happy, I could try. "Are you happy with him?"

She smiled. "Very."

Dad would want this. The thought had been in my head all along, but I didn't want to hear it. I'd been too selfish. I couldn't be that way anymore. I didn't want to be that girl. I smiled. "Then I'm okay with this."

Mom beamed back at me and kissed my cheek. "He doesn't have a lot of stuff to bake with here, but he did pick up some of those blueberry muffins you like from the bakery in town for breakfast."

"Tell him thanks for me."

She smiled and shut my door behind her on the way out. Once she was gone, I sighed and turned to grab the bag of new clothes my mom had picked up for me, but it wasn't there. *Crap.* Left them in the car.

I listened to the sound of cold rain beat on the roof like a drum, contemplating sleeping in my clothes rather than brave the rain outside. My need for comfort eventually won and I slid quietly through the house and out the front door.

I grabbed the bag and used it to shield myself from the icy rain and hurried back onto the porch. The rain had melted most of the snow, making a muddy, half-frozen mess of the rustic landscape. I reached for the front door—

"Emma?"

My breath caught in my throat and my heart thudded against my ribs. I turned around and found Finn standing in the rain. He didn't move and neither could I.

"Emma...I...I..." He couldn't finish. His teeth were chattering.

The sound of his voice sent panic flaring through me to the point of pain. I stumbled off the porch and into the rain, not caring about the ache in my leg or the stinging in my neck, or that the heavy droplets were practically freezing in my hair.

"Finn?" When I got closer enough, I stilled, paralyzed by disbelief. He was soaked. Rain dripped down his face, and his hands were clenched into shaking fists at his sides. I reached out and gasped when my fingers gripped a handful of his soaked T-shirt.

"Oh my God, Finn!" I grabbed him, not understanding, not thinking, only moving. I pulled him into the house behind me and prayed that Mom and Parker would stay in his bedroom as I dragged a strange boy through his living room.

Once we were in the safety of my room, I quietly shut and locked the door behind us, keeping my back pressed to the wood. I couldn't stop staring at him. Something told me that I should help the half-frozen boy in front of me, but I couldn't move. Finn couldn't be wet. He couldn't be freezing. Not my Finn.

He stared back, convulsions racking his frame, and smiled despite the pain showing in his face. "It hurts."

I slid away from the door and hesitated before grabbing his hands. They were freezing. I held them, perplexed by their solid fleshy feel. He felt like...me. "What hurts?"

"The cold. Everything."

I stripped his T-shirt over his head and tossed it to the floor. I wanted to ask how this was possible, but I couldn't. My hopes were already up, and I couldn't handle the disappointment that would smother me when he told me it was only temporary. So instead I kept moving, ridding him of his wet clothes. I unzipped his jeans and tugged them down over his hips, leaving him standing wide-eyed in only a pair of boxers.

I left him to start the bath, filling it with hot water, and hesitating to watch the steam roll off the top as I gathered my thoughts. When I came back, Finn grabbed me by the shoulders and ran his gloriously solid hands down my arms. Hands that had every part of me memorized before they'd ever even touched me. "How is this even possible? I don't understand."

He reached up to touch my face, his fingers trembling as they cupped my cheeks. "Emma, I'm a-a-a-live," he finally stuttered, then collapsed at my feet.

Chapter 39

Finn

When I opened my eyes, I was lying in a tangle of warm blankets. Emma was sitting on the bed next to me, her long legs folded Indian-style in front of her. She stared down at me, her brows drawn in thought, her blue eyes covered by a layer of unshed tears. Her gaze was focused on my bare stomach, so she didn't notice me awake. I lay still, wondering what she would do next. Her hand slowly stretched out. She ran her fingers along my chest and down to my stomach, sending my newly formed body into overdrive. I tensed, my fingers twitching, wanting to touch her. She jerked her gaze up to my face and pulled her hand away.

"Morning, pretty girl." My voice sounded gravelly. Every part of me throbbed as if I'd been thrown from a three-story building onto a slab of cold, unforgiving concrete. That might as well have been the case when I woke up in my new body on the slushy ground outside Parker's unfamiliar house.

She closed her eyes, kept them squeezed shut for several long moments, then opened them again.

"What are you doing?"

"Waiting for you to disappear." Her voice trembled. "Why haven't you disappeared yet?"

She looked up, her sapphire eyes holding me captive.

"I'm not going anywhere." I sat up, groaning with the effort and touched her chin. "Do you hear me? Never again. This is…" I was hesitant to say it. I was still waiting for the rug to be pulled out from under me. "This is permanent."

"This doesn't make any sense," she said. The sunlight streaming in through the window turned every wispy blond hair at the side of her face into threads of gold in its pale light.

"I know it doesn't, but it's real. I guess the best way to explain it would be to call it a gift." That wasn't exactly true. It was an exchange. When this life was done, I belonged to them…forever. But I wasn't ready to tell her that part. Not yet. Right now, I needed this moment with her to be perfect.

"I don't want to wake up from this," she whispered.

"You won't. Not this time."

Emma reached out, hesitant at first, and touched my hands. I looked down at them for the first time. They were full of blood, pulsing with life. The calluses I'd earned with Pop were painfully absent. I really was brand new. She ran her fingers silently over mine, then moved on to the lines of my chest. I inhaled sharply when her fingers reached my neck, grazed over the sensitive hollow of my throat.

"I need… I just need…" God, I needed so much my mind felt like it was in one of those medieval torture devices, being pulled in a thousand different directions, but I settled on her lips. I didn't even bother to take another breath. I leaned up and kissed her. Emma froze, making me doubt my action for a split second, but then she sighed into my mouth. It was a happy sound. A relieved sound. And in that moment I knew there was nothing more than this. Her smile on my lips. Her breath in my mouth. I wanted to live in this moment forever. I didn't want to think about tomorrow or the next day. Just here. Just now. Just this.

I pressed my palm into the warm small of her back, and lost myself in this kiss that was so much more than a kiss. This was Emma breathing the life back into me. I never knew it could feel like this, her skin against mine, my breath mixing with hers, our fingers tangled in a palm-to-palm embrace. It was like magic.

"Emma, why is the door locked?"

She broke away, her eyes wide as her mom jiggled the handle. She reached up to touch her lips, swollen from our kiss, and let her gaze wander silently over my half-clothed body. She didn't have to say it. I rolled off the bed, landed with a thud against the cool carpeted floor, and crawled under the bed.

"What was that?" Rachel knocked again. "Emma, are you okay?"

"I'm fine, Mom. What do you want?" The bed springs creaked and I watched her bare feet pad across the floor to the door. She opened it a fraction of an inch.

"Why is this door locked?" Rachel stuck her nose through the door but Emma pushed her back out. I listened to them prattle about locked doors and her mother's work schedule for the week. I was in heaven. Having to worry about my girlfriend's mom finding me in her bed was the biggest problem I had at the moment. Well, the biggest one I was willing to think about, anyway. I couldn't stop the stupid grin from spreading across my face.

"The coast is clear," Emma whispered. I rolled out from under the bed and climbed back on top to join her. We sat quietly until we heard the front door slam a few minutes later. Relief washed over Emma's face. She bounced up off the bed before I could reach out and touch her again. I flexed my fingers, wondering how they could suddenly feel so empty without her there to fill them.

"Where are you going?"

"To get food. Aren't you starving?" She pulled a pair of cotton shorts and a sweatshirt out of a duffel bag. When she gingerly pulled her pink silky camisole up over her head, navigating it around the stitches, and tossed it to the floor, something unraveled low in my stomach.

"Um… I can't blink out anymore. You have to ask me to leave before you do that." My mouth felt dry and I could feel my heart pounding in places it probably shouldn't. I should have looked away, but I couldn't tear my eyes away from her long, sunlit back.

"I never asked you to leave, Finn. You did that all on your own."

I swallowed and ran my hand over my mouth as I watched her pull the sweatshirt over her head, then slip out of her bottoms and carefully guide each long leg into her shorts. I had never once watched Emma change, but now that I had, I wouldn't trade the memory for anything in the world.

"Hungry?" She stopped at the door and blew a chunk of hair out of her eyes.

I laughed nervously, my adrenaline still rushing behind my ears. She had no idea. "Yeah, I think so."

Emma came back with two steaming cups of coffee with cream and sugar, and a plate full of blueberry muffins. The first bite of blueberry and warm pastry exploded in my mouth, leaving me almost dizzy. I hadn't tasted food in so long. I had to forcefully stop the moan from forming around the food in my mouth. Emma took a sip of her coffee and smiled, watching the expression on my face.

"What?" I asked wiping the back of my hand across my mouth and swallowing.

"You look like you're in Heaven."

Sitting here looking into her eyes, our knees touching and sending a shock wave of warmth up my thighs, I thought I might be. "Who says I'm not?"

I grinned and leaned across the small space between us to brush my lips against hers. And God help me, she tasted better than the muffin in my hand, so I abandoned it to pull her closer. Emma bit her lip and pulled out of my grasp.

"What is it?"

She held my hand in her lap. Ran the tip of her finger over the inside of my palm.

"Is my dad…" Pain flashed across her face.

"What is it? Tell me."

"Maeve told me my dad went to Hell." She looked up, eyes glossy. "Is it true? I won't blame you for lying to me if it is, but—"

"Emma." I grabbed her hands. "He's not in Hell. She was just trying to hurt you. I swear to you he's in Heaven. He's happy. At peace."

Emma nodded and her shoulders sagged, but there was still something fragile under the surface. "What happed in that house, Finn?"

I took a deep breath and sat back. "Why?"

"Because Cash is…something's wrong. He hasn't really talked to me since what we did that night, but it's more than that. I haven't felt her since the fire, but what if it's Maeve?"

"It's not Maeve," I said.

Emma's eyes opened wide. "Are you sure?"

I squeezed Emma's hand and closed my eyes. My retinas burned with the memory of watching the soul ripped out of the girl I loved. Watching Maeve crawl under her skin like it was a coat. I opened my eyes and smiled best I could. "I'm sure. She's never coming back."

"That's great, but Cash…" Emma shook her head. We have to help him. "

"We will. We'll fix it, whatever it is."

"Promise?"

I nodded and crawled up her body, gently pressing her into the mattress. "I promise."

The mattress springs creaked with the weight of both of our bodies. The blankets shifted and tugged beneath us. I smiled against Emma's cheek, wondering how something so small could make me so happy.

"We still have a lot to worry about," she said, banding her arms around my back to hold me close. "Like where you're going to live."

I nodded, breathing in her scent. "I know." The warmth of my breath made her shiver, a gentle rippling of heat that worked its way down her spine, then back up through mine like we were one being instead of two. I ran my fingertip up her leg, starting at her knee, then up, up, up, until my fingers gave in and closed over her hip. Emma closed her hand over mine, her eyes burning as blue as the hottest part of a flame.

I wanted to kiss her. Hell, I wanted to do a lot more than kiss her. But I didn't. Instead I brushed a strand of hair out of her eyes, and ran my fingers next to the stitches on her neck. Rage burned my insides like acid knowing that in spite of everything else, Maeve would always have her mark on Emma.

"You know you don't have to be with me, right?" she asked softly, her eyes finding my throat instead of my face. Her eyelashes brushed against the tender spot under my chin every time she blinked.

I lifted her chin so she'd look at me. "What are you talking about?"

"I don't want you to think that you owe me anything, or that you're obligated to be with me. You have a body now, a second chance at life. What if after a while you don't want this anymore?"

"Emma…" I swallowed through the emotions thick in my throat—twenty-seven years worth of them overwhelming me all at once. "I came back from the dead for you." Her eyes fluttered closed and I kissed her eyelids. They felt like satin against my lips. "If that doesn't prove how much I love you, then nothing will."

She sighed and her arms tightened around my waist. "I love you, too."

I kissed her. I'd meant for it to be soft, reserved, and respectful, but once her taste was on my tongue, there wasn't any going back. Maybe if I'd just finished the stupid breakfast, maybe if I'd let her come to me instead of me crawling on top of her, I could have held it together. But not now. Not when I was in a body that was all mine with the girl I wanted more than my next breath. I slid my palms up her sweatshirt, over her ribs, around to her back. I swallowed the whimper in the back of her throat. I kissed her until I wasn't sure where the air would come from if I didn't pull away.

I gasped for a breath when Emma finally broke the kiss. She laughed and ran her fingers through my hair.

"What?"

"I just thought of something." She wiggled away to sit up.

I kept my hands around her waist, wondering if I looked as confused as I felt.

"You said you never finished school," she said, smiling.

"So?"

"So, now you can finish. You can go to school with me."

The light in Emma's eyes was too much, glittering with possibility and happiness. I didn't say what I was thinking—that I'd rather reap a soul than go back to high school. Instead, I groaned and buried my face in Emma's stomach. "School? Really?"

Emma laughed and scratched the back of my head. "For me?"

I grinned and lifted up the hem of her shirt so I could rest my ear against her heart. Listened to it beat until my breathing matched its soothing rhythm. I knew in my heart, down to the pit of my soul, that I'd die for that sound. I'd die for this girl. I looked up at Emma and she arched a brow at me.

"For you?" I asked, brushing my lips against hers. "For you I'd do anything."

Acknowledgments

There are so many people involved in the process of getting a book from the mind of the author into the hands of the readers. And I have been blessed with the team that helped make this book a reality.

First, a big thank-you to my editor Heather Howland. When she made the decision to take a chance on me and this series, she made a dream come true. I will be eternally grateful for the hard work she put into this book. Also, hugs and thanks to assistant editor Tahra Seplowin and the entire Entangled team for helping to make this book shine. And to my publicist, Jaime Arnold, for helping me get *Inbetween* out into the world.

Never-ending thanks to my critique partners on this book, Mya Konstanti and Brock Adams. Mya, you are my writing rock and biggest supporter. I don't know what I'd do without you. And thank you to Brock for doing the math and helping me figure out that Finn, Anaya, and Easton couldn't do it on their own.

To my sister-in-law, Ashley, for reading my books before they are good enough to be called a book and cheering me on every step of the way.

To Elizabeth Yates and Julee Greenan. You were my best friends when I was a kid and you're still my best friends today. Thank you for supporting me and believing in my dream as much as I did.

Thank you to my mom and dad. There aren't enough words to say how thankful I am. I love you both more than words can say. Thank you to my grandmother. I wouldn't be the writer or woman I am today without her.

Thank you to my friends who cheer me on and keep me sane: Molly, Amber, Crystal, and Carolyn. And to some of the most amazing writers and friends I've ever known: Rachel Harris, Melissa West, Lisa Burstein, and the entire Entangled Teen crew. Thank you for your love and support. I seriously love you girls and am so lucky to have you with me on this journey.

And last but certainly not least, thank you to my husband, Jared, and my two sons, Colten and Caden. It's easy to write about an epic love when I have you to show me what that feels like every single day. I love you.

Keep reading for a sneak peek of Shea Berkley's

THE MARKED SON

*"Reading Shea Berkley is like watching magic unfold before
your eyes. THE MARKED SON is written with such intrigue and
depth, I could not get enough of this delicious tale."*
- Darynda Jones, author of *FIRST GRAVE ON THE RIGHT*

Seventeen-year-old Dylan Kennedy always knew something
was different about him, but until his mother abandoned him in the
middle of Oregon with grandparents he's never met, he had no idea
what.

When Dylan sees a girl in white in the woods behind his
grandparents' farm, he knows he's seen her before…in his dreams.
He's felt her fear. Heard her insistence that only he can save her
world from an evil lord who uses magic and fear to feed his greed for
power.

Unable to shake the unearthly pull to Kera, Dylan takes her
hand. Either he's completely insane or he's about to have the
adventure of his life, because where they're going is full of creatures
he's only read about in horror stories. Worse, the human blood in his
veins has Dylan marked for death…

Dreaming

I was eight the first time I saw the girl.

Mom freaked when I told her, said I was letting a girl terrorize my dreams, but I didn't get it. They were *dreams*, not nightmares. I don't remember ever waking up afraid. Not back then. So when the dreams kept coming, year after year, each one more vivid than the last, I held onto them like a skydiver clutching his ripcord. No way would I let Mom take them away from me.

It's been years since she's asked me about the girl, but lately Mom's been curious. I tell her I haven't had a dream in awhile. She eyes me like I'm lying.

So what if I am? I may not remember everything about my dreams when I wake up, but I do know when I'm about to have one. My scalp tingles, like tiny bugs zap, zap, zapping along my skin. The darkness behind my lids turns smoky. I've tried to pull away at that point but it's no use. I don't fight it now. Instead I sink into the thick air and come out the other side into a world that is nothing like the one I know...

Yet, it's familiar.

Tonight, the smoke fades, and the girl appears in a thin, white gown. I'm lying in a meadow surrounded by deep woods, one hand tucked behind my head—shirtless and shoeless and wearing a pair of old, ratty jeans. I can hear the TV I left on fading in the distance until only the sound of the meadow fills the air.

She's suddenly beside me, beautiful beyond words, her long, dark hair spilling over her shoulder as she bends to touch my hand. Her cool fingers rest more like mist than flesh in my palm. The rough corset she's wearing cinches the fabric snug to her hips. She's got a definite Victorian vibe going, but it suits her. I'd be lying if I said I didn't like it.

Her violet eyes darken, revealing the silent plea that carries a hint of desperation, and she tugs, urging me to get to my feet. She wants me to run, to escape. In the last two weeks, we've tried, running so long and so hard that we're sure we'll never find our way home again. We'll be lost together forever. It's what she wants. It's what I need. But it always fails. We eventually wind up back at the meadow.

Tonight, I'm content to pull her down beside me, lie in the soft grass, and stare at the sky. Our fingers intertwine, our shoulders touch. We've both gotten older since the first time we met. There were years when we rarely saw each other, but lately, our time together has intensified. There's a feeling of impending doom that wasn't there when we were younger, as if this perfect place of dreams is about to shatter, and we'll never see each other again.

There's so much I want to know. Why do I only dream about her when I need her most? Am I insane? I don't ask. I'm afraid to. I want her to be real. Just a few months more, maybe a year, then I'll grow up and cut this strange, imaginary cord. I can't lose her smile, not yet, or her lips against my cheek—one of her butterfly kisses that's gone before it's begun.

Her silence has never bothered me before. Tonight, all I want is one word.

My name.

I touch her hair, her cheek. I know the tilt of her head and the tip of her lips. I know when she's sad and when joy fills her to overflowing.

I've tried painting her in art class, but I've never been able to capture her perfection, because when I wake, her face dissolves with the dream. If she'd just talk to me, I'd remember everything about her. I would.

As we lie there, night and day flash by. One minute the sun warms my skin, the next the stars color it silvery bright. Flowers open and close. Birds sing. An owl hoots. The girl turns and lays her head on my chest. I wrap a protective arm around her and pull her closer, yet it's never close enough. She's my one comfort in life, but being with her is like holding onto sand that keeps slipping through my fingers. Time is running out, and I can't figure out why.

Suddenly, the darkness lowers and the dream grows cold, the woods sinister. She jerks upright. I follow. I ask her what's wrong. Her face shows her terror. Her mouth opens in an attempt to speak. No words follow.

The next moment, she's across the clearing. I call for her to come back. She doesn't. She can't. All I know is that she needs me. Now.

I slam back into consciousness, panting against the thudding of my heart. I peel off the scratchy covers and slip out of bed. The hotel room is dingy, but the night is laced with a full moon's light. I stand at the window and let the hopelessness overcome me as the dream fades away.

Heaving a sigh, I grip the windowsill and roll my forehead along the cool glass.

It's just a dream. Just a stupid, childish dream.

But how I wish it weren't.

AGAIN

I close my eyes, hoping to break free of this nightmare. Yet, when I open them, the hot breath of the southern summer is truly gone, replaced by a weakened sun and the cool breezes of the northwest. The car windows are open, and in the distance, the wooded foothills along the southern portion of the Cascade Mountains rise and fall like ripples in the earth. It's June. It should be sweat-rolling-down-my-spine hot. Instead, there's a damp chill outside. Not totally unpleasant, but not familiar. I slouch deeper into my seat and glare at Mom.

Her mouth pinches, her skin flushes, and she snubs out her cigarette in a tray overflowing with more than three days worth of ash and spent stubs. "Don't, Dylan. Just keep it to yourself."

She says I'm a petulant teenage boy. I am, but who wouldn't be in this situation? I'm disillusioned. Frustrated. Disgusted by life. I'm seventeen, on the brink of my senior year, and once again, I've been forced to leave everything familiar to me in order to appease another of her emotional breakdowns. Mom thrives on drama. She always has, and I've always played along.

Not anymore. I'm sick of playing the good son.

"All I'm saying is, we didn't have to leave."

"We did."

Same answer. Always the same.

"He left," I remind her for the hundredth time.

She shakes her head, and the few dark curls that have managed to stay bound in her messy ponytail suddenly bounce free to lash wildly in the wind. "His family lives there. You know how people are. Hateful gossips."

"So?"

Her jaw sets at a rigid angle. "I don't want to talk about it. Not to them, and not to you."

"So my life means nothing to y—"

"Shut it!" She blinks rapidly, still staring at the torn-up road. "I mean it. Not another word."

The tears are back. I look away, disgust searing my insides. The cool wind whips through my hair, pounding at my eardrums, drowning out her staccato gasps for breath. "I get it. Nothing's ever going to change."

She ignores me. I'm fine with that—at least, that's what I always tell myself—and soon she's lighting up again. She bought the ten-pack carton at the first gas station we saw on our way out of town. For eight months she didn't take a single drag. Not one. I'd been begging her to quit for years. Did she listen to me? No. But she listened to Jared, her latest ex-boyfriend. *Anything* for Jared. It's the one thing the walking dick did right, but now look at her.

Why did I think she would change? We're drifters, stumbling from small town to small town, staying a year or two until the man-pool dwindles, leaving the next. Mom changes men like some girls change their nail color. When she finally settles on one "special" guy, it's only a matter of time before he leaves, by way of the back door, with an armful of our stuff he can hock at the local pawn shop and a pocket full of what little money he finds in Mom's purse.

I've learned to lock my bedroom door.

The small evidence of our existence on this earth is behind us, rattling around in a rented trailer as it bounces in and out of deep ruts, shaking our rusty, old Plymouth Road Runner until I'm sure the rivets have come loose.

Mom curses as the car whines up another hill. She pumps the slab of steel with the ball of her foot like the hick she is, until the engine revs, re-engages, and spits us forward.

"You coulda at least slept your way into a better car," I mutter, pulling up the hood of my gray sweatshirt. Not likely. Mom's always been better at giveaways than bartering.

She doesn't hear, and it's probably for the best. A fresh round of tears would've been her answer. They're the answer for everything these days.

To the east, the hills climb into the mountain range. I stare out over the forested landscape, seeing but not seeing. My mind is on the girl in my dreams. Pale face. Dark hair. White gown. Eerie woods. Chills sweep my arms. It's just an impression, there and gone before I can capture it, but a strange, deep longing rises in my chest. I've dreamed about her every night for two weeks, and each dream is more intense than the last. Lately, I'm feeling desperate in a way I've never felt before, like I've been ripped out of the ground one too many times, and the next time will kill me.

My thoughts return to the present, and I see the road split. To the left, pavement riddled with water-filled potholes. To the right, dirt riddled with muddy potholes. We turn right.

I slap my hand on the outside of the door. "Seriously? A dirt road?" Trees quickly surround the car, and an unfamiliar thickness invades the air. Our soon-to-be-new home is fast losing its appeal.

"It's a sheep ranch, Dylan. Where do you expect it to be? In the middle of downtown Portland?"

"Not in the wilds of Oregon!"

The car shakes and rattles as we slowly make our way down the torn-up strip of dirt. Mom does all she can to avoid trouble spots.

"This is hardly—" She huffs when the car slams into an especially deep hole and mud splatters in a shower of gloppy brown. The undercarriage smacks the road hard, and she growls her frustration. "—out in the wilds," she finishes, but I can see even she's struggling to believe her own propaganda.

"Yeah, right. There's not even a damn Walmart out here, and Walmart is *everywhere*."

"Don't cuss," she says. "My mother hates cussing."

Good to know. Rattle off the seven unspeakable cuss words the first chance I get, and family or not, if she has any brains, her mom will send us packing.

Trees crowd the road, sucking the air out of the car. I'd forgotten how much I detest the great outdoors. I'd spent my whole life traveling toward the city, longing for a place where I belong, and now Mom slaps me back to square one.

Every so often, another dirt road forks off the main one, but try as I might, I can't see any signs of human life. The road looks like it leads to a campground. What is she thinking? She hates country life even more than I do.

"So, your mom… What am I supposed to call her?"

Her laugh is a short, bitter sound. "How about Granny? That'll rip her up."

"Using me to dig at your mom isn't very mature."

She pushes the dancing, brown curl out of her eyes. "Oh, shut up. You know I'm kidding. Anyway, what do you care?"

"I don't." I haven't cared about anything in a long time, but still. Someone has to be an adult, and it sure won't be her.

And she *isn't* kidding, regardless of what she says. It's good to know I'm not the only one who causes that particular look of resentment to flash in her eyes.

As we trundle over the hard-packed mud, a scruffy, tri-colored dog with a bobbed tail and spindle-legs shoots out of the trees and runs alongside the car, all barks and growls like it's never seen a rusted box on wheels before.

"Beat it, Fido." I swat at it, but it nearly bites off my hand. "Hey!"

"What?"

"The dog almost bit me!"

Mom looks at me like I'm the problem. "What are you, two? Don't touch a strange dog."

Yep. I'm the problem. I slouch back onto my seat. She would side with a mangy animal over her own flesh and blood. I guess that's what happens when you're the unwanted son of a teenage runaway.

The dog breaks away when we round a bend cluttered with trees. Mom mutters a few more cuss words. I close my eyes and sigh. That's Mom. Do as I say, not as I do.

The car veers to the left, and I crack my eyes open. The wall of trees separates to reveal a half-dozen strange, brightly-painted metal sculptures that belong in one of those modern museums only rich people go to. There's something disturbing about the way they rise up, twisting and stretching in a macabre, colorful dance.

Behind them, a huge, red barn overlooks a clapboard-sided house. When we bottom out near the top of the drive, a small woman, pail in hand, turns and watches us from her place on the front porch. I push my hood off to get a better look. "Yee-haw. There's Granny. So where's Uncle Jed, cousin Jethro, and Elly May?"

"Knock it off."

I can feel a headache coming on. "Let me get this straight. You can say whatever you want, but I've gotta behave?"

"Exactly. Nobody likes a smart ass."

"That would explain your lack of popularity."

She blows out the last of the smoke that's rotting her lungs. "For God sakes, would it kill you to be nice?"

The Road Runner rolls to a stop. Mom hops out with a big, yet wary, smile plastered across her face. I'm not at all eager to meet my maternal kin. Honestly, how great can they be? Mom left when she was barely sixteen. My life sucks and I'm still with *my* parental unit. What does that say about hers?

The woman drops the bucket, and when it lands on the porch's wooden planks, the expected clatter is swallowed by the surrounding forest. Her face pales. I recognize disbelief when I see it. Her hands shake as she rubs them down the sides of her worn-out jeans. Granny isn't exactly old. In fact, she's downright young-looking. A little weather-beaten, but still kind of attractive. An older version of Mom.

Mom hesitates. "Hey, Mama. Bet you didn't expect to see me."

I groan. I shouldn't be surprised that she's dragged us all the way up here without telling anyone, but I am. Mom's never been one to bother with practical matters like informing family we're coming to live with them indefinitely.

"Dylan," Mom yells, and motions me forward. "Get out of the car."

Grandma's attention shifts to where I'm still sitting in the passenger seat. Her eyes are big and pale blue, almost see-through. They're kinda creepy, actually.

"Who's that?" she asks. "Your boyfriend?"

I'm a big guy. Not, oh-my-God-look-at-that-giant-fat-boy big, but tall and muscular. I've been known to walk into a bar or two and not get carded.

"Beautiful," I mutter. Gritting my teeth, I get out of the car, one hand on the roof, the other on the door and glare at Mom. "She doesn't know who I am, does she?"

Mom's eyes widen. She looks like she's going to cry again, and burning anger starts to rise inside of me. I try to tamp it down, but I can't. It bubbles over, leaping into my eyes, my mouth, and my heart.

Without another word, I snatch an old army duffel stuffed with my things from the back seat and slam the door. I don't look back as I retrace my way toward the main road.

"Dylan!"

I ignore Mom's call.

"Dylan, stop."

I do, but it's got nothing to do with her. The crazy dog skids into my path. Its ears are down, and its teeth are showing. Long, mean teeth.

Mom's fingers clamp onto my shoulder, startling me. The dog leaps toward her, and I kick dirt at it and yell for it to go. Amazingly it does. I pull out of Mom's grasp, ignoring the pleading in her eyes. She latches on again. "You can't go. Please, don't do this."

Where does she get off, acting this way? "What do you care whether I'm here or not?"

"You have to stay! If you don't, it's going to get worse."

It *sounds* like she cares, but I'm not easily fooled. I turn away. "She doesn't know who I am. You never told her about me."

"Of course not. I haven't talked to her since I left."

I snap around and confront her. "Why are we even here?"

"There's no other place to go."

"Bullsh—"

"Don't cuss." She glances back and sees Grandma inching her way toward us. "We have to be smart about this. You promised me you'd behave."

The muscle in my cheek twitches. "People make promises all the time they don't intend to keep." Just like she'd promised to quit smoking and drinking and hooking up with men. Promises run cheap in our dysfunctional family.

I will *not* be like her. I will make something out of my life, even if it kills me.

Panic flushes her face. "Please, Dylan."

She's desperate. I can taste it in the air. I should relent, but an unquenchable need to hurt her like she constantly hurts me threatens to hijack my control.

The crunch of gravel stops me from saying something that would push her over the edge. Grandma's within hearing range, a look of suspicion on her face. "What's going on, Addison?"

"Addy," Mom says on a sigh as she turns to face Grandma. "My name is *Addy*. And nothing is going on. This is my son. Dylan."

"Your son?" The news is definitely a shocker for her. "But he's... How old is he?"

"Seventeen," I say.

Grandma appears dazed and more than confused.

"Yeah," Mom blurts out. "Do the math. Sixteen and pregnant. Daddy would've freaked—*I* freaked—so I left."

"What? Your father—"

Mom throws her head back and sways side-to-side like a nervous hen that's been pegged for Sunday dinner. "You know I'm right," she hollers at the sky.

Shadows flit into Grandma's eyes. "He would've been angry, yes, but that was no reason to leave like you did."

Mom's chin trembles, but she regains control. She looks toward the house and into the woods beyond, like she's searching for something. "Well, we can't change the past."

"No. We can't." Grandma glances at me. I can tell she wants to move closer for an inspection, but manners—and most likely shock—keep her back. "It's a pleasure to meet you, Dylan," she says.

Her gaze lances through me. I get this feeling like I should apologize, but I can't think what I've done wrong, exactly. I don't especially like the feeling. So instead, I thrust out my hand and throw her a smile laced with sarcasm. "Hey there, *Granny*."

There's a sudden void of sound, like the whole world stops for a millisecond, shocked by my rudeness. It whispers on the wind, "She's your grandmother. Have a little respect."

She blinks, and then her mouth cracks open into a wide smile, followed by a sharp laugh. She grabs my hand and squeezes. "You're your mother's child, all right."

I stiffen. She has no idea how deeply she's insulted me. Or maybe she does, because the sunlight suddenly splinters in her eyes, and her fingers squeeze mine.

Mom's fixated on the car, and she's as jittery as a crack addict. "Can we unpack, now?" she whines, and lights up a cigarette, sucking so hard the tip burns quickly into squiggly ash.

Grandma lets go of my hand to cup my face. There's an analytical slant to her stare—a "who's your daddy" look. I can see her mentally click through the slim White Pages of her acquaintances, searching for the culprit. A shadow of suspicion flickers before she gives my cheek a gentle pat. "You're a handsome boy, Dylan. I bet your girlfriend is still crying over you leaving."

Girls have been giggling and sighing over me since I hit the sixth grade. I won't lie. I like girls, and I like the attention they pour on me. A lot. But as soon as I get attached to one, we leave. Over the years, I've learned to adapt. To play the field. Life is less complicated that way.

I shrug and look at Mom. "I'm not strictly a one-woman guy, right, Mom?"

She blows out a thick stream of smoke before pitching the spent butt on the ground and grinding it out. "No, you're not."

Grandma's eyes twinkle. "A Romeo, huh?" When I start to pull away, her fingers intertwine with mine, and she leads me back up the dirt road toward the house. "Trust me. A time will come when one special person is all you'll want."

Mom snorts and lights another cigarette.

God, I hope not. The last thing I want is to become like Mom; chasing *the one* and always slinking away with the taste of burnt ash in my mouth.

To lose yourself in Dylan and Kera's romance, pick up

THE MARKED SON

online or in a bookstore near you!